WAR OF THE WORLDS
RETALIATION

MARK GARDNER & JOHN J. RUST

SEVERED PRESS
HOBART TASMANIA

WAR OF THE WORLDS: RETALIATION

Copyright © 2017 Mark Gardner & John J. Rust
Copyright © 2017 Severed Press

WWW.SEVEREDPRESS.COM

All rights reserved. No part of this book may be reproduced or transmitted in any form or by any electronic or mechanical means, including photocopying, recording or by any information and retrieval system, without the written permission of the publisher and author, except where permitted by law. This novel is a work of fiction. Names, characters, places and incidents are the product of the author's imagination, or are used fictitiously. Any resemblance to actual events, locales or persons, living or dead, is purely coincidental.

ISBN: 978-1-925597-66-0

All rights reserved.

PROLOGUE
THE SUDAN, 1898

Lieutenant David Beatty had had a bullet rip through his helmet and nearly had a ship's magazine explode right under him at Hafir. Neither of those near-death experiences filled him with the sort of horror the enormous, alien machines did.

A shudder went through him as he stood on *Fateh*'s gun deck, watching the three-legged metal monstrosities stomp across the desert. They had to be a hundred feet tall. He pressed his hand against the boat's rectangular, wooden bridge to keep it from shaking as he recalled the dispatches from London that spoke of the devastating heat rays. A stab of nausea plunged into his stomach, imagining the agony of his body being set afire.

How about killing them before they kill you.

Beatty turned away from the advancing Martian machines. "Sergeant," he called to the burly man standing by the six-pounder. "Bring all guns to bear on the enemy. Wait for my command to fire."

"Sir," blurted Sergeant Ellison, the royal marine in charge of gunnery. He barked out orders to the Egyptian gun crew, who swung around the big cannon in quick order. His next shouts carried across *Fateh*'s deck to the other gun crews, who quickly brought their weapons to bear on the Martians.

Beatty smiled. Ellison had drilled the men well.

"Morrison!" Beatty shouted up to the signalman atop the bridge.

"Sir."

"Signal the *Nasir* and *Metemma*." He gave Morrison the same order he'd given Sergeant Ellison.

"Aye, sir."

Beatty leaned toward the railing, staring past *Fateh*'s length to the other gunboats trailing him up the Nile. Beyond them was a lump of a ship laden with crates and dozens of refugees from upriver. The transport steamer *Blackwood*, making all of three knots.

He thumped a fist against the bridge, cursing the slower ship's presence. Now wasn't the time to crawl through the river. He needed all the speed his gunboats could muster. But he wasn't about to abandon an unarmed transport with terrified civilians.

Beatty turned back to the tripods. They had to be a half kilometer away. Still out of the range of his guns. What he wouldn't give to be back on the battleship *Trafalgar*, with its big guns and thick armor. Certainly, it would be more than a match for the Martians.

We're not exactly helpless. He looked at the *Fateh*'s guns, then at the enemy machines. He pushed down his fear, his anxiousness. It wouldn't be long before the Martians were in firing range, then he'd show the monsters what—

A yellow flash came from the lead tripod. Beatty tensed at the sizzling sound in the air. Something streaked to his right.

Nasir vanished in a geyser of flame and smoke. Beatty jerked at the *crash* of the explosion.

Metemma's guns thumped. One of *Fateh*'s six-pounders fired.

"Cease fire!" Beatty shouted, waving one hand. "Cease fire! You're wasting ammunition!"

Sergeant Ellison also yelled the order. The six-pounder fell silent. *Metemma* continued shooting. Plumes of smoke and sand kicked up far from the tripods.

"Morrison. Signal *Metemma* to—"

Another heat ray streaked from the lead tripod. A fiery explosion consumed *Metemma*.

Beatty clenched his jaw. Two gunboats were destroyed, and they hadn't so much as nicked the aliens. His eyes drifted to the *Blackwood*. Some of the refugees and crew gaped at the tripods in frozen horror. Others jumped over the side and swam to shore.

Letting out a slow breath, he looked back at the Martians. His insides went cold. This was it. One shot and he and his crew were done for.

"All guns!" he shouted. "Open fire!" Wasting ammunition didn't matter now. He may as well show the Martians they would go down fighting.

Sailors repeated the order throughout the *Fateh*. The guns boomed. Beatty watched the shells burst hundreds of feet from the tripods, throwing up clumps of sand. He clenched his fists, praying just one bloody shell hit those bastards before the end.

A heat ray flashed over the desert. Beatty closed his eyes.

A quake rocked the *Fateh*. Beatty cried out as he fell to the deck. Hammers of pain slammed into his back.

He blinked. *My God, I'm still alive.* Loud pops came from the boat's stern. Ammunition detonating. Smoke wafted above him. Tortured screams reached his ears.

Beatty grimaced, pushing himself up. Ellison and his Egyptian gunners lay in a heap on the deck.

"You all right?" Beatty called to them.

"Fine, sir." Ellison bared his teeth and rubbed his shoulder. Two of the Egyptians nodded to him.

Beatty clawed at the bridge, rising to his feet, then slipping. *Fateh* listed to port. Flames consumed the stern.

"Abandon ship!" he hollered. "All hands, abandon ship!"

He threw open the door to the bridge, ushering out the crew. Beatty ran below decks and into a cloud of smoke. His eyes burned as he checked for any sailors.

"Abandon ship!" Smoke stung his throat and lungs. "Aban—" A coughing fit rocked his body. He searched around him, his eyes narrow, watery slits. Beatty could barely see a foot in front of him.

The deck shifted under him. Beatty slid into the wall. A bolt of pain went through his shoulder. He thought about turning around and getting off this burning wreck.

Can't. Not until I know everyone's off safely.

At least, everyone who's still alive.

Two large forms burst from the smoke. Beatty grunted as they clipped his shoulder.

"Who's that?" asked a gruff voice.

Beatty recognized the man. Moffat, the Scottish civilian engineer, who serviced the boilers.

"Captain? That you?"

"It is." Beatty could barely keep his eyes open.

"You'd best get off this boat," said Moffat. "She's done for."

"Is anyone else belowdecks?" Beatty's face twisted in disgust from the stale taste of smoke.

"I doubt it." Moffat shook his head. "Fire swept through right quick. I barely got out of the boiler room with this poor bugger."

Beatty glanced at the man leaning against Moffat's side. One of the foreign firemen, he assumed.

He turned back to the corridor. An orange aura glowed through the smoke. The Scotsman hadn't been joking about the fire spreading quickly.

"Go. Go." He pushed on Moffat's arm, urging him to get topside. Beatty looked over his shoulder, biting his lip. If anyone below remained alive, he couldn't reach them.

Guilt clawed his soul as he raced up the ladder, pressing against the wall to keep his balance. *Fateh* listed at forty degrees.

He made it topside just as Moffat and the wounded fireman plunged into the Nile. Beatty half-ran, half-slid past the six-pounder and hurled himself into the water. He kicked away from the sinking gunboat, eyeing a nearby shoal covered in bushes. Sergeant Ellison and two of his gunners pulled themselves out of the river and crawled into the vegetation.

"The shoal!" he shouted to the survivors, jabbing a finger at the miniature island. "Get to the shoal!"

Beatty stroked and kicked so hard his muscles started to burn. He didn't stop until he reached the bank. Ellison waved him over to his hiding spot. Beatty checked around him. The brush seemed thick enough to prevent the Martians from seeing them.

He twisted around, peering through the branches. Moffat and the wounded fireman emerged next, the Scot dragging the foreign worker into the brush. Beyond them, smoke billowed from the sinking *Fateh*. Beatty's face tightened. He'd lost his ship. He didn't care that it wasn't a true warship like the *Trafalgar*, just a converted paddleboat with some guns stuck on it. It was his ship, and it had gone down with hardly a fight.

"Good Lord," Moffat stammered.

Beatty looked to the Scotsman, then followed his wide-eyed gaze.

The tripods were a quarter kilometer from the river. His mouth fell open. Their sheer size awed and terrified him at the same time.

The *Blackwood* floated into view, its deck devoid of people. Some of the refugees and crews swam for shore. Others had already climbed out of the water and run into the desert.

The tripods waded into the Nile. Beatty's eyes flickered between the enormous war machines to the people still in the water.

Faster. Faster!

A tentacle whipped out from the lead tripod. It snatched a man out of the river. Beatty barely suppressed a gasp as it lifted him high into the air and dumped him into a globular basket on the tripods rear.

More tentacles shot into the water, quick as a frog's tongue. Every time they came up with a struggling man or woman.

Tears stung Beatty's eyes. He pounded the ground with a fist. He couldn't do a damn thing to help those poor souls. Never in his life had he felt so helpless.

When all the swimmers had been plucked from the water, the Martians marched onto dry land, pursuing the remaining crew and refugees from the *Blackwood*. Beatty prayed at least some escaped those tentacles.

The tripods soon vanished from sight. Beatty and the others remained in the brush, tending to the wounded fireman, a Maltese named Grima. Half the man's face and torso were covered with dark scorches and bloody wounds. Beatty grimaced at the rank smell of copper and burnt flesh emanating from the man. Still, he ripped off the sleeves of his soaked uniform and used them as bandages. Ellison and one of the Egyptians did the same. Grima softly moaned the entire time. Beatty's chest tightened. Could they get him to a doctor in time?

Are there any hospitals left in the Sudan?

The small group remained hidden in the brush until nightfall. During that time, Grima passed. With no means to bury him, Beatty conducted a very short, impromptu service, and then led the others to the western bank of the Nile.

"So what do we do now, sir?" asked Moffat.

Beatty stared at the Scotsman. *Good question*. But he was in charge. He had to come up with some sort of plan.

"We find other survivors from the army or navy, and keep up the fight."

"How the bloody hell do we fight those things?" Moffat threw his arms out to his sides.

"We'll find a way," said Beatty. "We damn well better if we want to live, and when I say 'we,' I mean all of mankind."

He folded his arms and stared at the ground, thinking. Heading back to Atbara was out. The Martians burned the city to the ground. They could continue on to Shendi, twenty-five kilometers south. But what guarantee did they have the town wouldn't—or hadn't already—suffered the same fate?

Even if the Martians had destroyed Shendi, they should still be able to salvage some supplies and weapons, then he could figure out what to do next.

"We stay with our original plan," said Beatty. "South to Shendi."

They trekked through the darkness, staying along the river, but not too close. Beatty had no desire for him or any of his men to be dragged off by a crocodile.

When the sun came up, they rested. Beatty set up a watch, with each man, including himself, on duty for an hour. Not only did he have to worry about Martians and crocodiles, but the damn Mahdist rebels they'd originally come to Sudan to fight. He didn't think an alien invasion would quell their desire to kill any subject of the Crown they came across.

Too many damn things in this desert can kill us. They also did not have much in the way of weaponry to defend themselves against man, beast, or Martian. Beatty and Ellison carried their Webley pistols, though after a thorough soaking in the Nile he doubted whether they'd even fire. Even if they did work, what good would pistols be against those tripods?

What I wouldn't give for one of those heat rays.

They resumed their march south when the sun grazed the horizon. Beatty estimated they were nine or ten kilometers from Shendi. The absence of smoke or flames in the distance he took as a good sign. Perhaps the town remained intact.

Energized by renewed hope, he picked up his pace, striding up a small rise.

Beatty halted at the top, staring unblinking at the sight before him.

"Something wrong, sir?" asked Ellison.

Beatty didn't reply. He just kept staring, trying to digest what he saw.

"Sir?" Ellison marched up next to him. "What's the . . . Good Lord."

Three fallen tripods lay along the banks of the Nile half a kilometer from the rise.

"What happened to them?" Ellison wondered aloud.

"No idea." Beatty took a couple of deep breaths, summoning up all his courage. "Let's go find out."

Ellison drew his head back. His brow crinkled in an unsure expression. He then stiffened and said, "Yes, sir."

Webley in hand, Beatty led his men toward the tripods. Had the army in Shendi brought them down? The shadows of dusk prevented him from making out any damage.

He slowed as he neared the first tripod, half expecting it to rise and incinerate him. But the large machine remained still.

Beatty's heart beat faster as he came within a few meters of the tripod. He never expected to be so close to one and live. Its massive size overwhelmed his senses.

He also noticed something else. The tripod had no holes, no scorch marks, nothing to indicate it had fallen victim to artillery fire.

The group examined the second tripod. It, too, showed no signs of damage.

"Maybe they tripped over their own feet," quipped Moffat.

They made their way to the third tripod. Beatty tensed, gripping his pistol tighter when he saw a lump lying against the machine's turret-like top. One of the Egyptians gasped behind him.

Swallowing, Beatty took a cautious step toward it, then another.

The Martian didn't move.

He bent over running his gaze over the creature. It reminded him of an octopus, about four feet in length, a V-shaped mouth, and two large eyes, now closed. The skin was greenish-brown with gray splotches across its body. Beatty scrunched his face at the rank stench hovering around the alien.

"Hideous looking bugger, isn't it?" said Ellison.

"How did it die?" asked Moffat. "Doesn't look like it got shot."

Beatty stared hard at the Martian, concentrating on the gray splotches. They didn't appear to be part of its natural skin color. "I think it fell ill."

"From what?" Moffat took a step closer to the dead Martian.

"I don't know." Beatty shook his head.

"I guess the same happened to those two." Ellison jerked his head toward the other tripods. "You suppose the rest of these monsters got sick, too?"

"Let's pray that's the case." Beatty straightened up.

Ellison looked up and down the tripod. "Well, if these bastards are all off to the great beyond, they won't be needing these anymore." He patted the turret. "Imagine what we could do with them."

Hands on his hips, Beatty gazed at the heat ray and grinned. "I already am."

ONE
TWENTY-SIX YEARS LATER

Am I the only one on this planet that has not turned into a cowardly fool?

Supreme Guardian Hashzh aimed his large, dark eyes at the video screen. All eight of his tentacles trembled. He opened his mouth and unleashed a half-shriek, half-gargle of anger.

When the piercing sound stopped echoing off the curved walls of his chamber, Hashzh spread his tentacles along the floor and read the message from the Guiding Council.

Our most recent calculations show that the Shoh'hau race has more than adequate defenses to deal with any potential attack by the natives of Brohv. As we have stated previously, the Council has determined it is highly unlikely a primitive race like the Brohv'ii can replicate our technology to the point they are able to threaten our world. Thus, your request for more weaponry for the Guard Force is denied.

Hashzh's anger burned hotter as he continued reading.

Furthermore, Supreme Guardian Hashzh, your constant requests for more material for the Guard Force has not only grown tiresome, but wastes the time of the Guiding Council. We have stated numerous times that priority for resource allocation must go to the Final Project. Diverting those resources for armaments that will in all likelihood never be used means delaying the completion of the Final Project. You are to cease your requests for additional weaponry. Non-compliance of this directive will result in your removal as Supreme Guardian.

Hashzh wanted to cover all nine members of the Guiding Council in bodily waste. Did they truly believe the Brohv'ii not to be a threat? Had they forgotten what happened during the Cleansing Mission thirteen cycles ago? All the Brohv'ii needed was for one ship to land on Shoh, and just one of their race to set foot on this planet and spread their diseases.

That fear dominated his mind. He thought of the Shoh'hau in the Cleansing Force. How much pain did they endure as those alien microbes ravaged their bodies? How scared had they been, knowing they had no means to combat the sickness?

Would the same happen to him? To everyone on Shoh?

It will if fear continues to rule the Guiding Council. They wanted nothing more to do with the Brohv'ii. Hashzh sometimes believed the planet's leaders thought simply mentioning the word "Brohv'ii" would cause their diseases to spread throughout the world.

He thumped the tips of his tentacles on the floor, his frustration mounting. The probes he sent to the nearby blue and white planet of Brohv, or Earth as the natives called it, showed they had made huge technological strides in a short period of time. Their various nations had constructed large spaceships and equipped them with beam weapons and missiles. Satellites circled their planet. They even had artificial habitats on their solitary moon.

None of which would have been possible without the craft and machines left behind by the doomed Cleansing Force.

The Guiding Council, however, refused to admit the Brohv'ii posed any threat. After such a horrific failure, they decided the best way to deal with the Brohv'ii was to ignore them.

If the climate change doesn't cause our extinction, the humans just might.

Hashzh extended a tentacle to a panel and tapped the upper right corner. The reprimand from the Guiding Council vanished, much to his delight. Replacing it was the results from the planetary defense drills that took place during the early rotation period. What he read did nothing to improve his mood. Accuracy for more than half the tripod groups was atrocious. Many of the land guardian groups took longer than acceptable to reach their defensive positions. When he saw how the planetary defense batteries on the far moon performed, it made Hashzh shriek and gargle again.

Had the Guiding Council infected his Guard Force with their denial of reality?

That will change. He would make the Guard Force take their duties seriously. They would conduct drills from early rotation until final rotation. Perhaps he should banish some guardians to the bitter cold of the northern region. That would motivate the rest.

A short wail came from the circular door.

"Enter."

The door slid open, revealing a younger Shoh'hau with light brown skin and slim tentacles.

"Givrht. You have returned."

"Yes, Supreme Guardian. My shuttle landed a short while ago."

"Tell me of the progress being made," said Hashzh.

Givrht gave his report. A burbling sound came from Hashzh's throat. *At last, news I can take joy in.*

He thought back two-and-a-half cycles ago when he undertook this project. There were so many times when he wondered if he could actually make this happen. Now they were exactly sixty rotations away from completion. Sixty rotations until he could end the Brohv'ii threat for all time.

Hashzh felt his bitterness turn to hope. *The Guiding Council has their Final Project, and so have I.*

TWO

Colonel George Patton tightened his grip on the glass, glaring at the radio set perched on a shelf over the counter. He released a slow, growling breath as he listened to the interview.

"It makes no sense to spend so much money on spaceships and other weapons. The Earth is pure poison for the Martians. They're never coming back here. The money for our military should be used to provide food and adequate shelter for the poor."

"Yeah," Patton grumbled under his breath. "Then watch the damn Martians blow up all those 'adequate shelters.'"

"Settle down, George," said his wife, Beatrice, who sat across from him feeding little George IV his bottle. "People have a right to say what they want."

"And thanks to that damn radio contraption, anyone can say any stupid thing they want to the whole world." Patton waved a hand toward the offending piece of technology.

A few of the other customers in the diner turned toward him. Patton ignored them and took a huge bite out of his ham sandwich while he listened to the interview.

"But top generals and admirals at the War Department have said that the Martians are capable of attacking Earth from orbit," said the interviewer, Lowell Thomas. "They don't have to set one tentacle on the ground to exterminate us. How do you respond to that, Mister Cannon?"

"More propaganda by the warmongers in Washington. If the Martians wanted to bombard us from space, why didn't they do that in 1898? President Wood, Secretary of War Dawes, and all their generals and admirals want to keep this country, the entire world, in a state of fear. They want us scared of the Martian boogeyman to keep their fat cat friends in the war industry rich, while the people starve. If they want to make sure the Martians never attack us again, how about we try talking to them."

Patton slammed both hands on the table. "Do we have to listen to this commie jackass son-of-a-bitch?"

Everyone in the diner looked at him. None of them spoke. George IV broke the silence, crying in his mother's arms. Beatrice turned away from Patton, gently rocking the baby. Their daughters, Bea and Ruth, kept their heads down.

A fat, redheaded waitress behind the counter swallowed. "Um, I'll change the channel, sir."

"You do that." Patton's face twisted in rage.

Without a further word, the waitress reached up and turned the knob. Moments later, upbeat piano music came from the speaker.

Patton surveyed the diner. Many of the patrons looked away when his gaze settled on them.

"Any of you agree with that son-of-a-bitch? Any of you think the Martians are no longer a threat? Anyone here forget what those slimy bastards did to us twenty-six years ago?"

No one answered him.

Patton and his family finished their lunch in silence, at least once George IV finished crying. He paid the bill and stalked out of the diner, followed by Beatrice and the kids.

"Did you have to do that, George?" his wife scolded him. "That was so embarrassing. And what have I told you about using that kind of language in front of the children?"

"All right, I'm sorry." Patton tugged at the collar of his brown Army dress uniform. The damn summer heat was making him sweat like a pig. "But what am I supposed to do. Just smile whenever I hear some commie as—" He glanced at his daughters. "Um, some commie pig blather on about things he has no clue about?"

He stopped by the wall of a hardware store. His gaze settled on a colorful poster showing a woman and a young boy ensnared by a Martian's tentacles. In the background, tripods stomped through the burning ruins of a town. Big yellow words read, "Don't let this happen again! Enlist today!"

"Twenty-six years, Beatrice." Patton's shoulders sagged. "It's been twenty-six years since they almost wiped us out. Yet for some people, it's like ancient history. They have no idea what it was like."

Images of the charred rubble that had been his hometown flashed through his mind. He swallowed, remembering his parents pulling him by the hand through streets and hills, screaming people fleeing around them. He recalled the sight of tripods on the horizon, the orange hue in the night sky caused by the fires from Los Angeles. His jaw clenched, thinking of all the friends and relatives slaughtered by the damn Martians.

Beatrice rubbed Patton's arm. "Enough of us do remember what it was like. Let that man on the radio spew whatever nonsense he wants. People like him won't stop the rest of us from doing what needs to be done."

Patton patted her hand. "I hope you're right, dear."

They piled into the family's Buick Touring Car. The hydrogen fuel cell engine hummed to life. Patton pulled out onto the street. A breeze flowed through the open compartment. Patton glanced into the sky. His thoughts flew past the blue sky and puffy white clouds into the black of space, toward the red planet.

If I were in charge, we'd have already turned that damn world to ash. He'd heard rumors that the world's leaders were about to have another powwow to authorize the long-awaited invasion of Mars. Patton had heard similar rumors for the past five years and had yet to spill Martian blood on their miserable soil.

I'm going to have great-grandchildren by the time the damn politicians get off their asses and give the go-ahead.

Patton squeezed the wheel of his Buick, cursing the idiot presidents, prime ministers, and kings who ran the world.

Like the dunderheads at the War Department are any better. Fury surged through him as he thought about their latest rebuff of his ideas to improve the self-propelled artillery or SPAs.

Patton wound his way through the street of Anniston, Alabama, until he reached Camp Shipp. He drove past the bronze statue near the main gate, depicting artillerymen fighting a Martian tripod. It had been erected ten years ago to honor all those who died in the Battle of Anniston. Most cities and towns in the United States, and throughout the world, had some sort of memorial honoring the victims of the Martian invasion. Patton imagined a statue of himself at some army base, or better yet, West Point, honoring him as a great hero of the conquest of Mars.

If I'm still in the Army by the time we invade.

When they got home, Bea and Ruth went straight to their room, probably to avoid doing anything to anger their daddy. Beatrice put George IV in his crib while Patton went to his study, closed the door and sat down. He reached around the white, block-shaped device on his desk and flicked on the power switch. A steady hum came from the Electronic Brain Box, or "ebb." He had to wait five minutes for the damn thing to warm up. When it did, he hit Shift and one on the keyboard. His electronic address book appeared. Patton hit the down button until the hazy green bar settled on a name in the "R" section.

Dear Erwin,

I hope you are well on your side of the world. I also hope you are having better luck trying to convince your General Staff of the greater offensive capabilities of tracked armored vehicles than I am. Once again, I submitted a report to our War Department on how tracked vehicles, armed with a 37mm gun and two to four machine guns, can work in conjunction with battlewalkers in any offensive operations. This time, I felt I had recent history on my side. I cited thirty incidents from the Russian Civil War, the revolts in the Ottoman Empire, and my own experiences from the American Expedition to Mexico, which highlighted the shortcomings of battlewalkers. In all three conflicts, several walkers were lured into ambushes where the opposition dug camouflaged dynamite pits. The resulting explosions destroyed at least one leg, knocking them out of commission.

While battlewalkers carry plenty of firepower, their size makes it impossible to sneak up on an enemy. In Mexico, Pancho Villa's murdering bandits usually found a place to hide until our battlewalkers passed by, then ambushed our infantry and skedaddled before the walkers returned.

Patton stopped typing, the memories of bloodied American soldiers fueling his anger. Even more enraging was the fact after three years, the Army never captured that fat fucking bandito.

After a couple of calming breaths, he resumed typing. *Tracked vehicles are, of course, smaller and quieter than battlewalkers. They can use the terrain to mask their movements. They can scout ahead of the walkers for potential ambushes. They can encircle the enemy, cut off routes of escape, and let the walkers smash them into a bloody mess. If we wanted to be really underhanded bastards, we could have tracked combat vehicles lie in wait and pounce on the enemy, taking him by surprise. Try doing that with a battlewalker.*

Patton's fingers hovered over the keyboard. He knew the Army read all incoming and outgoing ebb-messages. What he was about to say could land him in hot water.

He shrugged. *I've been in so much hot water in my career; I feel like a damn tea bag.*

He continued typing.

As usual, the War Department, in all its infinite wisdom, rejected my proposal. I'm starting to think this doesn't have anything to do with their slavish devotion to doctrine. I believe it's personal. They feel I'm bitter that I failed to qualify as a battlewalker crewmember, and my proposals reflect that bitterness. I won't lie. It still pisses me off I failed in battlewalker training. But when I was assigned to self-propelled artillery, I vowed to make it the best branch in the Army. That meant coming up with new tactics and equipment.

But the people in charge of the War Department, it seems, have an aversion to anything new. Hell, some of their tactics date back to our civil war sixty years ago! Maybe if they got off their fat asses and left their cushy offices and watched real soldiers in the field, they would see the potential of tracked combat vehicles. Armored troop carriers can do more than just haul around soldiers. With enough machine guns or flamethrowers, they can provide fire support for the infantry. Our SPAs can do more than lob shells. With some modifications, they can be the lead element of an advance, smashing through enemy fortifications.

Have heart, Erwin. Whenever our leaders decide to send us to Mars to finish off those ugly squids, we will have our opportunity to show those generals we are right, and they are wrong.

Take care, my friend.

Yours truly,

George S. Patton, Colonel USA

Patton hit Shift and four to send the ebb-message. He then sat back in his chair. He thought of the numerous exercises involving his 214th Self-Propelled Artillery Regiment over the past year. More munitions and supplies had been stockpiled at Camp Shipp over the past month. The base commander had also canceled all leaves. He wanted to take this as a sign that this time the order would come down to take the fight to the Martians, but he'd had those hopes dashed before.

Patton bowed his head, praying this time it would be for real. That soon, he and his men would storm Mars, cover its rust-colored soil with the blood and guts of those murdering squid bastards, and in the process, revolutionize modern warfare.

RETALIATION

THREE

"Is this some sort of joke?" Admiral of the Fleet and Supreme Allied Space Commander David Beatty held up the piece of paper before the gathered heads of state.

British Prime Minister David Lloyd George made a guttural sigh. "Unfortunately, Admiral, it is not a joke."

The lean, round-faced Beatty tightened his grip on the offensive paper. "The Russians promised us twenty divisions, five hundred battlewalkers and up to three hundred combat spaceships. What's General Secretary Stalin playing at?"

"According to him, the Georgians are raising a bit of a fuss. He sees it as a threat to his rule."

The muscles in Beatty's face tightened as his anger grew hotter. "Is this more of their civil war rubbish? I thought that was over." Given what the Red Army and the Cheka secret police had done over the past six years, he was surprised there was anyone left to challenge the Communist rule in Russia, or the Soviet Union as they now called it.

"I assumed it was over, too," said Lloyd George. "Apparently, Stalin and the Georgians have other ideas."

Beatty glared at the paper in his hand. He had to read it two times before he could believe it. "Five hundred troops, two walkers and three space corvettes. No artillery, no space dreadnoughts, no spaceplane transporters. Belgium and The Netherlands are contributing more forces than this. Does Stalin truly need all those soldiers and walkers to put down a potential rebellion?"

"The man's paranoid," said a distinguished gray-haired American two seats down from George. "He sees enemies everywhere. He doesn't like to fly, which is why he never comes up here to Moon Base Alpha."

Beatty held back a snort of frustration, staring up at the domed ceiling of the conference room. President Leonard Wood was spot on about Stalin. The man only participated in these meetings of the Supreme Council of the Allied Space Expeditionary Force, or ASEF, through live ebb-messaging.

Except for today.

Unfortunate, thought Beatty. *Then I could give the crazy bounder what for.*

"Lenin was no prize, that's for certain," said Wood. "But at least he recognized the threat the Martians pose, even during his civil war. But Stalin? The only thing that matters to that man is staying in power."

French President Andre Maginot, Kaiser Wilhelm II of Germany, and Emperor Maximilian I of Austria-Hungary all nodded. Beatty gave his own slight nod, cursing the fatal stroke that befell Lenin earlier this year.

Now his death could jeopardize everything. He'd worked so hard, got himself in the good graces of the "right people," and dug in his heels against dunderheads in the government and military until he got his way to reach this point in his career. Now, on the verge of his greatest triumph, some Communist pillock was about to muck it up.

"My plan calls for the Russians to annihilate the cities in the Arcadia Plain. I can't accomplish that with five hundred of their soldiers and two walkers."

"I think that's painfully obvious, Admiral," stated Lloyd George.

"Then press Stalin." Beatty flung his arms out to the sides. "I need his full force for Operation Overlord to succeed."

"You think we have not tried?" groused Maginot. "We have pleaded with the man to put humanity's best interest ahead of his own. But he is unwavering." The French president grunted. "Stalin is more stubborn than you, Admiral."

"Then try harder." An edge crept into Beatty's tone.

Maginot sat up straighter. His oval-shaped face lit up in shock. He leaned forward, mouth opening.

Beatty glared at the Frenchman. If the president wanted to have a go at it, he'd oblige. It wouldn't be the first time he'd had a row with Maginot or any of the other leaders on the ASEF Supreme Council.

"Come now." Lloyd George held up a hand. "Let's just pause for breath."

Maginot looked at him, then settled back in his chair, a sour look on his face.

Beatty, though, went on the attack. "Gentlemen, we have been dreaming of this day, preparing for it for twenty-six years. The day when we take the fight to Mars and avenge the millions slaughtered by those bloody squids. We finally have enough ships and men for a full-scale invasion. We're four weeks away from launch, or we were until that buffoon in Russia ruined everything. This will set Overlord back a year, possibly two." Beatty said. "The world's nations will have to commit more troops, and build more warships and transport ships, to make up for the Russians reneging on their promise."

The leaders on the dais all looked to one another. Concern spread across their faces. Beatty furrowed his brow, wondering what could be going on.

Kaiser Wilhelm II leaned forward. "I am sorry, Herr Admiral, but that is simply not possible."

"I'm sorry, Your Excellency, but it is. We just don't have the troop strength now to invade Mars."

The German Emperor folded his hands. "It has been twenty-six years since the Martians nearly destroyed mankind. Twenty-six years. It is a very long time, correct?"

"Yes, Excellency." Beatty nodded, wondering where Wilhelm was going with this.

"It took us many years to rebuild our nations. It also took many years to learn the Martians technology and duplicate it for our own purposes. Then we needed more time to build up a military force large enough to invade Mars. In all that time, an entire generation had grown up without knowing firsthand what it was like when the Martians attacked us."

"I'm sure they have some idea," said Beatty. "They've heard stories from friends or relatives, learned about it in school, heard radio plays or seen films about it."

"Stories are a lot different than actually experiencing it," said President Wood. "We keep warning people that the Martians may strike again. We play up that fact every time a Martian probe or shuttle is detected. But with twenty-six years gone by without another Martian attack, how long will it be before those who didn't experience the invasion themselves think the Martians pose no threat? They'll think we're wasting money to build up our militaries."

"It is true," declared Maximilian I. "There are those in my empire, influenced by communists from Russia no doubt, that claim the Martians will never dare attack Earth again. They demand that we stop spending so much on our military and instead give more money to our poorer citizens for food and shelter. What makes this troubling is that these subversive elements are growing in number."

"That is the case in almost every nation," said Lloyd George. "Several colleges in the US have become breeding grounds for this anti-military movement."

Beatty nodded. He'd heard such grumblings from people in his native Britain. Even that famous writer chap, Wells, had said the government kept trumpeting the threat of a second Martian invasion as an excuse to expand the Empire beyond the stars.

You'd think he'd know better, having lived through that hell.

"What concerns us," Lloyd George continued, "is that in a few years, such people may achieve positions of power. When that happens, they will most certainly scale down our militaries and ignore Mars entirely. Many on the Supreme Council believe this is what the Martians want, for us to grow complacent and weak before they attempt a second go-round to end us."

"We must strike now." Wilhelm II thumped his fist on the table. "In another month, Mars will be closer to Earth than it has been in decades. The Overlord fleet will only require six days to cross the gulf of space and reach Mars. Our forces are sufficient for this operation. The survivors of the invasion have waited much too long for retaliation."

Beatty gazed at the Kaiser for several seconds, then looked at the other leaders. All of them had their own horror stories from the invasion. He was sure they all craved vengeance against the squid-like aliens.

Hell, he wanted vengeance. Beatty still got a lump in his throat whenever he recalled the Martian tripods destroying his entire gunboat flotilla in the Sudan. To this day, he considered it a miracle he'd survived the battle. Most of the men under him had not.

Lifting his chin, he said to the Supreme Council, "You wish to go forth with Operation Overlord, even with the Russians' participation now almost non-existent?"

"I don't think we have a choice, Admiral." Lloyd George gave him a supportive smile. "I'm sure you can find a way to make it work."

"Yes, Prime Minister," he replied, trying to hide his frustration.

He prayed to the Good Lord he could make this work.

FOUR

Was ist das?

Lieutenant Colonel Erwin Rommel leaned forward in the seat of his buggy, peering out the windshield. A dozen men in brown tunics and black pants stood in the middle of the road.

"Colonel, who are those men?" asked his driver, Corporal Kreutzer. "What are they doing?"

"They are getting in our way, that's what they are doing." A scowl formed on Rommel's hawkish face as the buggy neared the group. "You'd best stop, Kreutzer. We should find out what they want before we run them over."

"Jawohl, Herr Oberstleutnant."

The buggy came to a halt. Rommel checked over his shoulder. The rest of his self-propelled artillery regiment slowed to a stop. He got out of the tracked, bathtub-like vehicle and strode up to the nearest SPA. A stout, stone-faced man leaned over the side of the open compartment.

"Is there a problem, *Mein Herr?*"

"Perhaps," Rommel said to Sergeant Reimer. "There is a group of men blocking the road ahead of us. Have your crew break out their personal weapons and accompany me."

"Jawohl, Herr Oberstleutnant."

Reimer, along with the SPA's driver, gunner, and loader, jumped out of the vehicle, all clutching stubby MP-18 submachine guns. They walked with Rommel, who kept his hand close by the holster containing his Luger.

The brown-shirted men made no threatening gestures. It made Rommel wonder if they might be part of the anti-war movement. Their numbers had been growing over the years. Most of their activities were confined to protests or ebb-messaging campaigns. Sometimes, though, they blocked the entrances to military bases or covered recruitment posters with ones of their own, urging negotiations with the Martians.

The thought made Rommel's blood burn. He'd only been six when the Martians came. Still, he had vivid memories of the cities and villages of his native kingdom of Wurttemberg burned to the ground by alien heat rays. Men, women, and children had been turned into human matchsticks right before his eyes. His uncle Dietrich and cousins Luisa and Wolfgang lost their lives, and his aunt Bettina still bore the scars of the invasion.

Never once did he hear about the Martians attempting to negotiate with any human.

They can burn in hell. He'd see to it personally.

As soon as these fools got out of the way.

Rommel approached the apparent leader of the group. The man was similar to him in height, around five-foot-eight, with black hair combed predominantly to the left side and a small mustache.

"Are you in charge of these men?"

"I am," barked the dark-haired man. "Adolf Hitler, Chairman of the Nationalist Party."

Rommel had never heard of any Nationalist Party or of an Adolf Hitler. He regarded the men before him. They didn't have the look of anti-war advocates. For one, they all appeared old enough to have lived through the invasion. Most in the anti-war movement had been born after 1898. He also noted Hitler's eyes. They were dark and fiery. Rommel got the sense this was a man not afraid to use violence to achieve his goals.

He moved his hand closer to his Luger. "I am Lieutenant Colonel Erwin Rommel. You are impeding the movement of a regiment of the Imperial German Army. I order you to move off this --"

"We will not move!" Hitler screamed and practically lunged at Rommel. Reimer and his men brought up their submachine guns.

Hitler ignored the weapons. "We have heard the rumors. You are going to Mars. We cannot, we will not allow this."

Rommel fought to keep from frowning. ASEF had tried to keep Operation Overlord a secret. That proved difficult with so many troops, combat vehicles, and ships on the move.

"Since you do not rule Germany, Herr Hitler, you have no authority to tell us what we can or cannot do. Now I will ask you one last time to—"

"You will leave us to the mercy of the Jews!"

A bewildered look formed on Rommel's face. *What the hell is he talking about?*

"You are blind to the truth! The Martians are merely puppets of the Jews. While those monsters were destroying our cities, the Jews crawled into the underground like the rats they are. That is where they built their secret cities and raised their secret armies to reclaim the surface world once the Martians wiped out the human race."

Rommel drew his head back, stunned. Never in his life had he heard such mad ramblings.

Hitler carried on, yelling so loud the entire regiment could probably hear him. "The Jews bided their time, waiting for the day all our soldiers go to Mars!" He pointed a finger at Rommel. "But when you do, the Jews will spew forth from their sewers and take control of the world, because men like you will not be here to exterminate them!"

Rommel had had enough. "I do not have time to listen to your insanity. You will move aside and allow our regiment to pass, or we will detain you until we reach Osnabruck, then turn you over to the police."

"We will not move!" raged Hitler. "You will stay on Earth to deal with the Jews and their secret army!"

Rommel glared at Hitler. He then turned to the SPA crew behind him. "Sergeant Reimer. Go back and assemble more men to—"

A crazed scream erupted behind him. Something slammed into Rommel's back. The air exploded from his lungs. He fell to the asphalt.

"Stop them!" Hitler screamed. "Smash their vehicles! Do not let them pass!"

Footfalls pounded all around Rommel. He squirmed and thrashed, trying to throw Hitler off his back. A fist grazed the top of his head. Rommel glimpsed Hitler's hand passing over his right ear. He reached up and grabbed the lunatic's wrist. Rommel gritted his teeth. He squeezed and twisted with all his strength.

Hitler cried out in pain.

Rommel rolled to the right, throwing the madman off his back. He sprang to his feet. Brownshirts wrestled with Reimer's gunner and driver. Reimer and his loader swung their submachine guns. Hard wooden butts cracked against human skulls. Several soldiers jumped out of their vehicles and rushed toward the melee.

A roar of fury caught Rommel's attention. He turned to see Hitler charge him.

Rommel stood his ground and balled up his right hand. Hitler screamed louder. He drew back a fist.

Rommel punched him in the gut. Hitler doubled over. He gasped for air and collapsed to his knees.

A submachine gun chattered. Rommel dropped to the ground and looked around.

Sergeant Reimer fired another burst into the air. "Down!" he shouted. "Down on the ground or I'll kill you all!"

The brownshirts got on their knees, hands in the air, fear on their faces.

"Are you all right, *Mein Herr*?" Kreutzer hurried over to Rommel.

"*Ja, ja*, I'm fine." He dusted himself off and marched over to Hitler, who was still gasping for air. Rommel grabbed him by the collar and yanked him to his feet.

"You just assaulted an officer of the Imperial German Army. That will earn you a very long stay in prison."

He ordered Hitler and his followers tied up and put in separate transports, under guard. Five minutes later, the regiment was on the move again.

When they finally reached Osnabruck, hundreds of people lined the streets, cheering and waving black, white and red German flags. A few times he could make out individual shouts.

"Kill the Martians."

"Burn their cities!"

"Wipe them out!"

Rommel pressed his back into the buggy's passenger seat. So much for keeping this a secret. But then, he didn't see how that could be possible since Osnabruck hosted one of the largest spaceports in the German Empire. Someone at the base likely let slip what they were doing, damn them.

He spotted a policeman directing traffic at one of the city's intersections. When Rommel explained to him what had happened with Hitler and his Nationalist Party idiots, the policeman went over to a phone box mounted on a nearby light post. Several minutes later, a pair of boxy transports with the word *"Polizei"* emblazoned on their sides arrived.

"You stupid bastards!" Hitler shouted as two policemen pushed him into one of the transports. "You've condemned us to enslavement by the Jews!"

Rommel ignored him and climbed back inside his buggy. He checked his watch and scowled. They were fifteen minutes behind schedule thanks to that fool with the stupid mustache.

When the regiment reached the gates of the Osnabruck Space Forces Base, a portly senior sergeant ambled over to them. He looked old enough to have fought during the 1898 invasion.

"What is your unit, *Mein Herr*?" asked the sergeant.

"The Twelfth Schaumburg-Lippe Self-Propelled Artillery Regiment."

The unsmiling sergeant checked his clipboard. "This regiment was to have arrived seventeen minutes ago."

"You can thank a group of escaped mental patients for the delay."

The sergeant regarded Rommel in silence for a few moments. He then looked back at his clipboard. "The Twelfth Schaumburg-Lippe Self-Propelled Artillery Regiment has been assigned to the space troop landing ship Gothensee. She is located at Dock 51. Proceed straight for the next two kilometers, then turn right. There will be directors to guide you to your ship."

"*Danke*, Sergeant."

"*Mein Herr.*" The sergeant saluted Rommel. He returned it, then ordered Kreutzer to drive on.

The SPA regiment hummed along the road, turning right at the appropriate point. From there, soldiers waving flags directed them toward the space docks. Rommel noticed most of them were women. Germany, like many other nations, utilized female soldiers in support roles, freeing up more men for combat units.

Rommel's regiment joined the flow of many other vehicles. He mused how they looked like ant columns, all moving toward enormous, breadbox-shaped vessels. Tingles raced up and down his body.

We're really doing it. We're really going to Mars.

The vehicles of the 12th Schaumburg-Lippe SPA Regiment drove up the rear ramp of the Gothensee and into the cavernous cargo hold. Members of the ship's crew lashed them to the deck with chains. A fair-haired spaceman who couldn't be older than eighteen led the soldiers to their quarters. As a senior officer, Rommel rated his own cabin. The junior officers would bunk three or four to a cabin, while the non-commissioned and enlisted ranks, as usual, got stuffed into a hold like sardines.

Hands behind his back, Rommel stared out the porthole. Transports, armored troop carriers, self-propelled artillery, and buggies made their way into other landing ships. He paid particular attention to the SPAs. It brought to mind the ebb-message he received a few weeks ago from his friend, George Patton, on making SPAs a viable fighting vehicle. The American had many good points but neglected one key element. The gun could only go up and down. If you wanted to fire in another direction, you had to turn the entire vehicle. That would be impractical in the close-in fighting he and Patton envisioned. Rommel felt that problem could be remedied by putting the gun on a turret, similar to a battleship or cruiser. But when he presented this idea to the German General Staff, they regarded him similarly to the way he had regarded Adolf Hitler.

What do they know?

He hoped George was right, that Mars would provide them the opportunity to prove their theories on armored warfare.

Two hours had passed when a voice blared from the *Gothensee*'s loudspeakers, "*Achtung! Achtung!* All personnel are to secure themselves in preparation for liftoff. Liftoff to take place in twenty minutes."

Rommel groaned. He'd always hated this part of space travel.

He dug into his knapsack and pulled out his g-suit. It took a couple of minutes to strip out of his fatigues and put on the gray, one-piece uniform. He then sat in the chair at the plain metal desk, both of which were bolted to the deck, and strapped himself in.

Nothing to do now but wait.

"*Achtung! Achtung!*" the loudspeakers blared. "One minute until liftoff. Repeat, one minute until liftoff."

Rommel tensed, his hands clenching the armrests.

The ship's fusion engines rumbled, growing louder every second.

"Five . . . four . . . three . . . two . . . one. Liftoff!"

A noise like a hundred thunderstorms surrounded Rommel. Giant, invisible hands pressed down on him as *Gothensee* rose higher and higher.

It seemed like forever before he took his next breath. By that time, he felt lighter than air. The ship had passed beyond Earth's atmosphere.

He relaxed and undid his straps. A smile spread across Rommel's face as he floated out of his chair. He reached out to the ceiling, pushed off, and corkscrewed in mid-air. He let out a chuckle. Amazing how weightlessness could make one feel like a child.

Not that he had had much of a childhood, thanks to the Martians.

Sighing, Rommel pushed off the bulkhead and headed for the hatch. He opened it and floated into the bland, steel corridor. Several other soldiers also made their way down the corridor, using handrails mounted on the bulkhead to pull themselves along. Rommel figured they were headed to the same place as him.

A retching sound came from behind him. It was followed seconds later by another one. Rommel felt a bit of sympathy for the poor soldiers. He, too, had thrown up his first time in zero gravity. Luckily, he had grown used to it. Some soldiers never did.

Rommel floated up a companionway and found himself facing a brown, chunky substance hanging in the air. His nose wrinkled at the stale odor it emitted.

Someone had not reached his vomit bag in time.

Now Rommel felt nauseous. He managed to calm his stomach by the time he reached the observation deck.

Men crowded around the long window, oohing and aahing. Rommel's eyes widened, overwhelmed by what he saw. He'd been in space many times before for zero gravity training or combat exercises on the Moon. Still, the sight of the blue and white orb of Earth hanging in space never failed to amaze him.

He floated closer to the window. Many of the soldiers gaped at the Earth in silence. Others made comments like, "They'll never threaten it again," or, "Let's see how the Martians like having their cities destroyed."

Rommel passed a sergeant who held a grainy photograph of a plump, dark-haired woman in his palm. Tears glistened in his eyes. "This is for you, *Mutti*. I will avenge you."

Rommel wanted to tell the sergeant, "Yes, you will avenge her," but decided to leave the man to his thoughts. Instead, he looked back at the Earth, thinking of the losses to his own family. His uncle, his cousins, and in some ways, his aunt, too. She had been confined to a mental asylum for the past twenty-five years. Ravaged by time and insanity, his withered Aunt Bettina spent her days looking out the window, whispering to herself, "They're coming back. They're coming back."

Rommel's face tightened in a determined look. *No, they won't.*

FIVE

Arms folded, Admiral Beatty stared at the large screen mounted on the front bulkhead of HMSS *King Edward VII*'s Battle Management Compartment. Thousands of electronically generated dots merged into several green blobs. The sight of so many ships made him shudder in awe.

This is really happening.

"United States Space Forces Task Force 44 arriving," announced the combat coordination officer from a console to Beatty's right. "Royal Australian Space Forces First Flotilla arriving."

More green dots popped up on the screen. The blobs expanded in size.

Will it all be enough? Beatty clenched his jaw. He cursed the worry that had nagged him since that meeting with the ASEF Supreme Council a month ago. He'd altered Operation Overlord best he could, tried to believe the desire for revenge by the soldiers and spacemen in the armada would make up for the lack of Soviet participation.

It had to. He'd be damned if he would go down in history as the man who oversaw humanity's defeat on Mars.

"Astro-Hungarian First Space Battle Group arriving," said the combat coordination officer, a short, stocky lieutenant named Porter. "French Space Forces Sixth Fleet arriving."

More dots flickered across the screen.

Beatty caught movement out the corner of his eye. A portly man with receding black hair appeared at his side.

"Impressive, isn't it?" said Matthew Gibbons, the space dreadnought's captain.

"It would be even more impressive with the Soviets here," Beatty grumbled.

Gibbons cocked his head to the side. "Perhaps. But look how their forces fared against the Japanese a few years back. Not very impressive. I don't think we'll miss them much on Mars."

Beatty chuckled. He had known Gibbons for years. A man after his own heart, the captain was a man of good humor who eschewed the rigid discipline of the Royal Navy and Royal Space Forces and was not afraid to exercise initiative. Gibbons proved this as a young midshipman during the Martian invasion. His battleship, HMS *Repulse*, had bombarded enemy tripods along the coast of Dublin when a volley of heat rays severely damaged the vessel and killed most of the officers. Gibbons took command and used the ship's remaining battery to destroy a tripod before *Repulse* went under. He had been one of just twenty men to survive.

That was the sort of man Beatty wanted in command of his flagship.

"Perhaps you're right." Beatty turned to Gibbons. "Still, always nice to have numbers on your side."

"You'd think the other ASEF countries would scrape up some more ships and soldiers to make up the deficit."

"I did put in such a request, but the Council wants to have some of our forces Earthside in case the Martians attempt a counter-attack." Beatty sighed, his shoulders sagging. "Plus we also have to worry about potential human adversaries. Some on the Council worry the Russians, Japanese, or Ottomans might take advantage of Operation Overlord to attack their neighbors."

"British Royal Space Forces Third Fleet arriving," announced Porter. "Royal Canadian Space Forces Second Flotilla arriving."

Beatty shook his head. "Remember the years after the invasion?" he asked Gibbons. "All those articles in *The Times* and other newspapers about how the invasion would bring mankind together? It was the talk of many a party my wife and I attended. No more countries or borders, just one, united Earth. I guess we know the truth now, Captain. That was sheer fallacy."

"Yes, sir." Gibbons nodded. "Hard to change human nature. For chaps like Stalin, maintaining their hold on power is real. Another invasion by monsters who haven't set foot on Earth in over twenty years, not so much."

"Well, if they do come again, Stalin won't have any power, will he?" Beatty gave a dismissive wave. "To hell with him. The man belongs in an asylum with the other loons." He thought of the Georgians who were rebelling against Moscow, forcing Stalin to keep most of his forces on Earth.

A pox on both their houses. Beatty scowled, hoping both sides bloodied one another. Served them right for putting their selfish needs ahead of the good of mankind.

"Soviet Space Forces Two Hundred Twenty-Second Squadron arriving," said Porter.

"So nice of them to join us." Beatty glared at the dots on the ebb screen representing the tiny Russian space squadron. He thought about how much he had to change Operation Overlord because of Stalin's paranoia. He couldn't reallocate enough forces to adequately secure the Arcadia Plain, which was to have been the Russians' area of responsibility. The best he could do was shift some dreadnoughts, spaceplane transporters, and escort vessels to bombard the area. Still, even the most effective bombardment wouldn't annihilate all the Martians and their machines in the Arcadia Plain. There'd be plenty for human ground troops to contend with when they marched in there.

In addition, intelligence reported quite a bit of activity there over the past year and a half. Their analysis—*more like a guess, really*—was that the Martians had underground weapons factories in that region. Beatty didn't like neglecting what could be a vital enemy installation, but Prime Minister Lloyd George told him to "make it work." He had to do the best he could with what he had, and pray it didn't come back to bite him and the rest of the ASEF in the bum.

"Imperial German Space Forces Fourth Fleet arriving . . . Italian Royal Space Forces Second Fleet arriving." Lieutenant Porter turned to Beatty. "Sir, I can now report the entire Allied space fleet has assembled."

"Thank you, Lieutenant." He pronounced it "leftenant." Beatty took a seat and strapped himself in. "Alert the rest of the First Fleet. Tell them we lift off in five minutes."

"Yes, sir."

Beatty continued to eye the screen with its thousands and thousands of dots, each one representing a ship. So many of them.

Would it be enough to take Mars?

King Edward VII's fusion engines roared to life. The space dreadnought, and the other ships of the Royal Space Forces First Fleet, rose from the docks of Moon Base Alpha.

Beatty gripped his armrests, excitement and dread dueling for control of his soul. Six days from now, they would be in Mars orbit.

RETALIATION

SIX

Hashzh never believed he would witness a scene such as this.

The Guiding Council, who had ruled Shoh with their great wisdom for hundreds of cycles, now devolved into frantic ramblings.

"How could the Brohv'ii have done this?" Councilor Rezdv's tentacles flailed. "They are primitive, unenlightened. They could not have possibly built so many spaceships."

"The Brohv'ii ships are certain to have defects," proclaimed Councilor Ehjah. "They will fail, and thus, never reach Mars."

Hashzh did not know whether to be angry with Rezdv and Ehjah or to pity them. How terrified of the uprights must the two councilors be to make them deny reality?

"It is useless to debate what is fact," said Councilor Dvemt, who in Hashzh's opinion was the only rational member of the Guiding Council. "The Brohv'ii are coming to Shoh."

"And they will bring their diseases with them." Councilor Yrvul spoke in a rapid, panicked tone. "They need no beam weapons or missiles. All they need to do is open their mouths and exhale, and they can exterminate us."

"The humans will not be able to do that," said Hashzh. "Our atmosphere has less nitrogen and oxygen than theirs. They will have as much difficulty breathing the air of Shoh as the Cleansing Force had breathing the air of Brohv. Much of the surface of our planet is colder than the Brohv'ii can tolerate. They will need environmental protection suits to survive."

"Surely some of the Brohv'ii will gladly sacrifice themselves to kill us off."

Hashzh had to admit Yrvul's argument had merit. The Cleansing Force had reported several acts of self-sacrifice among the Brohv'ii, especially in the Ottoman and Japanese Empires. It was not implausible to think a few uprights would shed their protective suits to spread their deadly germs throughout the population.

"We shall distribute protection suits to all Shoh'hau," suggested Supreme Councilor Frtun, who lay on the center mat of the large, tubular Hall of the Guiding Council.

"Supreme Councilor," said Dvemt. "There are not enough suits to give to every Shoh'hau."

"Then we shall inform them to stay in their dwellings in the event of a Brohv'ii invasion. They must inspect their dwellings for any openings and seal them." Frtun paused. "We must also hasten our selection process for the Final Project."

"The Final Project is not anticipated to be ready for another fourth of a cycle," Yrvul pointed out. "The Brohv'ii will be here well before then. Supreme Guardian Hashzh, you must dispatch every warship available to intercept the enemy fleet and destroy it."

"Councilor Yrvul, we do not have enough warships to destroy all the Brohv'ii ships. Our fleet will be vastly outnumbered." *All because you would not allocate the necessary resources to the Guard Force to construct more ships.* Hashzh wanted to say that aloud, but no matter how furious he was at the Guiding Council, such disrespect was inconceivable.

"What does that matter?" Rezdv blurted. "Our technology is superior to the Brohv'ii. We can defeat them."

"The Brohv'ii are much more advanced than they were thirteen cycles ago when the Cleansing Force was sent to their planet," Hashzh pointed out. "They will overwhelm our fleet with sheer numbers. We cannot defeat them in space. At most, we can slow their transit to Shoh."

"Then slow them," ordered Frtun. "We must have more time to complete The Final Project."

"You must also send the entire Guard Force to protect the Final Project," Yrvul told Hashzh.

The Supreme Guardian kept his tentacles from trembling in anger. "Councilor Yrvul, if the Brohv'ii adopt the same strategy as the Cleansing Force, they will not land in one region. They will strike all our large cities at once. They, too, must be defended."

"The Final Project must be defended at all costs!" Yrvul's tentacles rose above him.

"It is well defended, I assure you." The words shot from Hashzh's mouth. He wearied of Yrvul's state of fear. "Many of our tripods and guardians are positioned underground. If we position all our forces around the Final Project, the Brohv'ii will know something important is there. That is where they will concentrate their forces. Even if the Guard Force is successful in repelling the enemy, the Final Project could sustain damage, perhaps irreparable damage. The majority of our forces positioned there should stay hidden from view. The rest of the Guard Force must be spread throughout Shoh to wear down the Brohv'ii and ultimately defeat them. That will give us the time needed to complete the Final Project."

The Guiding Council said nothing. They all looked to one another. Supreme Councilor Frtun pushed himself up as high as his tentacles would allow and gazed at the other Councilors. "I approve of Supreme Guardian Hashzh's recommendation. What say the rest of the Guiding Council?"

Yrvul and Ehjah dissented, with Ehjah adding, "The Brohv'ii ships will not reach Shoh. They will malfunction."

Hashzh left the Hall of the Guiding Council immensely satisfied. Frtun and the others could actually use their intelligence, though only when the threat was rocketing across the gulf of space toward them. Ehjah, though, proved to be the exception. That concerned him. A few Shoh'hau had been so shocked by the annihilation of the Cleansing Force their brains, for want of a better term, malfunctioned. He sensed the same thing happening to Councilor Ehjah. If true, he would have to suffer the fate of the others with brain malfunctions. Death. There was no place in Shoh'hau society for those who could not use their intellect.

Hashzh would welcome Ehjah's death. Then another Shoh'hau, one more intelligent, without any brain malfunctions, would replace him. The Guiding Council would be stronger and better able to deal with the coming Brohv'ii invasion.

Hashzh took an underground transport tube back to his headquarters. When he entered his chamber, he called for Givrht. The Guard Commander Third Order soon appeared.

"The Brohv'ii fleet will reach Shoh in a few rotations," said Hashzh. "Gather all the engineers and resources you are able to, then depart for *our* Final Project. Complete it quickly. If you have to work the crews to death, do so."

"I will, Supreme Guardian. If I may, I wish to bring a concern to your attention."

"You may."

"My subordinates have reported that while our guardians are diligently preparing for the Brohv'ii invasion, many are expressing fears of succumbing to the same diseases that killed our Cleansing Force."

"The Guiding Council also expressed the same fears. I believe those fears to be warranted. But know this, Guard Commander Givrht. Should the Brohv'ii eradicate our race, it will be your duty to make sure they all perish as well."

RETALIATION

SEVEN

"Finally, we're prepared for you." A grin slowly formed on Admiral Beatty's face. He leaned back in his chair, staring at the large ebb screen in *King Edward VII*'s battle management center, heart pumping quicker as the four hundred sixty dots representing the Martian fleet closed with the ASEF ships. This would not be like the slaughter of his gunboat fleet in the Sudan. This time, they'd fight the bloody squids on equal footing.

Fight and win. Beatty closed his eyes. The faces of the young lads from his gunboats floated through his mind. A slight shudder went through him as he recalled the heat of the explosions, the screams of the wounded, the sight of men vaporized.

A lump formed in Beatty's throat. *I'll make them pay. I swear it to all of you.*

"They're splitting up." Captain Gibbons pointed at the screen. "Looks as though they're sending most of their bigger ships to hit our flanks."

Beatty nodded, watching large groups of dots break off and make for different parts of the ASEF fleet.

"Lieutenant Porter," he said to the combat coordination officer. "Have US Task Force 44 and the German Eighth Fleet reinforce our left flank. The British Third Fleet and French Sixth Fleet will reinforce the right flank. US Task Force 34, the Brazilian First Fleet, and the Norwegian Third Flotilla will reinforce our rear."

"Aye, sir." Porter repeated the order to the appropriate fleet commanders.

"Also," Beatty held up a finger, "move up the Canadian Second Flotilla, the Spanish First Fleet, and the Italian Second Fleet to protect the transports and support ships."

"Aye, sir." Porter relayed that order as well.

Anticipation grew within Beatty. He yearned to give the order to fire. He looked around the BMC, thought of the thousands of human ships at his command, all built from the technology the Martian invaders left behind when they died.

Technology about to be turned against you monsters. Oh, the delicious irony. Perhaps he'd pen a poem about it one day.

"Lower projection screens. I want complete 360-degree coverage of the battle area."

"Aye, sir," replied Porter. "Lowering projection screens."

Four large gray screens, similar to those found in a cinema, descended from the ceiling, two on each side of the ebb screen. Images transmitted by four ASEF space corvettes appeared, each one showing a multitude of allied ships spread out across the blackness of space. Before long, the moving picture cameras spotted the cylinder ships of the approaching Martian fleet.

Beatty's eyes flickered between the ebb screen and the image from the British corvette HMSS *Pegasus*, which covered the front of the ASEF fleet. More than a hundred Martian ships headed straight toward them.

He reached out for the console, switched on his radio, and grasped the steel, circular-shaped microphone. "All forward fleet elements, line up behind your flagships. On my mark, turn to starboard, and bring all guns to bear on the enemy."

Beatty watched the various allied ships maneuver into compact formations of parallel lines. He drew a slow breath, watching the two fleets close, almost in firing range.

Almost . . .

"All forward fleet elements," Beatty said. "Hard to starboard, ninety degrees. Bring all guns and rocket launchers to bear."

Beatty felt the maneuvering thrusters kick in, nudging *King Edward VII* to starboard. The other ships followed right behind his flagship. They formed a long line in front of the Martian fleet, "crossing the T," a tactic used to great effect by Japan in its war with Russia in 1911. Beatty hoped it would be just as effective in space warfare as it was at sea.

"New contacts!" Porter hollered. "Numerous small contacts around the forward element of the Martian fleet."

"What are those buggers playing at?" Gibbons stared at the ebb screen.

Beatty watched as tiny dots, like a swarm of gnats, formed around the Martian ships.

"Readout from the ebb identifies new contacts as shuttles," Porter reported.

A puzzled look came over Gibbons's face. "Why would they use shuttles against us? Boarding parties?"

Beatty shook his head. "Can't be. Not practical in a zero gravity environment, especially with their bodies."

He straightened in his seat when the realization hit him. "They're armed."

Anger flashed through him. Curse the damn intelligence people. They always maintained Martian shuttles were only used for transport and reconnaissance.

Maybe if those arrogant fools worked a bit harder . . .

Beatty grunted. Being angry wouldn't change their situation. He reached out for his microphone. "All corvettes, concentrate your fire on the Martian shuttles. Cruisers and dreadnoughts, concentrate fire on the larger vessels."

He checked the picture from the *Pegasus*. A mass of small, oblong craft with stubby wings streaked toward the ASEF fleet. Nervousness slithered through Beatty. There were so many of them, and so small. Could they prevent everyone from slipping through to attack the transports and support ships?

Beatty clenched the microphone. "All ships . . . open fire!"

More than a hundred beams of light flashed across the projection screen. Balls of light burst and faded as dozens of shuttles exploded. More beams reached out to the bigger Martian ships. Several of them vanished in brilliant fireballs.

The Martians returned fire. The image from *Pegasus* filled with countless beams slicing through the black void. A rumble and shudder went through *King Edward VII*. Beatty's muscles tightened. He flashed back to the Sudan.

"Impact portside, aft," stated the ship's systems analyst, Petty Officer Douglas. "Damage is superficial. No loss of hull integrity."

Beatty's muscles unwound ever so slightly. He thanked God for the dreadnought's thick armor.

Heat beams and missiles filled space. Explosions flared non-stop.

"Four shuttles on an intercept course with us," reported Porter.

"Target them with secondary batteries," ordered Captain Gibbons. "Main Guns One and Two, target large Martian cruiser, coordinates zero three five, range one hundred ten kilometers."

Pencil-thin beams shot from *King Edward VII*'s smaller ray guns just beneath the superstructure. One shuttle exploded. Then another. The remaining two fired their heat rays. Beatty barely felt the jolts from their impact. Those ray guns had less punch than the ones carried by the Martian tripods and cruisers.

At least against a space dreadnought. Corvettes and transports had much weaker armor.

A flurry of beams lashed out at the remaining two shuttles. Both exploded. A bright flash erupted further away. Beatty watched a Martian cruiser slew to port, its entire fore section ripped away.

"Main Guns One and Two, hit that cruiser again," Gibbons ordered. "Finish it off."

Heat rays streaked from *King Edward VII*. Both struck the wounded Martian cruiser. It vanished in a ball of white light.

Beatty checked the other screens. Beams and missiles crisscrossed between the ASEF and Martian ships on the flanks. Here and there little suns winked in an out of existence.

Shuttles soared around the ASEF ships at the front of the fleet. A rain of heat rays fell onto dreadnoughts, cruisers, and corvettes. Beatty tensed as he watched two of his ships flare and disappear.

"Corvettes *Ariadne* and *Medusa* destroyed," stated Porter. "American cruiser *Atlanta* damaged."

More quakes rocked *King Edward VII*. The straps dug into Beatty's torso, keeping him in his seat.

"Damage to Decks Four and Five," Douglas said. "Damage control parties responding."

The flurry of beams and missiles never let up. Martian shuttles zipped around the human ships, peppering them with their heat rays. The cruisers HMSS *Bedford* and USSS *Independence* fell out of line, gaping holes in their sides. The corvette HMSS *Argonaut* exploded. More beams slashed through space at the Martian shuttles. Several vanished in flashes of light.

More poured through a gap in the ASEF line.

Beatty held his breath. He checked the armada's inner defensive ring, then grabbed the microphone. "German cruisers *Konigsberg* and *Emden*. Move up and plug the gap between British ships *Minotaur* and *Good Hope*."

He watched the two German vessels rush toward the gap. Heat rays and missiles burst from their launchers. A few Martian shuttles exploded. Others flew on, firing at the Germans. Beatty cringed when a bright flash erupted on the bow of the *Konigsberg*.

Dammit. Beatty pounded his fist on the armrest. *We should have armed our shuttles, too*. Better yet, they should have built jets that could operate in space instead of solely within the atmosphere.

Now ASEF might pay for that oversight.

King Edward VII's heat rays fired again. A Martian cruiser flared and disappeared. Another cruiser appeared and opened fire. Beatty grunted as a hammer blow rocked his dreadnought.

"Damage to multiple decks!" hollered Douglas. "Main Gun Turret Four destroyed."

"Severe damage to American dreadnought *Chester Arthur*," blurted Porter.

Another tremor shook *King Edward VII*. Beatty glimpsed two of their escorts firing on the Martian cruiser. Heat rays sliced into the cylindrical hull. The alien ship turned into an orb of white light.

An explosion blossomed among the Allied fleet.

"American cruiser *Albany* destroyed," Porter reported.

Beatty held his breath when he saw another flash, then another.

"French dreadnought *République* and British cruiser *Furious* destroyed."

Two more explosions appeared.

"British corvette *Erebus* and German cruiser *Seydlitz* destroyed."

Beatty looked at Lieutenant Porter, eyes narrowed. He then swiveled his chair to face *King Edward VII*'s commanding officer.

"Captain Gibbons, there seems to be something wrong with our bloody ships today."

EIGHT

I am not going to die on this blasted ship!

Unfortunately, *Commandant* Charles de Gaulle couldn't see what he could do to prevent that. Martian heat rays had taken out the bridge of the landing ship *Agadez*. That meant they had no captain, no way to steer, and no control over the vessel's limited weaponry.

The tall, narrow-faced Frenchman looked around at the soldiers in his battlewalker company, all clad in spacesuits and fishbowl-shaped helmets. Fear radiated from their faces. Even worse than fear. De Gaulle saw hopelessness in their eyes.

"Follow me!" He floated toward the troop compartment exit.

"What are we going to do, sir?" asked one of the men.

"We will not stand here and wait for the Martians to finish us, that is what!" de Gaulle snapped. "Now move!"

Many of the men turned to one another. A few nodded or clenched their fists. They propelled themselves through the air and followed de Gaulle into the corridor.

Two crew members floated toward him. He was about to stop them when he noticed one of the men clearly injured. He let them pass so they could get to sickbay.

Not that it will do them much good if the Martians blow us up, he thought maliciously.

De Gaulle pressed on. He attempted to stop three other crewmen.

"We are damage control!" shouted one of them. "We have no time for you!"

The trio moved on

Frustration boiled inside de Gaulle. He needed to talk to someone, preferably an officer, and figure out what to do to save this ship, or at the very least go down fighting.

He kept floating through the corridors, his men behind him. The klaxons blared. He tried to fight off the paranoia that any second, Martian heat rays would tear through the *Agadez* and end them.

De Gaulle turned down another corridor. He spotted a man in a spacesuit gripping a handrail and floating in place. He took off toward him.

The man was practically hyperventilating. De Gaulle took note of his young, round face. The man couldn't be more than twenty-one. His name tag read MANAVIAN, and his shoulder boards indicated he was an Ensign Second Class.

De Gaulle scowled. He finally found an officer, only to have him be the lowest ranking one on the ship, meaning he was useless.

Still . . .

"What is being done to fight the Martians?" de Gaulle demanded.

"Huh?" Manavian turned to him, his eyes wide with fear.

"Can we still use the heat ray or machine guns? Can this ship maneuver?"

Manavian's mouth opened, but he didn't speak. He kept staring at de Gaulle with that terrified gaze.

"You are useless!" De Gaulle shoved Manavian. The young ensign floated away, making no attempt to stop himself.

De Gaulle pressed a fist against his helmet and closed his eyes. He couldn't rely on anyone on this ship to help him. If he and his company were to survive, they'd have to find a way themselves.

And how do we fly a crippled spaceship and fight off Martians?

There had to be a way. All problems had solutions.

What do we have? What works?

The engines worked. They could move, but not steer. Was there a way to fix that? As for weapons . . .

De Gaulle's head snapped up. He looked back at his men. "Lieutenant Deschamps. Go to the engine room. See if they can still maneuver this ship."

"Yes, sir."

"Sergeant Giroux. Go to the observation deck. Find the nearest warship and radio its position to the engine room. We will attempt to move closer to it so its weapons can protect us."

"Yes, sir."

"The rest of you, follow me to the cargo hold."

"The cargo hold?" A quizzical look formed on the face of *Caporal-chef* Bosquier, the driver of de Gaulle's battlewalker. "Why there?"

"So that we can fight the Martians ourselves. Move!"

The men followed him toward the rear of the *Agadez*. A quake rocked the landing ship. Fear surged through de Gaulle. For a moment, he expected the *Agadez* to explode. When it didn't, he pulled himself through the corridors quicker than before.

The ship shook again as de Gaulle and his men reached the cargo hold. He looked to the right and found a small compartment used by the loadmaster. De Gaulle floated over and found a cherubic man hovering beside a bolted down desk.

"Who is in charge of the ship, then?" the man asked into a microphone.

"We are not sure," a voice came from a boxy speaker connected to the microphone. "Everyone is too busy trying to repair the damage."

"Dammit, somebody find out. We have to have a captain for this ship. Now find out who is the most senior officer alive and report back to me."

"Yes, Lieutenant."

The lieutenant clipped the microphone to the side of the speaker, then turned to de Gaulle. "What do you want . . . um, sir?"

De Gaulle glanced at the lieutenant's name tag. It read JOBERT. "I need you to open the cargo hatch."

Jobert's eyes bulged. "You what?"

"We can use the heat rays on our battlewalkers against the Martians. It is the only option we have."

"*Mon Commandant*, I don't know."

"Do it! On my order, open the hatch!"

De Gaulle turned away from Jobert. He barely heard the lieutenant say, "Yes, sir," before barking out orders to his men. His crew and another led by *Sergent-chef* Aumont would board the battlewalkers closest to the ramp. Another senior sergeant, Degats, would stand near the edge of the ramp, tethered by a safety harness, and use hand signals to alert them to approaching Martian ships. The rest of the company was sent out of the cargo hold.

De Gaulle and his men floated up to their walkers. His eyes took in the three legs ending in round feet. A metal arm with pincers protruded from each side. The pod resembled a snail's shell, with several machine guns around it and eight tubes in the rear. Mounted in the nose was the dish-shaped heat ray.

Once they reached the top, de Gaulle and his men floated into the cramped pod. He took his place as commander/heat ray gunner in the rear seat. At the horseshoe-shaped console just below him sat the driver Bosquier, and the secondary gunner, Ponge.

De Gaulle looked out the thick, wraparound windshield. When Degats was in position, he looked up and saluted. De Gaulle nodded and got on his radio.

"Lieutenant Jobert."

"Here, sir."

"Open cargo bay hatch."

There was a pause, followed by a worried-sounding, "Yes, sir."

De Gaulle drew a deep breath and held it. He heard a loud *clunk*. The hatch cracked open. A strong wind buffeted the tied-down battlewalker as the air vented into space. Several seconds passed before the walker stopped shaking.

De Gaulle stared out into the black void. A flash of light consumed a nearby troop ship. Two shattered corvettes tumbled through space. Small, oblong shapes darted back and forth.

Shuttles. So the Martians had armed their shuttles. He would applaud their cleverness if he didn't despise the ugly squids.

De Gaulle tapped a button on his console. An ebb-generated targeting scope appeared on the windshield. He narrowed his eyes on a pair of shuttles circling an ASEF support ship. He gripped the heat ray's control stick and squeezed the trigger. A yellow beam streaked from the nose of the battlewalker.

De Gaulle spat out a curse when it missed.

He fired again. So did Aumont in the other battlewalker. Both heat rays missed. The shuttles darted to the left and vanished from sight.

De Gaulle ground his teeth, the right side of his face twisting in anger. He gripped the control stick tighter and glanced at Degats. The sergeant peered around the edge of the open cargo hold. De Gaulle waited, and hoped, to see Degats signal more shuttles were coming.

No such signal came.

They will come, he thought despondently. *They have to*. He was not going to die until he killed one of those monstrosities. He owed it his grandparents who died when the Martians razed his hometown of Lille. He owed it to every French citizen who died in the invasion.

Degats held up one arm and pointed to the left with his other.

"Aumont. Do you see Degats?" he radioed the other battlewalker commander.

"Oui, Mon Commandant."

De Gaulle tensed, his eyes flickered between Degats and the void of space. His finger caressed the trigger of his control stick.

Degats' right arm came down. De Gaulle stared straight ahead.

There! Two shuttles zipped by. De Gaulle squeezed the trigger. The beam sliced through space. A second beam flashed from Aumont's walker.

Both missed.

The shuttles disappeared from view before they could fire again.

De Gaulle felt his face turn red. He closed his eyes, fighting down his rage.

You can do this, Charles. You will destroy one of them. You will show them that a true Frenchman fights to his last breath.

He opened his eyes.

Two shuttles appeared, rocketing straight at them.

De Gaulle grinned. As sometimes happened in warfare, the enemy provided you with an opportunity to defeat him.

He barely took the time to aim before firing. The beam shot past the shuttle.

Take your time. Take your time.

De Gaulle rotated the pod slightly to starboard. The targeting scope came to rest on one of the shuttles just as Aumont's battlewalker fired, and missed.

He started to squeeze the trigger.

The Martian shuttles fired.

"Shit!" Bosquier cried out.

Both beams streaked past De Gaulle's battlewalker. Every hair on his body stood on end. He pushed aside the fear and fired.

The heat ray struck one of the shuttles. A brilliant white light blotted it out.

The remaining shuttle fired.

De Gaulle caught a flash to his right.

"No," *Soldat* Ponge gasped.

Chunks of metal from Aumont's battlewalker floated out of the cargo bay and into space.

De Gaulle refocused on the approaching Martian shuttle. The craft grew larger by the second. Was it going to ram them?

I won't give it the chance.

De Gaulle fired. The Martian fired.

Both beams missed.

De Gaulle fired again.

The Martian shuttle exploded.

"*Viva la France*," he blurted.

Bosquier also cheered, while Ponge let out a sigh of relief.

De Gaulle started to ease back in his seat, then stopped when he saw movement far beyond the cargo ramp.

Four more Martian shuttles formed up in a staggered line and headed straight for him.

Fear came and went, replaced with acceptance and bitterness. His desire since childhood had been to go to Mars and make those revolting monsters pay for the devastation they wrought on France.

Staring at the four shuttles bearing down on him, de Gaulle knew that would not happen.

RETALIATION

NINE

"That's it! Plow through them! Don't let up!"

Beatty leaned forward in his chair, his eyes glued to the moving picture transmission from *Pegasus*. Deciding the best defense was a good offense, he abandoned his "crossing the T" formation, massed the armada's forward element, and had them plunge into the approaching Martian fleet. A vicious storm of heat rays and missiles blazed across the screen. Ships burst into little white suns. Beatty smiled when the ebb readouts indicated more of them were enemy than friendly.

Two blows pounded the *King Edward VII*. Captain Gibbons constantly called out targets. Beatty watched two of the dreadnought's main batteries rip through a Martian light cruiser.

His eyes darted around the screen, noting the positions of all his ships. The cruiser USSS *El Paso* and the corvette USSS *Flusser* vanished in huge balls of light. Four Martian ships soared past their remains. Beatty ordered the dreadnought USSS *Zachary Taylor* and the cruisers USSS *Akron* and USSS *Rockford* to intercept the aliens. A barrage of heat rays from the American warships tore into the Martian ships.

Shuttles converged on the *Danzig*. Beatty grimaced as heat rays tore into the German cruiser. White flashes flickered up and down its length. The ship's nose dipped as it fell out of formation.

Another explosion blossomed on the screen, where the corvette USSS *New Orleans* had been.

Beatty gripped the armrests of his chair. The outcome of this battle was still very much in doubt.

* * *

Charles De Gaulle readied himself as the four Martian ships converged on the open cargo bay door. *I shall take what small measure of revenge I can get,* he thought as he gripped the control stick.

Heat rays tore through the Martian formation. All four shuttles exploded.

De Gaulle blinked in surprise. *What the hell?*

Several ships appeared, diving through the debris from the Martian shuttles. Corvettes, a couple of cruisers, and a dreadnought. It was on the bigger ship that de Gaulle spotted a red, yellow, and red-striped ensign and the name *Arrogante* on the hull.

Saved by the Spanish, he bristled. Their war with the Americans, coupled by the Martian invasion, had left the Spanish Empire a shadow of its former self.

At least they're good for something.

De Gaulle felt the *Agadez* move to starboard. He nodded in satisfaction. Apparently, the engineers had found a way to pilot the landing ship despite the loss of the bridge.

He stared through the open cargo hatch, watching both human and Martian ships pass by. A few times he fired at enemy shuttles but failed to hit one.

The *Agadez* slowed. De Gaulle checked around. To starboard, he caught sight of the blunt bow of human warship. Probably a cruiser, given its size.

"*Mon Commandant*," a voice blurted from the radio. "It is Sergeant Giroux."

"Yes, Sergeant?"

"The engineers have maneuvered us beside the Canadian space cruiser *Hamilton*. She can protect us from any further Martian attacks."

De Gaulle's lips curled. *"Oui,"* he responded in a flat tone. He would rather be next to one of his own warships. How could he trust a nation within the British Commonwealth to put every ounce of effort into protecting a French ship?

Unless the captain is Quebecois. He prayed that was the case.

Quebec native or not, the *Hamilton* did not allow any more Martian shuttles to attack the *Agadez*.

More of de Gaulle's attention shifted to the three severed legs still secured to the cargo deck, all that remained of Aumont's battlewalker. His chest tightened as he thought of the debris and bodies floating out into space minutes ago. Aumont and his crew had all been good men. And in a flash, they were gone. Unfortunately, that was the nature of war.

De Gaulle looked hard at the legs, wondering how many more men he would lose.

* * *

Beatty's head swiveled from side to side, taking in all the screens in the BMC. The number of Martian ships dwindled by the minute.

Soon, there were none.

Beatty froze, overwhelmed by the sudden stillness. He shook, satisfaction swelling inside him. Were it not for the fact it would appear unseemly in front of his subordinates, he would have thrown up his arms and cheered. Twenty-six years after his gunboats were sent to the bottom of the Nile, he'd finally repaid the Martians. Repaid them in spades. Hundreds of their ships were destroyed, along with thousands of those soulless beasts.

This is only the beginning, old boy. We still have their entire planet to deal with.

He picked up the microphone next to his chair. "Capricorn One to all ships," he used his code name to communicate with the ASEF armada. "The void is clear of Martians. Splendid job, all of you. Take stock of damage and casualties, and transmit them to me. Out."

He replaced the microphone and turned to Gibbons. "Captain. Fine job fighting the ship. My compliments to you and your crew."

"Thank you, sir, though from initial reports, it would appear those squids gave us quite a bloody nose."

"A bloody nose is preferable to floating around space surrounded by chunks of steel that used to be this ship."

Gibbons smiled and nodded. "I won't argue that, sir."

Beatty looked back at the screens and redeployed the armada back to their standard formations.

"Admiral." Lieutenant Porter called to him. The combat coordination officer bit his lower lip before continuing. "The ebb has compiled initial losses, damage, and casualties for the armada."

Beatty felt his shoulders knot up. He nodded and forced himself to reply. "On screen."

The hazy green cursor flew along the ebb screen, leaving behind trails of data. Beatty read the information, the swirl of anger, worry, and sorrow growing larger with each line he read.

TOTAL SHIP LOSSES: 235
101 SPACE CORVETTES
48 SPACE CRUISERS
28 SPACE DREADNOUGHTS
21 SPACE TROOP LANDING SHIPS
16 SPACEPLANE TRANSPORTERS
12 SPACE SUPPLY SHIPS
6 SPACE MUNITIONS SHIPS
3 SPACE HOSPITAL SHIPS

The number of damaged ships was nearly three times as high. The dead and wounded surpassed 100,000. Beatty pressed his hands against his legs to keep them from shaking.

Two hundred-plus ships, more than 100,000 souls. They hadn't even reached Mars and already they had suffered staggering casualties.

ASEF may have defeated the Martians, but the aliens had hurt them. Beatty swallowed as he looked at the support ships that had been destroyed and damaged. Invasions could be rather difficult when the enemy took a good bite out of your ground troops, food stocks, and ammunition. The long supply line didn't help matters. The time it took a support vessel to head back to Earth, take on supplies or reinforcements, and return to Mars would come out to roughly three weeks.

In war, a lot could happen in three weeks.

Beatty lowered his chin to his chest. He had to meet with his planning staff. Operation Overlord would have to be revised—again—to compensate for their losses.

Make it work. Again he heard Prime Minister Lloyd George's words echo in his head.

Between the Russians all but pulling out and the losses from this battle, Beatty wondered if the prime minister might be asking for too much.

T E N

Ugly.

That was the first word that came to Patton's mind when he gazed at the dark red orb that was Mars. The world looked scarred and dreary, the complete opposite of Earth. He'd never seen blues and whites so vibrant as when he looked upon his home world from space. It strengthened Patton's faith in God, for only He could have created something so beautiful.

No wonder the slimy bastards down there wanted Earth.

He narrowed his eyes as he floated near the large observation window of the space troop landing ship, USSS *Fossil Creek*. How long had the damn Martians been watching Earth before they invaded? Decades? A century or two? And all that time mankind had been fighting amongst themselves, completely unaware that a bunch of space squids the next planet over spied on them, probing their strengths and weaknesses.

Patton's fury burned hotter by the second. His anger wasn't just directed at the Martians but at his own race. Why hadn't they done more to build better telescopes and rockets? Mankind could have detected the Martians years before their invasion. The nations of the world could have banded together and made plans to kill these sons a'bitches. Instead, their ignorance nearly brought about the extermination of all life on Earth.

Now you're the ones who are going to be exterminated.

Patton hovered over the deck along with the rest of his 214th Self-Propelled Artillery Regiment. All their eyes were aimed at Mars and the ASEF armada that surrounded it. He glanced down at his watch, now set to Mars time. The face was a bit wider than on a normal watch. It had to be since a day on Mars was thirty-nine minutes longer than a day on Earth.

Anticipation built within him. It wouldn't be long before the bombardment began before mankind exacted its revenge.

Patton lowered his head and closed his eyes. *Lord, please look after all Your children and keep them safe as we do what must be done to safeguard Your creation, Your Earth. Grant us the strength to accomplish our mission and smite any and all who would defile Your world.*

Amen.

He opened his eyes, looked up and waited.

"Look! There!" One of the enlisted men nearby pointed at the window.

Patton stared out into space. Two pinpricks of light move away from one of the ASEF ships. Soon more specks of light appeared around the armada. It looked like a swarm of fireflies, all of them rushing toward Mars.

Cheers went up throughout the observation deck. Patton looked around. His men raised their arms and slapped each other on the back. A few even cried tears of joy. Not a very manly thing to do, but in this case, he'd make an exception.

He turned back to Mars, his lips pulling back in a wicked smile. Each of those little blobs of light represented a space-launched ballistic missile, carrying about two-thousand pounds of high explosive. He pictured huge balls of fire obliterating Martian cities. The last time anything had made him this happy was the day George IV was born.

Streaks of light shot from the ASEF ships. Heat rays, all of them slicing through the Martian atmosphere.

"Yeah!" one of the soldiers shouted. "Now we're giving it to 'em!"

"Fry those bastards!" Another soldier raised his fist.

The cheers and shouts continued. Patton's smile grew wider as more missiles and beams bombarded the planet. Now it was their cities burning. It was them dying by the thousands, hopefully, millions.

One of the ASEF ships vanished in a ball of light. Another followed seconds later. The cheering diminished. Several of the soldiers gasped.

"Dammit!" one cried out. "They're taking out our ships."

Patton snapped his head toward the panicked soldier. "What the hell's wrong with you? What the hell's wrong with all of you? They blow up one or two of our ships, and you think we're beat? What the hell kind of Americans are you?"

He floated up to the window and faced the regiment. "Our nation was born out of war and blood. We've brought empires to their knees. Every time our country has faced a great challenge, we have risen to the occasion and triumphed. This time will be no different. Now I won't have any defeatist attitudes in my command."

He gazed around at the men of the 214th SPA Regiment. All of them stared at him in rapt attention.

Patton drew a deep breath and continued. "If any of you start to lose faith, if any of you doubt we will win the day, remember what it was like twenty-six years ago. Remember our cities in ruin. Remember the millions who died, burned by heat rays, choking to death on the black gas, crushed like bugs by the tripods. Remember the parents and siblings and other family members butchered by those slimy, butt-ugly Martian bastards!"

Patton glanced behind him. Ray beams and missiles continued to blaze between the ASEF fleet and Mars.

"We will not lose this fight because we cannot afford to. If we don't wipe out the Martians now, you can damn sure bet they'll come back to Earth and wipe us out. Well, that's not going to happen. You're all fine soldiers. I know this because I trained you. I know I was a son-of-a-bitch, and I know you hated my guts for some of the things I made you do, but it was all in preparation for this." He pointed to the barrage behind him. "I had to turn you into hard-asses, into killers, to not only survive, but to win. And how do we win a war?"

As one, the entire regiment said, "You win not by dying for your country, but by making the other son-of-a-bitch die for his!"

"Exactly. Now you cheer on those space navy limp dicks out there. You cheer them on like you were at a baseball game. And you start salivating at the chance to go down to that piece-of-shit planet, tear out the hearts of every one of those Martian bastards, and eat them like they were damn T-bone steaks!"

A roar went up from the men. Patton raised his fist and turned around, watching the ASEF ships continue to rain death down on the Martian.

"Pound those sons-of-bitches into the damn ground!" he shouted. "Just save some for us!"

* * *

Hashzh lay still, his eyes locked on the monitor before him. He watched the stubby missile with rectangular wings, and a tubular engine mounted on the rear falling toward the great city of Rvunr. Or rather, what remained of it. Pillars of flame consumed its domes and obelisk-like structures. A thick cloud of gray-black smoke hung over the city. The Brohv'ii missile plunged into that smoke. Seconds later, an orange flash lit up the blackness.

Hashzh's tentacles quivered. Another part of Rvunr destroyed. More Shoh'hau dead.

He clicked from one screen to the next. Each one showed the same image. A Shoh'hau city in flames.

His anger split between the Brohv'ii slime obliterating his world and the Guiding Council that allowed this to happen. Part of him hoped one of those Brohv'ii missiles struck the Council's shelter and incinerated everyone of those incompetents.

Hashzh mentally scolded himself. How could any Shoh'hau with even a trace of logic and respect wish death on the leaders of this world? He briefly worried that his brain might be malfunctioning.

No. You are simply allowing anger to dictate your feelings. He purged those vile thoughts from his mind.

A blue light flashed on the panel embedded in the floor of his command shelter.

Just when I was thinking about them. Had he been a Shoh'hau from tens of thousands of cycles ago, those who believed in superstition over science, he would have feared the Guiding Council could read his thoughts. It was fortunate they couldn't. Otherwise, he would likely be incinerated.

Hashzh pushed a button on the panel. The monitor expanded and showed all nine members of the Guiding Council.

"Councilors. How may I serve you?"

"Exterminate the Brohv'ii!" Councilor Yrvul exclaimed. "Our telescopes show their ships approaching the atmosphere. They will soon land and contaminate our world. You must blast them out of the sky!"

"Our planetary defensive batteries have destroyed several of their craft."

"Yet Brohv'ii missiles and energy beams continue to strike our world. You were given the responsibility to protect Shoh from attack, and you have failed."

Fury surged through Hashzh. With great effort, he restrained himself from lashing out at Yrvul. "I did all I could with the resources available to me. As I have stated on prior occasions, the Guard Force does not have sufficient ships and planetary defense batteries to deter a full-scale invasion by the Brohv'ii. All our efforts must now be focused on fighting and defeating them when they land on our world."

"The Brohv'ii cannot land here. It is impossible," Councilor Ehjah said in a distant voice, as though he were talking to himself. That would be an obvious sign of brain malfunction.

Many of the Guiding Council looked at Ehjah with suspicion. Perhaps they suspected the same as Hashzh.

"The Brohv'ii are coming," Councilor Dvemt stated. "That is a certainty. Therefore, we must take precautions to safeguard ourselves."

"What do you suggest?" asked Councilor Rezdv.

"We should proceed to the facility housing the Final Project. It has managed to withstand the Brohv'ii bombardment. We will be safe there until the project is completed."

"Unless the Brohv'ii find a way to enter the facility." Yrvul's large eyes bore in on Hashzh. "Supreme Guardian. You must increase the security for The Final Project."

"The Final Project has sufficient protection, Councilor."

"Then you will increase security for the Guiding Council. You will assign ten tripods and fifty Guardians for each of us."

The order shocked Hashzh. They wanted ninety tripods to protect them? Did they not realize that would require him to leave entire regions without any tripods? The Brohv'ii would easily overwhelm the infantry.

Those tripods would better protect the Guiding Council by fighting the Brohv'ii, not by sitting deep underground.

"Agree," Ehjah spoke in a hurried manner.

"Agree," said Rezdv.

The other members of the Council also voiced the same word, including Supreme Councilor Frtun.

Hashzh considered telling them how this could negatively impact Shoh's defenses but contained his words. As infuriated as he was with them, they were still the Guiding Council. How could the Shoh'hau cope if all their leaders were killed?

"It shall be done," Hashzh responded.

"Very well," said Frtun. "Send those protection forces to our shelter. They will escort us to the Final Project."

The screen showing the Guiding Council went black.

Hashzh fought off his frustration and issued the necessary orders. At least the tripods and Guardians could travel to the Council's shelter and to the Final Project underground, avoiding Brohv'ii surveillance. The climate change had resulted in a large network of underground tunnels and facilities being built all over Shoh.

That network might also give them the advantage necessary to defeat the Brohv'ii.

RETALIATION

ELEVEN

"One minute to touchdown."

Every muscle in Rommel's body tightened when he heard the announcement. He drew a slow breath as he sat in the commander's seat of his SPA. One more minute until he set foot on Mars. One more minute until he was in the middle of a war again. Only this time, it would be *as a soldier*, not a refugee fleeing from Martians, as had been the case when he was six.

He gazed around the open interior of his SPA. Corporal Ehelechner, the lanky driver, stared down at his lap, clutching his hands. Private Frosch and Private Kopitz, the gunner and the loader, had their eyes on the *Gothensee*'s rear hatch, leaning forward in eager anticipation. Truth be known, *he* was eager as well. He just hid it better than the two privates, as would any man who had seen firsthand the destruction the Martians were capable of.

"Thirty seconds to touchdown," the loudspeakers blared.

Frosch turned to Kopitz and slapped him on the shoulder. "Soon, *mein freund.* Soon."

Kopitz grinned wide. "Time to see how the ugly bastards like having their planet invaded." He tacked on a hearty laugh.

Ehelechner shivered, still staring at his hands.

The *Gothensee* shuddered. For a split second, Rommel feared a heat ray or a missile had struck the ship. When flames didn't rush through the cargo hold, he let out a sigh of relief.

That relief vanished in an instant. Even with the ASEF armada bombarding Mars for a full day, some of the enemy's defenses had to have survived. They had to be firing at the landing ships.

Rommel's stomach tightened. He thought back to the attack on the ASEF armada. Several landing ships had been destroyed, including one carrying his good friend, Colonel Heinz Guderian.

He shifted in his seat. He wanted to get out of this damn ship now! He did not want to die like Guderian and those other soldiers. Trapped in an oversized steel box, unable to fight back.

Land. Land!

"Ten seconds to touchdown . . . Five, four, three . . ."

Rommel stifled a sardonic laugh. What a great injustice it would be if the moment they landed, a Martian heat ray blew the *Gothensee* sky high.

"Two, one. Touchdown."

A *thump* reverberated through the ship. Crewmen scrambled around the deck, removing the chains that kept the SPAs in place.

The cargo hatch lowered. Rommel stood and clicked on the radio in his spacesuit. "Twelfth Schaumburg-Lippe Regiment. Forward."

He gripped his console as the SPA lurched forward. It rolled down the ramp, followed by several others. Rommel held his breath as he took in the landscape. The sky had a brownish-orange hue. There was no vegetation, just dark red sand and rocks. Large mountains, also dark red, stretched across the horizon.

I'm actually on Mars.

Something orange flashed in the corner of his eye. A landing ship fell from the sky, flames gushing out its side. His mouth fell open as he watched the vessel smash into a hill less than a kilometer away. A ball of fire rose from it. He braced himself for an ear-shattering explosion. Instead, what he heard sounded more like the rumble of distant thunder. That's when Rommel remembered. The lower atmospheric pressure of Mars muffled sound, preventing it from traveling very far.

He turned away from the burning ship, trying not to think about the soldiers who would never have a chance to fire a shot at those tentacled swine. He had a regiment to lead.

"All vehicles," Rommel radioed. "Move to first prearranged positions."

The SPAs split into groups of four, their hydrogen fuel cell engines almost silent in the Martian atmosphere. More landing ships touched down as Rommel's regiment took position behind rises and boulders and in gullies.

Streaks of light flashed from the western horizon. Heat rays. The beams shot overhead. Two of them found their marks. A pair of landing ships crashed to the surface in flames.

An angry breath shot out his nostrils as he stared at the burning wrecks. More heat rays slashed across the sky.

They needed targets, and they needed them now.

"*Windhund Sieben*, this is Fox One," he radioed. "What is your status? Over."

"This is *Windhund Sieben*. We are coming down the ramp as we speak."

Rommel looked at the landing ship *Dummersee*. Battlewalkers of the *Windhund* Division marched onto the Martian soil. The walker designated *Windhund Seven* had been assigned as his regiment's artillery spotter during the initial landing.

"Take the high ground and locate those Martian heat ray batteries. We have to take them out now."

"*Jawohl*, Fox One."

Rommel watched the battlewalker break off from the others. It strode up to a hill a half kilometer away and easily scaled its way to the top. Meanwhile, more troops, vehicles, and battlewalkers streamed out of the landing ships. Once each vessel disgorged its cargo, it lifted off toward space.

"*Windhund Sieben*. Do you have a—"

"Incoming!" Ehelechner shouted.

Rommel looked up. White contrails arced across the sky and descended toward them.

"Missiles!" he hollered. "Take cover! Take cover!"

Rommel dropped to the deck of his SPA, as did Ehelechner, Frosch, and Kopitz. Heat rays flashed above them. They had to be from German ships and battlewalkers, trying to shoot down the enemy missiles.

Bass drum-like thumps rippled through the air. The ground vibrated. Every muscle in Rommel's body froze. Would his SPA be hit? Would it hurt, or would it be over quick? The face of his wife, Ilda, appeared in his mind's eye.

The noise and shaking subsided. Rommel peered over the side. Smoking craters marred the ground. Fear clenched his heart when he saw a plume of the black cloud gas drift toward them. He quickly shook off that fear. Their spacesuits would keep out the gas.

None of his SPAs had been hit. He offered up a silent prayer for that.

Other units, however, hadn't been as lucky.

Burning nausea went up Rommel's throat when he saw bodies and parts of bodies lying around newly formed craters. Two battlewalkers had fallen on their sides, smoke billowing from their domes. Flames rose from the bow of a landing ship. One soldier knelt over another, moving his hand back and forth over his wounded comrade's torso, probably using an emergency adhesive spray to seal a tear in the spacesuit.

Rommel fought the urge to bang his fist against the side of his SPA. He hadn't traveled millions of kilometers across space just to watch his fellow Germans get blown to pieces before they could fire a single shot at the damn squids.

He was about to radio *Windhund Sieben* when the voice of its commander echoed in his helmet.

'Fox One. Targets sighted. Three heat ray batteries and two missile batteries, eleven kilometers to the east, coordinates two-five-seven."

"Dammit," Rommel hissed. The 15cm guns his SPAs carried had a maximum range of just under five kilometers. Probably a bit further here on Mars, with its lighter gravity, but certainly nowhere close to eleven kilometers.

He switched his radio to the command frequency.

"Fox One to Hermod."

"This is Hermod. Over."

"We have spotted enemy heat ray and missile batteries. Request permission to advance and bombard."

"Standby, Fox One."

The seconds dragged by as Rommel waited for the order. *Standby*. Why should he standby? Their job was to attack. They needed to move forward now. Drive into the Martian lines before they knew what hit them. *Mein Gott,* what he could do with SPAs and battlewalkers moving forward and attacking in tandem.

His thoughts were interrupted by shouts of, "Incoming!"

More missiles arced across the sky.

"All guns! Move to secondary positions!"

He felt the slight vibration of the engine start. Ehelechner backed up the SPA, wheeled it to the left, and shot across the red sand. Rommel pulled out his topographical map, then looked out at the landscape. A pile of boulders lay a quarter kilometer from them, just as the map indicated. So far it had been accurate.

So far.

Dull thumps came from behind Rommel. He turned around. A wave of cold swept over his body.

One of his SPAs flipped over. Flames licked the tracks and underbelly. A second SPA had been reduced to a twisted, smoking wreck.

Rommel trembled with fury. Now *his* men were dying.

And he wasn't doing a damn thing to stop it!

What's taking those idiots at division so long to respond?

"Hermod! Hermod, this is Fox One! We need to get within range of those enemy batteries and lay down suppressing fire."

No response.

"Hermod! Answer me, now!"

"Fox One, this is Hermod. Hold your position."

Rommel drew his head back in astonishment. "Say again, Hermod?"

"You are to hold position."

"Hermod, we are taking casualties. Those heat rays and missiles must be destroyed now before we all die."

"They will be dealt with. Out."

Rommel clenched his teeth. *They will be dealt with*. When? Five minutes from now? Ten? When half the landing force had been wiped out?

Spouts of flame and dirt flew into the air around the rolling SPAs. Rommel scanned around him, a lump in his throat. It vanished when he saw all his SPAs had survived the barrage.

The lump returned when he saw more dead German infantrymen and a burning battlewalker.

Rommel toyed with the thought of disobeying orders when Frosch pointed to the sky. "Look!"

Stubby dark shapes with large swept wings hurtled above them. Fokker 15s, probably from the spaceplane transporter *Helmuth von Moltke*. While their jet engines would make a thunderous roar on Earth, on Mars he couldn't even hear them.

The Fokkers streaked toward the Martian batteries. Heat rays flashed through the sky. Three of the planes vanished in balls of fire. The others dove toward the ground. Tiny dots fell from their bellies. More heat rays zipped past them. Two more fireballs winked on and off in the sky.

Fire and smoke rose in the distance. The surviving Fokkers banked right and flew off. Only a few heat rays fired at them.

The second wave of Fokkers bombed the Martian batteries. This time, there was no return fire.

A bitter feeling swelled within Rommel. He knew he shouldn't feel that way. He should be grateful to the Fokker pilots for destroying those heat rays and missile batteries. Well, he was grateful. He just wished his regiment could have done it.

It took an hour for the landing force to form up. A very, very long hour for Rommel. An hour that the Martians likely used to strengthen their defenses. When they finally did move out, the battlewalkers took the lead, with the infantry bounding along behind them, and the 12th Schaumburg-Lippe Self-Propelled Artillery Regiment bringing up the rear.

Rommel couldn't help but shake his head. Before 1898, the world's militaries could never dream of a mobile force like this. Walkers and tracked vehicles could move faster than horses and carry more armaments. Infantrymen could ride them into battle instead of marching as they had done for thousands of years. That meant battlewalkers and SPAs had to go at a snail's pace for the foot soldiers to keep up.

How can I be the only one to see the potential here? The army had speed. They should utilize it. Hit the enemy hard, from multiple directions. Don't give them a chance to recover. Battles would end quicker, with fewer German casualties.

Despite all the great technological leaps of the twentieth century, the old fools who ran the General Staff remained stuck in a nineteenth century mindset. Mass your troops and march straight at the enemy.

They will be the death of us . . . literally.

Four kilometers from their objective, a city designated Huygens Seven, Rommel received orders from division HQ to halt.

"Our scouts have found a regimental-sized force of Martian infantry in a series of trenches with heat ray and missile batteries supporting them." The soldier at HQ read him the coordinates. They would bombard the Martian positions for a half hour before moving forward.

Rommel shook. The walkers should be on the move under cover of the artillery barrage to smash through the Martian lines. The infantry could follow on and take care of any survivors. Then they would keep moving to their next objective, and the next and the next, not stopping until they took the entire planet.

At least, that's what he'd do if he were in charge.

But he wasn't. All he could do was lob shells at whatever target HQ wanted.

Rommel's regiment did just that. Hearing the *boom* of his gun, watching columns of smoke and dust rise in the air, proved therapeutic. His anger lessened every time he barked out the word, "Fire!" The gun went off and a shell flew through the air. Seconds later it exploded, killing Martians, making them pay for all the lives lost, all the cities burned to the ground twenty-six years ago.

When the bombardment ended, the battlewalkers and infantry moved forward. The SPAs stayed put, waiting for the ammunition carriers to arrive and replenish their magazines. Rommel watched the advance through his binoculars. Heat rays spat from the battlewalkers. Not as many beams as he expected. Had the bombardment killed most of the Martians?

"Ah!" Frosch blurted. "Here come the carriers."

"*Sehr Gut.*" Kopitz smiled. "More shells. More Martians to kill."

Rommel turned and saw the bulky tracked vehicles rolling toward them. He nodded and switched to the regimental frequency. "This is Fox One to all SPAs. Ammunition carriers are en route. Check your magazines and see—"

A tremor rippled underneath his SPA.

"What the hell was that?" Ehelechner whipped his head from left to right.

The tremor continued.

Rommel saw no telltale sign of artillery. Could it be an earthquake? Did Mars even get them?

Best be prepared in case it isn't natural.

"Kopitz. Do we have any high explosive rounds left?"

"Just one."

"Then load it—"

Rommel's radio burst to life.

"Fox! Fox! Request artillery support!"

"Enemy all around us!"

"They're coming out of th—"

Rommel raised his binoculars. Puffs of reddish dust shot up around the distant battlewalkers and infantry.

"Fox One to *Windhund Sieben*. Our advanced forces are under attack. I need targets . . ."

His mouth hung open when the ground ahead of him collapsed.

Again his radio became clogged with multiple, panicked voices. Three more sections of ground caved in.

"*Mein Gott.*" Ehelechner pushed himself back in his seat. Kopitz looked up from the gun and froze, the shell still not pushed through the breech.

Four Martian tripods emerged from the holes.

TWELVE

"Pull back! All units, pull back!"

Rommel's SPA rolled backward. His wide eyes locked on the tripod rising out of the Martian soil. Chills swept over his body as he remembered the alien machines laying waste to his native Wurttemberg.

He pushed away the memories. He had to concentrate on the here and now if he, and his regiment, had any hope of survival.

The SPAs continued to roll backwards. The four tripods towered over them.

"Split up!" Rommel radioed. "First and Second Battalions right. Third and Fourth Battalions left. Now!"

Corporal Ehelechner yanked the control handles. The SPA jerked to a halt, rotated to the right and sped off. Rommel checked around him. Several other SPAs followed.

Yellow beams spat from the tripods. Fireballs blotted out two SPAs. More beams streaked from the tripods. Three more SPAs exploded.

Sweat coated Rommel's face. His heart hammered against his chest. *Schnell! Schnell!* He mentally urged on his vehicle.

He saw the ammunition carriers spinning around and rolling back to the division's staging area. One of the tripods stomped after them. A white beam cut through the air. It touched one of the bulky tracked vehicles. A pillar of flame and smoke erupted, accompanied by a deep *thud*. Seconds later, the other ammunition carriers blew up.

Rommel thumped the armrest of his command chair. How the hell could they fight four tripods with just a handful of shells?

He radioed Division HQ for support. They explained several other units also encountered Martians emerging from underground but promised them help as soon as possible.

Rommel looked behind him. Two tripods turned toward the fleeing SPAs.

"As soon as possible" is too long.

He scanned the terrain. To his left the ground dropped off, leading to a long, twisting canal. Too confined. The Martians could pick them off with ease.

About two kilometers away was a row of hills. An idea formed.

"First and Second Battalions. Follow me. We're getting behind those hills two kilometers in front of us."

Rommel heard what sounded like a heavy footfall behind him. He checked over his shoulder. Flames tore through one of his SPAs. More heat rays streaked from the tripods. Several beams struck the ground, throwing up smoke and clumps of dirt. Three struck SPAs. Fire and smoke consumed them.

"All units," Rommel radioed. "Swerve! Swerve! Don't give them an easy target!"

Ehelechner threw their SPA into a tight right turn. After about five seconds, he swung to the left. The other SPAs zigzagged as well. For a split second, the sight amused Rommel. It looked as though all the drivers had spent too much time in a beer hall before getting behind the controls.

But if it kept them alive, so what if it looked funny?

The SPAs veered and twisted. Heat rays struck the ground around them. Rommel grinned briefly, wondering if the Martians were getting frustrated.

Two SPAs to his right smashed into each other. One continued on, its left front end crumpled.

The other stood still.

Move. Move! Rommel urged them.

A heat ray hit the stalled SPA. It burst into flames.

Rommel turned away, putting the deaths of the SPA crew out of his head. He stared at the hills. *Mein Gott*, they looked so far away.

An SPA to his left exploded.

Rommel clenched his armrests, staring at the hills. *Schnell!*

A heat ray struck the ground near the SPA. Smoke and dirt burst into the air.

SCHNELL!

The hills loomed before him. The SPAs climbed the slopes. Chunks of ground exploded around them from enemy fire.

Rommel's SPA crested the hill. He bounced and pitched forward in his seat as the vehicle descended the slope. More SPAs surged over the hill. They were shielded from the Martians' view.

But not for long.

Rommel surveyed the terrain, scowling. He wished that Martian "red weed" had been present. That would have provided them with excellent cover. But there was no sense in wishing for what he couldn't have.

There was only one thing to do. Stand and fight.

Rommel ordered seven other SPAs to turn and face the summit. Six more were positioned at the base. The other vehicles sped away from the hill.

I pray this works.

He rid his mind of doubt. It would work. Finally, he could utilize the SPAs mobility like he'd always wanted.

The domed top of the first tripod appeared just beyond the hilltop.

"Hard right! Ninety degrees."

Ehelechner swung the SPA around. The other self-propelled artillery vehicles followed suit. Private Frosch sat by the 15cm gun, ready to fire.

Rommel watched the first tripod walk into the clear. He looked over the gun. It was pointed straight at the domed cockpit.

"Fire!"

The gun thumped. The other SPAs opened fire. Three geysers of flame sprouted from the tripod.

"Fall back!"

The SPAs raced back down the hill. The others at the bottom also opened fire. One shell exploded against the tripod's front leg. The machine wavered. Fire and smoke gushed from its dome.

Rommel ordered Kopitz to load one of their two remaining shells. A shrapnel one. It wouldn't do the sort of damage as a high explosive round, but some damage was better than none.

The burning tripod stumbled. The second one walked around it and fired its heat ray. It missed the SPAs.

"Swing around. Fire at will, then retreat."

The SPAs made sharp U-turns. Tension gripped Rommel as they came to a stop. What he wouldn't give to have these things fire on the move.

The SPAs jerked left and right, trying to sight up the tripods. A heat ray tore into one vehicle. Flames swept over it. Another SPA exploded. Three others fired and drove off. All the shells detonated far away from the tripods.

"Target sighted!" hollered Frosch.

"Fire!" Rommel ordered.

The gun thumped. The recoil vibrated the SPA. The shell exploded on the ground a kilometer behind the second tripod.

"Dammit," Rommel hissed.

Other SPAs opened fire. A shell hit the burning tripod in one of its green portholes that looked like eyes. The undamaged one advanced and fired. Another SPA turned into a fireball.

Rommel ordered the surviving SPAs to retreat. He checked left. The rest of his regiment, which he had sent away from the hills, turned around and drove toward the tripods. Hopefully, they could—

"Jets!" Frosch pointed to the east.

Rommel looked up. Four Fokker 15s rocketed toward the tripods. Flames flickered from their wings and noses. Rockets and cannon rounds raked the alien war machines. Flames and sparks shot up from their domes and legs, as well as the ground around them. The second tripod fired its heat ray at the Fokkers. It missed.

Bombs fell from the jets. Fireballs surrounded the tripods.

"All units," Rommel radioed the regiment. "Fire at will. Don't let up on them."

"*Ja*," said Kopitz. "Why let the flyboys have all the fun?"

The loader shoved in their last shrapnel shell. Frosch fired the gun. The round burst near the side of the second tripod. Shells from other SPAs tore up the ground around it. One struck a foot on the second tripod.

The Fokkers came in for a second attack run. Streaks of red and yellow spewed from the aircraft. Shells and rockets rained down on the Martian machines. A fireball ripped apart the dome of the first tripod. One of the legs on the second tripod blew apart. It toppled onto the red sand. The SPAs fired their remaining shells at the downed tripod. Flames washed over its dome.

"*JA!*" Kopitz raised his arms in triumph. Frosch followed suit. Ehelechner just slumped in his seat, drawing a long breath and closing his eyes, looking relieved.

One of the Fokkers flew overhead, waggling its triangular shape.

"Fox One, this is Blue Dragon Three. Over."

"This is Fox One," Rommel replied to the Fokker pilot.

"Fox One, all tripods in your area are neutralized."

"Acknowledged, Blue Dragon. *Danke.*"

The Fokker swung left and sped off.

Rommel examined his topographical map, picked out a rally point, and ordered his regiment to proceed there. Next, he contacted division HQ and requested additional ammunition carriers. They told him it might be a while, as the security of their supply lines was in doubt.

"Just remember," Rommel replied. "Artillery is not very useful without shells to fire."

He led his SPAs around the burning tripods. He wanted to feel satisfied at the sight of the wreckage. It was proof that SPAs could be used not just for fire support, but as a mobile, offensive weapon.

The deaths of so many of his men tempered his personal triumph.

THIRTEEN

The soldier next to Captain Georgy Zhukov flung out his arms. He slowly fell to the ground, three holes in the back of his spacesuit.

Zhukov pumped his legs as hard as he could. With the Martian gravity, it felt as though he were moving through molasses.

He heard low hums around him. Spouts of red dirt shot up from the berm in front of him. Impacts from Martian bullets.

Zhukov grunted and pushed off the ground. He felt like he was hanging in mid-air, a perfect target for the Martians. He clenched his teeth, expecting rounds to tear through his spacesuit.

Gravity finally took hold. Zhukov dropped behind the berm. He twisted around, gripping his Mosin-Nagant rifle. Other soldiers from his company also dove behind the berm. Two of them landed hard on the ground and did not get up.

Zhukov peered over the top. Dozens of Martians slithered out of the hole in the ground, each one carrying slender tubes with boxes attached to the bottom.

They also wore a form-fitting, brown coverall with a glass faceplate and a cylindrical tank on their backs. Their version of a spacesuit he guessed.

Maybe survival suit is a better term. He imagined the Martians would want to take precautions so as not to expose themselves to the same human bacteria that killed their comrades who had invaded Earth.

Zhukov sighted the nearest alien and fired. A spray of red liquid burst from its head. The Martian's body sagged and didn't move.

He worked the rifle bolt back and fired again. Again. Again. Other soldiers joined in. Several Martians stopped moving. Others took cover behind rocks or in small ditches. They methodically moved their guns back and forth. Bullets hummed overhead or kicked up spouts of dirt. A soldier nearby pitched backward. Half of his glass visor had been shattered. He lay on his back, hands covering his helmet. The soldier went into spasms and wheezed, straining to draw in what little oxygen the Martian air had to offer.

Zhukov grimaced as the soldier's shaking grew more intense. With bitter cold air seeping into his spacesuit, it wouldn't be long before he froze to death.

There's nothing you can do for him.

Zhukov turned away from the dying soldier and fired, picking off another Martian. He glanced around at his company. What he saw both frightened and angered him.

Two of his machine gunners swung their weapons back and forth, never easing up on the trigger. How many of those rounds missed? A few soldiers fired a shot and looked up to see if they hit anything. Two were struck by the Martian bullets. Other soldiers just pressed up against the berm, not even attempting to fight back.

More than a dozen soldiers didn't even run for the berm. They scattered in all directions, trying to escape the Martians. Some even dropped their rifles as they fled.

Inexcusable!

Several fleeing soldiers stumbled and fell. They lay on the ground motionless. One soldier turned and raised his arms above his head. A Martian brought up its sleek rifle and shot him in the chest.

Fools! Useless fools! Zhukov scowled, cursing his superiors. They had saddled him with the dregs of the Red Army. When he mentioned this to the colonel in command of his regiment, the man told him, "We cannot send our best troops to Mars, not when enemies of the Revolution still threaten us here on Earth."

If they weren't going to provide me with good soldiers, they should have never sent us to this ball of shit!

But he was here on this "ball of shit," and if he ever wanted to see Earth and Mother Russia again, he'd better get these men fighting like real soldiers.

Zhukov shoved a fresh five-round stripper clip into his Mosin-Nagant, bent at the waist, and stomped down the line.

"Fight!" Zhukov kicked one of the cowering soldiers. "Fight, damn you!"

He went up to one of the machine gunners and punched him in the back. "Stop spraying the air with bullets! You're wasting ammunition, and you'll overheat the barrel. Aim and fire short bursts."

Zhukov eyed a group of soldiers huddled together, crouched as low as possible. None of them dared to rise an inch and fire.

"Up! Get up and start shooting at them!" He pointed toward the Martians.

A young soldier looked up at him, a private named Isakovsky. "B-B-But they'll kill us."

"Of course they want to kill you, you idiot! They're the enemy. It is your duty to fight them."

Isakovsky shook. "I-I... I can't! I don't want to die!"

The young soldier dropped his rifle and bounded away as fast as Martian gravity would allow.

Zhukov bared his teeth. He watched with unblinking eyes as Isakovsky ran away, deserting his post, his comrades.

His country.

Zhukov brought up his rifle. He put the sights on Isakovsky's back and fired. The 7.62mm round tore through the spacesuit. Isakovsky stiffened, then collapsed face first onto the ground.

Zhukov swung around to the other soldiers. A few cringed.

"If the Martians do not kill you, I will! You will either fight and live or fight and die. But you *will* fight! Understood?"

The soldiers nodded, their eyes wide with fear.

Zhukov directed them around the berm, making sure they had interlocking fields of fire. He took a couple of shots at the Martians himself. He didn't hit any, but in a way, it didn't matter. Troops were more willing to follow an officer who fought side by side with them.

He spotted one of his lieutenants, a narrow-faced, brown-haired young man named Morgunov, kneeling in a cluster of half a dozen other soldiers.

"Morgunov. Take ten soldiers, including a machine gunner." Zhukov pointed to the left. "Go around the berm. There are some boulders by the edge there. Use them for cover, and attack the Martians' flank."

Morgunov just gawked at him.

Scowling, Zhukov stuck the barrel of his Mosin-Nagant inches away from Morgunov's helmet. "Do I need to repeat myself, Lieutenant?"

"N-No, sir."

Under Zhukov's glare, Morgunov and his squad bounded off. Zhukov assigned another squad to hit the Martians' other flank, this one led by a senior sergeant named Zinchenko. The man had been disciplined several times in the past for brawling and drunkenness, but in combat, he killed the enemy with unbridled enthusiasm. Zhukov could work with that.

His company kept up a steady stream of fire. The Martian advance slowed, despite their rapid-fire weapons. Zhukov shot at a Martian poking out of a ditch. The round kicked up a spout of dirt. He ducked down as mini dirt geysers erupted along the berm. Zhukov glanced left and right. Morgunov's and Zinchenko's squads neared the edges of the berm.

He plucked a metal stick grenade from his weapons belt. "Grenades!" He held it up and waggled it. "Grenades! Machine gunners, keep firing!"

The Lewis Guns belched out a steady *punch-punch-punch* while the riflemen yanked out their grenades.

"Pull pin!" Zhukov ordered.

The soldiers obeyed.

"Now!"

Zhukov reared back and flung his grenade. Dozens of other steel sticks tumbled through the air. Much too slow for Zhukov's taste. Damn Martian gravity. He ducked down behind the berm. So did most of the soldiers. A few watched the grenades.

"Get down!"

The soldiers looked at him, then lowered their heads.

Low groans filled the air. Zhukov furrowed his brow. It took a couple of seconds to realize it was the grenades detonating. The lower atmospheric pressure on Mars dulled sound.

Zhukov peeked over the berm. Frustration burned inside him. The grenades didn't seem to have hurt or killed any of the Martians. They probably all exploded before they reached their targets.

Damn lighter gravity.

Zhukov brought up his rifle and fired until he exhausted his five-round clip. He shoved another one into the Mosin-Nagant and searched for a target.

That's when he noticed movement out the corner of his eye. A smile flashed across his face.

Lieutenant Morgunov's squad had taken up a position among the boulders. One of the soldiers rested the bipod of his big-barreled Lewis Gun on a rock and opened fire. The riflemen around him joined in.

A few Martians hiding behind boulders sagged. Others turned toward Morgunov's squad and peppered them with bullets. Two soldiers fell.

Sergeant Zinchenko's squad then opened up on the right flank.

"Keep firing!" Zhukov ordered.

The deep pops and thumps of rifles and machine guns never let up. Dirt spouts sprang up around the Martian positions. Chips of rock flew off the boulders they used for cover. The volume of enemy fire tapered off as they became more concerned with staying down than shooting.

Zhukov could feel it. They were gaining the upper hand.

To hell with gaining the upper hand. It is time to seize the initiative.

"Fix bayonets!"

The soldiers pulled out their bayonets and attached them underneath their rifle barrels. Zhukov let the machine gunners unleash another barrage before shouting. "Charge!"

He jumped over the berm without hesitation. A war cry burst from his mouth as he bounded across the red sand.

Some of the Martians fired. Two of his men collapsed. The other aliens turned and slid their potato-like bodies over the ground. A few twisted the tentacles holding their rifles and fired. Bullets hummed through the air but didn't strike anyone.

Zhukov pulled the trigger, never breaking stride. The Martians continued to retreat, moving faster than he thought possible with those bulky bodies.

Zhukov continued to bound over the soil and yell, though it became a yell more of frustration than bloodlust. No matter how hard he pumped his legs, he never seemed to gain on the Martians.

The aliens took a few more shots at them before slipping into the hole they'd crawled out of just a few minutes ago. When Zhukov finally reached it, he stuck his rifle into the darkened maw and fired until he emptied the magazine. Other soldiers also fired into the hole. Then they tossed in some grenades. If any Martians were near the entrance, they'd be nothing but bloody chunks of meat.

Zhukov saw Morgunov's squad approaching. "Good work, Lieutenant. Good work all of you."

"Thank you, sir." Morgunov nodded to Zhukov.

"I want your squad to establish a perimeter around this hole. If the Martians so much as stick out a tentacle, kill them."

"Yes, sir."

"How can you allow them to escape?"

Zhukov stifled a groan when he heard the nasally voice. He turned to find a man with thin lips, cold eyes and a weasel-like face walking toward him.

"They are enemies of the Revolution. They would use their science and wealth to slay the people and exploit our resources. Surely you cannot allow them to live."

Zhukov took a deep breath, trying to control the anger that always arose in the presence of this little shit.

"Comrade *Politruk*," he said to Lavrentiy Beria, the company's political commissar. "Surely you can see the tunnels are too cramped for a man to walk through them upright. Martians are built low to the ground, and thus do not need as much clearance to move through interior spaces. The most practical approach is to call in our engineers to dig holes through the tunnel ceilings, then drop in grenades or burn them with flamethrowers. It may take a while, but the result will be the same. Their extermination. It will also not cost us as many lives, which is crucial as we do not have many Red Army soldiers on Mars." He couldn't help but get that back-handed dig in at his superiors.

Beria crinkled his nose, making him look even more like a weasel. Finally, the *politruk* snorted and muttered, "Very well."

Zhukov restrained himself from grinning in triumph. Political commissars. Could a more useless position have ever been dreamt up? Very rarely had he ever seen these vermin fight. Instead, they slinked off to some hole when gunfire erupted, then crawled back out to spew the philosophies of Marx and Lenin and ensure every soldier's loyalty to the Party.

Not only was the position useless, but Zhukov also took it as a personal insult. He had turned his back on the Tsar and readily joined the Bolsheviks. He had fought with distinction throughout the Civil War. How dare anyone in the government question his loyalty to the Party and the Revolution?

He shook off the bitter thoughts. There were more important things to do.

Zhukov sent out scouts to search for any more Martian tunnels. The last thing he wanted was to have the squids springing up somewhere else and attacking them.

He went over to one of the dead Martians and picked up its rifle. Sergeant Zinchenko also joined him. So did Beria, much to his annoyance.

"I do not recall such guns being found among the dead Martians on Earth," said Zinchenko.

"Nor do I." Zhukov held up the weapon and ran an appraising eye over it. "Perhaps they did not think they needed it since they did all their fighting from their tripods. Still, it is a good design. It feels lighter than our Nagants, but fires like a machine gun."

"Perhaps the imperialist nations did find such weapons when the Martian invaders died." Beria nodded to the alien rifle. "That means they are hoarding them and will use them on the Soviet Union once they are done here on Mars."

Zhukov frowned. Even though he didn't trust the British, Americans, French, or Germans, he doubted they would keep a Martian rifle a secret when they had shared the technology from their tripods and spaceships with the rest of the world.

"Collect these rifles." Beria swept his hand out toward the dead Martians. "When we return to Earth, our scientists can examine them."

Zhukov didn't move. He just locked his narrowed eyes on Beria. He hated it when this arrogant ass barked out orders. Unfortunately, there wasn't much Zhukov could do. *Politruks* had the same amount of authority as the company commander. More so, in fact. Zhukov couldn't order Beria to do a damn thing, but that rodent could tell him to attend a lecture on the virtues of Marxism or countermand an order in the middle of a battle.

Or tell him to collect Martian rifles.

Which I would have done anyway. I am not an idiot.

Zhukov ordered three squads to pick up the rapid-fire rifles, then contacted headquarters to send out a buggy to transport them back to base. He and the rest of the company headed back to the berm. When Zhukov neared the top, he halted. His eyes widened at the sight before him.

Five soldiers knelt on the ground. One of the machine gunners covered them, holding his weapon at the hip.

"What is going on?"

The machine gunner, Corporal Golubev, turned his head slightly, one eye on Zhukov, the other on the kneeling soldiers. "Captain. These riflemen stayed behind during your charge. I detained them so you may punish them for their cowardice."

Zhukov glared at the men. He felt his blood pulsate with fury.

"Good work, Corporal." Zhukov spoke in a low, deliberate tone. He stomped over to the kneeling soldiers. None of them dared look up at him.

"So. You five decided to stay here, skulking behind a pile of dirt, while your comrades braved death and fought the enemies of Mother Russia, enemies who would kill them, our families, and all our fellow citizens back on Earth with the same regard as a man who steps on an ant. Have you men no pride in your country? Have you no honor?"

One soldier lifted his head. "P-Please, sir. I'm... I'm sorry. I was scared."

"You are worthless!" Zhukov roared. "You are a disgrace to your uniform. I require soldiers who will fight, who will do what is necessary to protect our country. If you cannot do that, then I have no use for you."

He pulled out his M1895 Nagant revolver and stuck it inches away from the sniveling soldier's helmet.

"No, Captain! Please! I beg you!"

Zhukov's finger tightened on the trigger. The seconds passed slowly. The soldier's sobs grew louder.

Zhukov moved the pistol to the next soldier in line. The young man's mouth fell open in shock and horror.

Crump!

The helmet's glass visor exploded. A dark red hole appeared above the bridge of the soldier's nose. He crumpled to the side, brushing against the soldier Zhukov spared at the last second. The young man yelped and scrambled away.

"That is the second time I have had to shoot a man for cowardice." Zhukov holstered his revolver, then glared at the remaining four soldiers. "Do you require another lesson on the consequences of refusing to fight?"

"No, sir," they all muttered.

"Then next time I order a charge, you will get off your asses and rush the enemy with—"

Beria stepped past him, pistol in hand. He took aim at the soldier Zhukov had spared.

The young man threw up his hands. "No!"

Beria shot him through the helmet. He moved the pistol down the line and did the same to the other three soldiers.

"Comrade Beria!" Zhukov snapped his head from the *politruk* to the five dead soldiers. "What is the meaning of this?"

"I should ask you that question, Captain. You were actually going to spare these men?"

"An example was made of one of their number. There was no need to execute the others."

"They are cowards! They refused to fight for their country, for the Party. They had to be punished."

"We do not have many men on Mars. We must be selective if and when we mete out executions."

"You would defend these weakling scum?" Beria marched up to Zhukov. His voice was low and menacing. "There is no place for cowardice in the army. It is your duty to punish any soldier unwilling to fight. If you are incapable of doing that, I will inform the Party, and they will replace you with someone who can."

Beria turned and walked away.

Zhukov's eyes bore in on the *politruk*'s back, wishing a bullet would tear into it. He then looked around at his men. Many fidgeted as they glanced between him and Beria.

"Dammit," he cursed under his breath. Thanks to this victory, Zhukov felt he was well on his way to turning these men into real soldiers, ones that would follow his orders without hesitation.

But Beria had destroyed all that progress.

Zhukov wondered how he could be an effective leader with that little shit undermining him.

FOURTEEN

Commandant de Gaulle held his breath as the battlewalker wobbled to the right. He half expected it to fall over.

Just a little further. He stared out the windshield. A half-dozen rectangular support ships sat little over a kilometer away. Numerous gray, oblong shapes surrounded the vessels. Portable habitats.

De Gaulle tensed as the walker dipped to the right. He let out a slow breath of relief when the driver, Bosquier, managed to keep it upright. The *Caporal-chef* gripped the controls so tight his knuckles turned white. He slowed the walker's pace, trying to nurse its damaged right leg.

Sweat soaked de Gaulle's body as he willed Bosquier, and the walker, to keep going. The headquarters for the French Third Army now lay half a kilometer away. Was the shaking in the right leg getting worse?

Don't fall apart.

The battlewalker made it to the base perimeter, wobbly but still upright. A soldier below waved a green flag in each hand, pointing them to the repair ship *Rochebrune Peak*.

Easy... easy. The battlewalker limped through the base. De Gaulle's eyes locked on the ship's open cargo bay. Several other walkers were inside, many in worse shape than his.

Bosquier guided the battlewalker up the ramp. It tilted far to the right. De Gaulle gripped his console and swallowed. *Stay up!*

The battlewalker did just that. Another soldier inside the *Rochebrune Peak* directed them to a space in the cargo bay. Bosquier locked the legs in place.

De Gaulle's muscles unwound, and he slumped in his seat. Both Bosquier and Ponge let out audible sighs of relief.

"Well done, Bosquier," said de Gaulle.

"Merci, Mon Commandant," the driver replied, sounding out of breath.

"We should give thanks to the Lord for getting us back here safely, and to Renault for building a tough battlewalker."

"Oui, Mon Commandant," said Bosquier, while Ponge nodded and crossed himself.

De Gaulle pressed a button on his console to lower the ladder in the rear of the cockpit. The trio climbed down to the deck, where a stocky senior NCO looked over their walker. He scowled and shook his head.

"Look at this leg. Ruined! We'll have to replace the whole thing. As if we don't have enough battlewalkers to fix."

De Gaulle grunted at him. "My crew and I are fine, thank you for asking."

The NCO faced him, his expression neutral. *"Oui, Mon Commandant."*

He walked away from de Gaulle and examined another damaged battlewalker that had just entered the cargo bay.

"What now, sir?" asked Ponge.

"There is not much we can do without our walker, is there? Get cleaned up, get something to eat, and get some rest. Tell that to everyone else in the regiment."

"Oui, Mon Commandant," they both replied.

The trio headed out of the ship, with de Gaulle going to his habitat. There wasn't much to it. A cot, a desk, a trunk, and a small bathroom he shared with another regimental commander who lived on the other side. At least the habitat came equipped with a generator that provided him with an Earth-like atmosphere. He could take off his spacesuit without worry of lack of air or deathly cold temperatures.

And take it off he did, much to his relief. The damn thing reeked of sweat and day-old farts. De Gaulle drew in a long breath of fresh air, or at least, the mechanically generated oxygen from the habitat's life support system.

He shuffled into the bathroom, grateful to piss in an actual toilet and wash the sweat and stench from his body in the cramped shower. After changing into fresh fatigues, he sat at his desk and turned on his ebb. He typed his after-action report, his fingers tapping the keyboard slower and slower as memories of the battle played out in his mind. It still seemed unbelievable, watching those tripods rise out of the ground. Machines on both sides battled at point-blank range. De Gaulle had even used his walker's arms to knock down a tripod. He and his crew had given a good accounting of themselves, destroying three alien machines.

The same could not be said for the rest of his regiment. They lost eleven battlewalkers, with many others, including his, damaged. Their advance on Tharsis City had stalled, and HQ ordered his regiment to withdraw.

Withdraw? We ran away.

De Gaulle's fingers stabbed at the keyboard. Anger lines etched his narrow face. There had been too many French defeats over the past fifty-four years. The Franco-Prussian War, which led to the downfall of Napoleon III and the demise of the Second French Empire. The Second Mandingo War in West Africa. He even considered the Fashoda crisis in East Africa a defeat since the French did not provide enough naval forces to deter the British from laying claim to that region. Both empires had been trying to defuse the situation when the Martians invaded. After those monsters succumbed to Earth's bacteria, the French government, in the interest of international cooperation, just handed over Fashoda to the British.

And now we're being led by a damn Englishman. Thinking of Supreme Allied Space Commander Beatty made de Gaulle even angrier.

It took nearly forty minutes to finish his report, which he transmitted to his division commander. Not wanting to put his spacesuit back on to go to the mess hall, de Gaulle took a ration tin from his trunk. He regretted that decision when he took his first bite of the bland boiled beef.

At least it is better than the paste I have to suck through my spacesuit's food tube.

He grimaced as he chewed on his beef, then bit into a dry biscuit.

Not by much, unfortunately.

When he finished his horrific meal, de Gaulle laid down on his cot and closed his eyes. Just before he drifted off to sleep, he prayed the mechanics repaired the damage to his battlewalker—all the battlewalkers—quickly. He was anxious to get back to the front and restore the honor of the French army.

Two days passed, and his battlewalker still hadn't been repaired. The same was true for many others. De Gaulle had gone to the lieutenant in charge of *Rochebrune Peak*'s maintenance section and demanded that he hurry with the repairs.

"We had more damaged battlewalkers than expected," the lieutenant explained. "We must wait for more parts before repairs can be completed."

De Gaulle glared at him. "That will be of great comfort if the Martians attack us."

Another concern involved his men. He didn't want them lazing around and losing their edge. De Gaulle made them exercise. Not doing so in the lighter gravity would lead to muscle atrophy. He set up a firing range so they could have target practice. He even assigned them books to read, most of them accounts of the 1898 invasion. De Gaulle wanted to make sure they remembered why they were on Mars and what might happen should they fail.

Another day passed, then another. De Gaulle's aggravation grew every hour he was stuck at the damn base instead of fighting Martians. He finally marched over to the tent of the 41st Division commander, General Couturier.

"*Mon General.* How long must we sit here and do nothing? Every day we waste, the Martians are fortifying their positions around Tharsis City. That means more losses for us, and we already lost many men during that ambush on the Amazonis Plains."

The paunchy, mustachioed officer stared at de Gaulle in annoyance. "Jets from our spaceplane transporters are conducting bombing runs on the city to weaken their defenses."

"For whatever good that will do."

Couturier narrowed his eyes. "You are out of line, *Commandant.*"

De Gaulle bit back an angry retort. He took a slow breath before continuing. "What I mean, *Mon General*, is the Martians likely have the bulk of their combat forces hidden underground. Our bombs will not affect them. We must go in with battlewalkers and infantry, draw them out into the open, and destroy them."

"The last time the Martians came out into the open, they nearly destroyed us. Most of the ASEF ground offensives have stalled because of that. The only armies making any kind of progress are the British in the Isadis Plains and the Americans in the Aeolis Region."

De Gaulle scowled. "So back on Earth, they look like heroes, and everyone thinks the French military impotent… again. How long must we continue to surrender our national honor to the British and their American cousins? We must get back in this fight."

Couturier leaned forward, eyes narrowed. "What you must do is remember your place as a *commandant*. Perhaps you believe your actions on the *Agadez* make you special, make you think you can demand things of superior officers. I assure you, it does not. Your idiocy jeopardized that entire ship. It was sheer luck you shot down those Martian shuttles, which is the only reason you were not brought up on charges of gross negligence."

The general's expression grew harsher. "You will fight when *I* tell you to fight. Is that understood, *Commandant*."

"*Oui, Mon General,*" de Gaulle replied through clenched teeth.

"You are dismissed."

De Gaulle saluted, then stormed out of the habitat. He muttered a stream of expletives, many of which called into question General Couturier's intelligence, manhood, and sexual preferences.

He took out his frustration on his men, drilling them mercilessly. They probably hated him for it, but so what? Sometimes the most effective commanders were also the most hated.

Six days after the ambush on the Amazonis Plains, General Couturier called all of the 41st's regimental commanders to the command habitat for a meeting.

"Do you think they have a new plan to fight the Martians?" *Commandant* Alphonse Juin, another battlewalker regiment commander, asked de Gaulle.

"Either that or we have been ordered back to Earth so the other empires can have Mars to themselves."

Juin gave him a queer look. De Gaulle just looked down, brooding.

When he and the other commanders entered the habitat, he noticed a map of Tharsis City mounted on an easel. Unit symbols and arrows were drawn on it.

Dare I hope?

Everyone came to attention when General Couturier entered.

"Gentlemen, I know this waiting has been intolerable to you, some more than others." Couturier's eyes lingered on de Gaulle. He did not flinch from his superior's gaze.

Couturier continued, "But this wait was necessary. Our scouts and engineers have searched the Amazonis Plains for any more tunnels the

Martians can use to ambush us. The ones that were found have been caved in. We now have clear paths to our objective, Tharsis City."

A smile formed on de Gaulle's face as General Couturier laid out the battle plan. It would be a three-pronged assault, with the Third Army entering the city from the south while the Fifth Army came in from the west. The eastern part of the city had been assigned to a combined army group made up of Belgians, Dutch, Danes, and Norwegians. De Gaulle bristled at that. He'd rather have another French unit head up the eastern advance instead of four nations whose militaries, he felt, were suspect.

Couturier informed everyone of their objectives. Some battlewalker regiments would provide direct support to advancing infantry. Others would secure the manufacturing facilities in the western part of Tharsis City. De Gaulle's regiment, along with Juin's, would drive north and seize the spaceport. That brought a smile to his face. Tharsis City had one of the largest spaceports on Mars. To capture it would be vital to future operations in the northern hemisphere.

It would also look good on his record.

Unfortunately, de Gaulle would have to wait some more before leading his regiment into Tharsis City. The plan called for a twelve-hour orbital bombardment by ASEF ships, followed by bombing runs and an artillery barrage.

But knowing that he and his men would play a major role in the attack, de Gaulle figured he could be patient just a little longer.

RETALIATION

FIFTEEN

De Gaulle felt as though he was walking toward Hell itself as he stared out the windshield of his battlewalker. Pockets of fire sprouted all over Tharsis City. Thick black smoke hung in the sky. It turned the Martian dawn dark as night, to the point they needed the walker's searchlights to see ahead of them.

"Stay alert," he told his crew. "In this darkness, it would be easy for a tripod to sneak up on us."

"Oui, Mon Commandant," replied Bosquier. "It appears our bombardment was a little too successful, wouldn't you say?"

"I would. I am beginning to wonder if there are any Martians left for us to kill."

The thought made de Gaulle frown. His thirst for vengeance was still not quenched. Far from it. The closer they got to Tharsis City, the more he thought about the fires that swept through his hometown of Lille when the Martians came. On a more personal note, he thought of his father's vast library. As a child, he loved reading those books. The poems and essays of Charles Peguy. The philosophy of Plato. The history of the Hundred Years War.

Gone. All of them. De Gaulle remembered how he cried when his family returned to the charred remains of their home and he stood in the ashes of what had been the library.

Fury built up inside him. He stared at the trigger for the heat ray.

There had better be some Martians left alive for me.

De Gaulle's regiment marched into Tharsis City. Or rather, the smoldering rubble that had been one of the Martians' largest cities. Clouds of black smoke consumed entire sections of the city. Here and there a building had miraculously survived the bombardment. De Gaulle aimed the heat ray at one and fired. The domed structure erupted in flames.

Maybe some Martian's prized library was just destroyed. He smiled at the thought and radioed the rest of his regiment. "Red Wolf One to all walkers. Destroy any buildings that are still standing. I want this city completely leveled."

The other battlewalker commanders acknowledged him.

De Gaulle continued to lead the regiment through the burning city. He had to use his compass to make sure they headed north toward the spaceport. With all the smoke, it was impossible to see at any distance.

They tramped over the rubble, crushing it beneath their walkers' feet. De Gaulle hoped a few Martians got crushed as well. He continued looking around, searching for any targets.

There! On the street just ahead of him. A group of potato-shaped, tentacled aliens. He was about to tell Ponge to open up with the machine guns but stopped. None of the Martians moved.

De Gaulle pulled up the viewing scope from his console and pressed his eyes against it. He twisted the knobs on the side, increasing the forward spyglass's magnification. Gray splotches covered the aliens' greenish-brown hides. It reminded him of the old photos he'd seen from after the invasion of dead Martians. Had they picked up human germs? Maybe from a dead soldier whose space suit had been ripped open?

Then he remembered. The artillery units had special shells that contained cultures of anthrax and bubonic plague. It made sense. If diseases on Earth killed the Martian invaders, why not bring those diseases to Mars?

De Gaulle moved back from the viewing screen, grateful those "germ shells" were being used on aliens. The thought of human armies hurling those things at one another made him grimace.

The regiment went on for a kilometer. Two kilometers. A few times one of the other battlewalkers blew up an undamaged building. Had all the Martians been killed? Or maybe they fled this inferno. Those able to, anyway.

"Red Wolf Twelve!" one of the walker commanders blurted over the radio. "Tripod spotted, coordinates zero-zero-six, six hundred meters!"

De Gaulle looked to the left. A tripod rose from behind a pillar of flame. Its tentacles flailed. The heat ray on its domed cockpit extended higher.

De Gaulle turned his walker's cockpit toward the tripod. The crosshairs just swept over it when three white beams struck the Martian machine. Its cockpit vanished in a ball of fire.

He grunted in annoyance. *Next time.*

"Another tripod!" Ponge called out. "Coordinates zero-two-zero, eight hundred meters."

More urgent shouts came from the radio. Three more tripods had been spotted.

De Gaulle swung the cockpit to the right, aiming for the tripod Ponge spotted. The Martian fired its heat ray at one of the other battlewalkers. It missed.

The crosshairs settled on the tripod. De Gaulle held his breath and pulled the trigger.

The beam struck the alien machine in its green "eyes." Flames gushed out of the front. The tripod shuddered and pitched forward. It crashed into the ground and threw up a grayish debris cloud.

Another tripod exploded. The remaining two fired their heat rays, missing. They turned and fled into a huge smoke cloud.

"Fire into the smoke!" de Gaulle ordered.

Dozens of white beams sliced into the hovering blackness. He scanned the smoke, looking for any flashes of orange that would indicate a direct hit.

None of their beams hit.

The regiment fired again. Again. Still no telltale sign of an explosion.

"Follow me into the smoke," ordered de Gaulle.

The battlewalkers advanced. The smoke swallowed them up. The only thing the searchlights did was better reflect the blackness around them. Nervousness clutched the pit of de Gaulle's stomach. A damn tripod could be right in front of him, and he wouldn't know it.

He gripped the trigger, staring straight ahead, ready to fire.

"It looks like the smoke is clearing," said Ponge.

Indeed it was. De Gaulle saw more rubble ahead. A hundred meters away another thick cloud of smoke hung in front of them. He saw no sign of the two tripods. They had to have gone into the smoke. He grinned momentarily. It was nice to see those alien bastards running away for a change.

"All walkers. Fire into the smoke."

A barrage of heat rays slashed through the smoke cloud. Something flashed out the corner of de Gaulle's eye.

"Was there an explosion in the smoke?" he demanded. "Did anyone see that?"

"Red Wolf Seven. I saw it. It looks like we hi-"

Heat rays burst out of the smoke.

"Shit!" Ponge blurted.

De Gaulle's chest tightened as a beam missed his battlewalker by just a few meters.

"Red Wolf Ten is hit!" someone radioed. "Repeat, Red Wolf Ten is hit!"

"Spread out!" de Gaulle ordered. "Don't make yourselves easy targets. Fire at will!"

De Gaulle fired twice into the smoke. More heat rays came back at them. None hit his battlewalkers.

"*Mon Commandant!*" Bosquier pointed at the windshield.

De Gaulle's eyes widened as twenty Martian tripods charged out of the smoke.

RETALIATION

SIXTEEN

De Gaulle's stomach shot into his throat. The battlewalker's cockpit dropped toward the ground. Martian heat rays streaked all around him. He glimpsed fire erupting from the side of a nearby walker. How many others had been hit?

His battlewalker now sat like a crab. Bosquier maneuvered it to the left. Standing still only made them an easy target. De Gaulle saw another battlewalker topple over, smoke spewing from its cockpit.

He looked back at the charging tripods. More heat rays lashed out at them. One zipped over de Gaulle's walker. Several panicked voices burst from the radio. Fear seized de Gaulle. He could feel the initiative slipping from his grasp. Within seconds, his regiment would break and retreat.

There was only one way he could think of to prevent that.

"This is Red Wolf One! All walkers, charge the enemy! Engage at point blank range!"

Bosquier looked back at him. *"Mon Com-"*

"Do it!"

Bosquier turned back around. The cockpit swiftly rose, and the battlewalker surged forward. A Martian tripod filled the windshield. De Gaulle almost fired the heat ray but stopped himself. At this close range, the explosion would damage his walker.

Only one thing to do.

De Gaulle extended the battlewalker's pincer-like arms. He drew the right one back, ready to strike.

The tripod's tentacles shot forward. One wrapped around the right arm, another around the left. Two other tentacles slammed down on the cockpit. A quake ripped through the entire walker. Ponge gasped. De Gaulle glanced up. Part of the hull had caved in.

He wrestled with the controls, trying to break the arms free. Bosquier also strained at his controls, attempting to pull out of the tentacles' grasp.

The battlewalker shook again. Two of the tentacles drew back, ready for a third strike.

Think. Think!

The arms were useless. Firing the heat ray would be suicidal.

But...

"Bosquier! The front leg. Kick that damn Martian."

The driver turned halfway toward de Gaulle, then said, *"Oui, Mon Commandant."*

De Gaulle felt rather than saw the forward leg rear back. It swung forward. The impact of metal on metal sounded like a muffled clap. A tremor shook the walker.

"Again!" de Gaulle slammed a fist on his console.

The battlewalker kicked the tripod in its front leg a second time. A third. De Gaulle felt the tentacles' grip on the arms slacken. He pulled at the controls, teeth clenched.

The tripod bashed the walker with its tentacles. The cockpit hull caved in even more. The walker kicked the tripod's front leg a fourth time. De Gaulle groaned and pulled at the arm controls.

The walker's arms broke free. De Gaulle drew back the right arm, then thrust it forward. The metal pincers smashed through the tripod's "eyes."

"Back up!"

Bosquier did as ordered. The tripod stood still for a couple of seconds, then fell forward. Bosquier twisted the battlewalker to the left. The tripod fell right past them and crashed into the smoldering rubble.

De Gaulle rotated the cockpit, surveying the battle around him. His wasn't the only battlewalker going toe-to-toe with a tripod. One walker used its pincers to rip open a tripod's cockpit. Another walker ripped out a tripod's tentacles.

To the left, de Gaulle saw a tripod stomping on a battlewalker. He triggered the heat ray. A fireball tore through the tripod's dome-like cockpit. He barely watched the burning Martian machine fall, most of his attention on the downed battlewalker. Anger and sorrow swirled within him. The cockpit had been utterly crushed. No one inside could have survived.

He shoved his emotions aside. A battle was no place to mourn. He would do that later.

If I'm still alive.

De Gaulle searched for more targets. Very few tripods remained standing. Those that did were being pummeled by battlewalkers. One by one, the tripods fell. For good measure, the battlewalkers blasted them with their heat rays.

De Gaulle ordered his battlewalker commanders to check in. All but eleven failed to do so, including his regimental executive officer, *Capitaine* Lhenry.

He closed his eyes and said a quick prayer for the dead. There was no time for anything else.

"All battlewalkers forward. We're far from finished here."

The regiment stepped over the fallen tripods and continued north through the ruins of Tharsis City. De Gaulle spotted an obelisk-like tower half a kilometer away that had, for the most part, survived the ASEF bombardment. He brought it down with the heat ray.

"I don't want a single building left standing in this damn city," he growled.

On they went, blowing up any intact buildings they came across.

"Black Wolf One," *Commandant* Juin radioed. "We are being engaged by two company-sized tripod units and are taking heavy casualties. Sector Seven; coordinates one-one-five. Request assistance."

"Black Wolf One, this is Red Wolf One. I am detaching two of my companies to your position."

"*Merci*, Red Wolf One."

De Gaulle issued the order and watched several of his battlewalkers lumber off to the west to aid Juin's regiment. That and the losses from their earlier engagement left his regiment severely depleted. Still, he gave no thought to halting his advance. He had the advantage and had to press it.

The remaining battlewalkers marched north. At one point four tripods attacked them, destroying one of the walkers. The others made short work of the Martians.

De Gaulle checked his compass, then looked at the map of Tharsis City taped to the left side of his console. By his estimate, the spaceport should be six kilometers away.

He monitored the regimental and divisional radio bands as his walkers moved further north. His two companies had hit the tripods attacking Juin's regiment from the rear. The infantry was engaged in heavy fighting and making slow progress through the southern and western parts of the city. The combined European army group to the east had been held up at the city limits by stiff resistance. De Gaulle cursed their lack of aggressiveness.

Numerous calls went out for fire support. Unfortunately, the thick smoke over Tharsis City made accurate bombing and orbital bombardment impossible. The artillery units ran into the same problems, as many of their shells landed far from their targets.

Then it will be up to us to take this city.

De Gaulle had no problem with that.

The battlewalkers tromped over rubble and through smoke clouds. He saw another undamaged Martian tower and zapped it with a heat ray.

A break came in the smoke. De Gaulle leaned forward and peered through it. He saw a large, relatively flat expanse before him. A smile spread across his face. They had reached the spaceport.

That smile vanished when he saw forty tripods along the perimeter.

"All walkers! Fire at will!"

White beams sliced through the smoky air. Flames blossomed on three tripods. The cockpit of a battlewalker turned into a fireball.

"All walkers!" de Gaulle radioed. "Fire your rockets. Use the smoke for cover. Try to get closer to the Martians."

Contrails shot over the smoldering ruins as the battlewalkers fired their rear rocket launchers. De Gaulle waited for the *whoosh* and rumble from the launchers on his walker.

None came.

"Ponge! Fire rockets."

"I cannot. The launchers must have been damaged when the tripod struck us."

"Shit!" De Gaulle scowled. Columns of fire and smoke billowed up around the tripods. A few collapsed, covered in flames.

De Gaulle gripped the trigger for the heat ray and fired, rotating the cockpit left to right. Dozens of beams cut through the smoke and flames. Most missed. Here and there he caught flashes of explosions. Two on the Martian side, one on his side.

He ordered a platoon of battlewalkers to continue their frontal assault, while he led half the regiment toward the enemy's left flank. *Capitaine* Giraudeau, now the unit's most senior officer behind de Gaulle, led the rest of the battlewalkers toward the right flank. They ducked into the smoke every chance they got, firing constantly. De Gaulle saw one of his walker's beams clip a tripod, slicing off two tentacles.

A few tripods moved along the perimeter, shadowing de Gaulle's force. He fired. Missed. Fired again. Missed. Another walker blasted a tripod. Seconds later a battlewalker erupted in flames.

De Gaulle's eyes flickered between the tripods shadowing them and the ones still positioned at the front of the spaceport. He concentrated on the ever-increasing gap between the two forces.

"Red Wolf Twelve," he radioed.

"Twelve here," replied Lieutenant Simenon.

"Take your platoon and Red Wolf Thirteen's platoon. Penetrate that gap on the right and attack the Martians in their rear."

"*Oui*, Red Wolf One."

"We will give you covering fire on my mark. Three, two, one… mark!"

De Gaulle squeezed the trigger as fast as the heat ray's batteries could recycle. The battlewalkers around him also unleashed beam after beam in rapid succession. The worry of overheating the heat ray niggled at the back of his mind. He tried to ignore it. He needed to keep the Martians focused on him so Simenon's walkers could enter the spaceport.

The number of tripods engaging de Gaulle's force dwindled. Two beams connected on the cockpit of one Martian machine. It blew apart in a maelstrom of orange and black. De Gaulle aimed at the last tripod and fired. A miss. Another walker connected with its heat ray. The tripod exploded.

De Gaulle drew a deep breath and leaned forward. Simenon's battlewalkers entered the spaceport, and the entire western perimeter was wide open. He could send half the regiment through with ease. One of the main objectives of the Tharsis City assault would be achieved.

He would achieve it.

"Forward!"

De Gaulle's walker lurched forward. His chest swelled with pride. Their bitter defeat on the Amazonis Plains would be avenged.

The battlewalkers were roughly fifty meters from the edge of the spaceport.

"Red Palace to all units."

Shock gripped de Gaulle when he heard General Couturier's voice over the radio.

"Red Palace to all units. Break off the attack and withdraw at once. Repeat, all units, withdraw at once."

De Gaulle went numb. He could not have heard right. His regiment was about to seize the spaceport. They couldn't withdraw now.

"Red Palace, this is Red Wolf One. Say again."

"I said withdraw, dammit," Couturier snapped.

"We are about to seize our objective. Enemy resistance has crumbled. We cannot leave now."

"Our eastern army group is being pushed back, and our other groups have lost many men and battlewalkers. We have reports of sizeable Martian reinforcements coming from the north and west."

"We are inside the city," de Gaulle said. "We can establish defenses and hold them off until we get reinforcements."

"Enough, *Commandant*. You have your orders. Obey them."

Fury exploded inside de Gaulle. His entire body shook. "This is asinine! We are on the verge of the greatest triumph of this war, and you would have us run away? France has done enough running over the past fifty years! It is time we stand and fight!"

Couturier stayed silent for several seconds. When he finally spoke, he did so with a deliberate tone. "*Capitaine* Lhenry. *Capitaine* Lhenry, respond."

"Lhenry's dead!" de Gaulle stated.

"*Capitaine* Giraudeau "

"*Oui, Mon General.*"

"*Commandant* de Gaulle is relieved of command for insubordination, effective immediately. You are now in command of the Forty-Fifth Battlewalker Regiment. Withdraw immediately."

"Um, *Oui, Mon General.*"

De Gaulle narrowed his eyes at the radio. White hot rage paralyzed him. Relieved of command? General Couturier had actually relieved him? Because he had more balls than that useless weakling?

Giraudeau cleared his throat over the radio. His voice then took on a more confident tone. "Forty-Fifth Regiment, withdraw and regroup outside

Tharsis City, coordinates three-zero-seven." A pause. "Sorry, *Mon Commandant.*"

De Gaulle just grunted.

"Sir?"

He lifted his head to see Bosquier staring at him, an expectant look on his face.

"Do as *Capitaine* Giraudeau ordered." De Gaulle scowled.

"Oui, Mon Commandant."

De Gaulle ground his teeth as the battlewalker turned and marched south. He looked over his shoulder, imagining the ruined city behind him, and the spaceport, the great victory, that had been within his grasp.

Now he and the entire French military had to endure another inglorious defeat.

SEVENTEEN

"Bloody hell." Admiral Beatty thumped a fist against the observation window on the *King Edward VII*. He watched a red glow form over Mars, growing brighter by the second. It was the wreckage of the dreadnought *USSS Robert Morris*, burning up in the atmosphere.

Four ships. He'd lost four ships in the last hour from Martian planetary defense batteries. Just when he thought they'd rooted out the last of them, others popped up. The same with those damned armed shuttles. Beatty wondered if the squids had an endless supply of that craft.

Little by little, they're whittling us down.

ASEF still had a large fleet, but if these attacks continued, it would soon be a not-so-large fleet. He'd sent repeated requests to the Supreme Council asking for more ships. Unfortunately, the majority of Earth's space forces were already here at Mars. As French President Maginot rebutted, "We cannot snap our fingers and instantly create spaceships for you."

"No, but you can pressure the Russians and Japanese to commit more of their forces to Mars," he had countered.

Last he heard, ASEF representatives were still negotiating with Stalin and Emperor Taisho. But Stalin remained paranoid that enemies, real and imagined, would try to overthrow him. As for Taisho, well, the Japanese were so mysterious and isolationist, who knew what went on inside their heads.

Beatty continued to hover near the observation window. To his left, heat rays spat from several ASEF ships, directed at enemy targets on the Martian surface. To his right, missiles flew from the tiny moon of Phobos, which had been seized by his forces early in the invasion.

Heat rays shot up from the surface. A blazing miniature sun appeared and faded. Another ASEF ship destroyed.

Beatty scowled and clenched a fist. His mind flashed back to his meeting with the ASEF Supreme Council on Moon Base Alpha nearly two months ago when he mentioned the impact of Stalin's near-withdrawal from Operation Overlord. Prime Minister Lloyd George had told him, "I'm sure you can find a way to make it work."

That could be hard to do if the Martians keep blowing up our ships and killing our soldiers.

He rubbed his hands over his face and drew a slow breath. His attention returned to the space around Mars. ASEF heat rays and missiles rained down on the red planet. The Martians on the surface responded in kind. Another ASEF ship exploded.

Beatty folded his arms and stared at the deck. If Earth sent reinforcements, he doubted it would be anything significant. Deep down, he knew if he were to make it work, it would have to be with the men and ships he had here and now.

He turned away from the battle and floated through the corridors. Men saluted him as they passed. He propelled himself up three decks before reaching a hatch that read "Command Staff Compartment. Authorized Personnel Only." The marine on guard saluted Beatty, then opened the hatch for him. He grabbed the frame and propelled himself inside.

The entire ASEF command staff floated around a finely polished oak table. They came to attention as Beatty maneuvered himself toward the head of the table.

"Right then." He looked to the chubby, balding man to his right. "What's the latest from the Arcadia Plains?"

French General Gaston Ducreux, the head of ASEF intelligence, answered, "The Martians have deployed two more tripod regiments to the region. That brings the estimated number there to two thousand."

"What about Martian infantry?"

"Aerial reconnaissance spotted more troops to the west. At least a division's worth. We believe they moved underground. No one saw them until they appeared in their trenches. The Martians now have at least five army groups in the Arcadia Plains."

"We're getting reports that the Martians are pulling tripods and troops out of several other fronts," explained a gray-haired, distinguished-looking American, General Charles Summerall, commander of ASEF ground forces. "I think it's obvious those forces are being sent to the Arcadia Plains."

"This is only further proof that the Martians have something important there," pointed out a stocky German with a bushy white mustache. General Hans von Seeckt, the Deputy Supreme Allied Space Commander.

"Yeah, but we still don't know what it is." Summerall gave Ducreux an accusatory look.

"We are still trying to determine that." Ducreux glared at Summerall. "We have intercepted several communiqués to and from the Arcadia Plains. Some our codebreakers have been unable to decipher, and others are merely routine messages."

"Do you at least have any theories what the Martians could be hiding there?" asked Beatty.

"They could be building new weapons. It could also be the new headquarters for their Guiding Council. The Martians would go to any length to protect them."

Beatty pressed his palms down on the table and gazed at the map of Mars before him. He took in all the symbols around the Arcadia Plains that denoted Martian units. Good Lord, there were a lot of them.

What is so important to you blighters?

He looked at other areas of the red planet. British and American forces were close to securing the Isadis Plains and Aeolis Region respectively. Other ASEF forces had made significant breakthroughs in the Thyle Region, Hellas Plains, Sinus Meridiani, and Cassini Land. Beatty figured a lot of it had to do with the Martians siphoning off forces from those theaters to aid in the defense of the Arcadia Plains.

His eyes came back to that spot on the map. Ideas took form in his head. Many of them caused his stomach to tighten. *What choice do you have, David?*

"There's only one way to know what the Martians are up to in the Arcadia Plains. We have to take it."

The veins in General Summerall's neck stuck out. "That's going to take a lot of troops and battlewalkers. We still have a lot of other regions of Mars we need to secure before we can launch an offensive there."

"No." Beatty shook his head. "I don't believe we can wait for the action to wrap up in the other theaters. What if the Martians are building new weapons there? Weapons we can't begin to conceive of. They could defeat ASEF, force us to head back to Earth. It will take years to rebuild our forces. By that time, the Martians could use those weapons on Earth itself. No. We need to take the Arcadia Plains as soon as possible."

"Admiral," Summerall began. "There are over a million and a half Martians there. We don't have sufficient forces in the region to take them on."

"Then we'll have to do what the Martians are doing. Pull units from other theaters and send them to the Arcadia Plains."

Shock flashed over Summerall's face. "That means giving up most of our gains on Mars. What's to keep the squids from retaking them?"

"They may not have the numbers to do that," said Beatty. "We've already degraded their military capability. The bulk of what they have left is being concentrated in the Arcadia Plains. We could be looking at *the* decisive battle of Operation: Overlord right here." He thrust his hand out toward the map.

"An offensive of such size requires a lot of munitions." General von Seeckt turned to a tall, brown-haired American. "Admiral Thurman, do we have sufficient stores?"

The head of ASEF logistics let out a slow breath. "I don't know if I can say yes to that. We have been going through ammunition at a faster rate than I expected. We're getting low on ship-launched ballistic missiles, as well as replacement batteries for our heat rays."

"How long will it take to get more munitions from Earth?" asked Beatty.

"Loading operations for the replenishment fleet should take two more days to complete. Then another six days to travel to Mars, and three to four days to transfer munitions and supplies to our ships."

Beatty let out a slow breath. His face scrunched in frustration. That was nearly two weeks! Who the hell knew what would happen in two weeks? The Martians could spring whatever new weapon they had on them.

He closed his eyes, composing himself, then looked up at the command staff. "Begin drawing up plans for an offensive against the Arcadia Plains. Any and all ASEF units are at your disposal. In the meantime, General Summerall, I want you to call a halt to all ground operations."

Summerall's jaw fell open. "A halt, Sir? You want us to stop fighting the Martians?"

"In effect. I want all ground forces to hold their positions until further notice."

"If we do that, we're inviting the Martians to attack us. We have the advantage on several fronts. We need to keep pushing forward and gain more territory."

"Which will cost us more lives, battlewalkers, artillery, and jets," said Beatty. "We can't count on significant reinforcements from Earth, so we must conserve what we have here on Mars. And we certainly can't mount an attack on this scale without sufficient stocks of munitions. Therefore, we have to restrict ASEF to defensive operations only until the replenishment fleet from Earth arrives."

"And that gives the Martians two weeks to recover and build up their defenses," said Summerall. "Or launch an offensive of their own. How many of our forces will we lose then?"

Beatty narrowed his eyes at the American general. He had allowed the man some leeway to make his point, but now he risked crossing the line.

He was about to address the matter when von Seeckt spoke up. "Admiral, I do think General Summerall has a point."

Beatty whipped his head around to his number two man. Anger billowed inside him. He started to open his mouth when the German general continued.

"I agree, we must wait until we have more munitions before we begin this offensive. But we should not, um, what is the term, 'let up' on the Martians. We should try to disrupt them in some way. Raids, probes, harassment fire."

Beatty mulled it over. Such attacks meant using valuable ammunition. Still, he didn't like the idea of giving the Martians a complete respite. "Very well. You have permission to conduct small-scale operations against the Martians until the Arcadia Plains offensive. We must let them know we haven't forgotten about them."

A few soft, brief chuckles went up from the command staff. General Summerall gave a half-smile and a slight nod. It seemed this order satisfied him to some degree.

"We should also conduct more bombardments with our germ shells," said the American. "That ought to disrupt any Martian operations during our . . . break."

"That may not do much good," Ducreux pointed out. "Most of the Martian infantry are equipped with protective suits."

"Most of their civilians aren't."

Beatty turned to Summerall. "We have had reports of significant outbreaks in and around Tharsis City and Hellas Plains thanks to our germ shells. More such outbreaks could cause the Martians to concentrate more on stopping the spread of those illnesses than on launching any new offensives against us. See to it, General."

"Yes, sir."

"Once we're resupplied," said Beatty, "we'll begin moving our forces into position."

"We're risking a lot here, Admiral," said Summerall.

"True, General, but in war, one must take risks."

"Of course. But if we fail to take the Arcadia Plains, it's going to be very costly regarding men and material. It may not be the battle we lose, but the entire war."

Beatty locked eyes with Summerall, feeling his face go rigid with determination. "Well then, General, we'd best not fail."

RETALIATION

EIGHTEEN

We should not be doing this.

Supreme Guardian Hashzh's concerns grew the longer he stared at the screens in his chamber. Computer generated images of tripods, automated batteries, armed shuttles, and land guardians stretched across the northern part of Shoh. So many of them.

All visible to the Brohv'ii.

His tentacles trembled. He had warned the Guiding Council, told them putting large numbers of guardians around the Final Project would alert the Brohv'ii that something of great importance was happening here. They were sure to attack.

But once again, panic usurped reason. The Council ordered much of the Guard Force to the Final Project. Even with their network of tunnels, they could not keep such a large force hidden from the Brohv'ii. They would come, with as many soldiers and fighting machines as they could gather. He only hoped he had sufficient numbers of Shoh'hau to defeat them.

We must. The consequences are unthinkable.

That last word caused him to shift his vision to a screen on the right. A row of tripods blocked a group of more than five hundred Shoh'hau fleeing the fighting in the Toivi Region, a region where the sickness released by the Brohv'ii had killed thousands. This had been his fear, his and many other Shoh'hau, that the Brohv'ii bacteria that wiped out the Cleansing Force would contaminant this world. Now that it had…

His eyes remained fixed on the monitor. He hated what was about to happen, but it was necessary.

The tripods fired their heat rays. Flames and smoke swept over the Shoh'hau. Disbelief and anger surged through Hashzh. They were killing their own people! Yes, it was necessary to keep the Brohv'ii diseases from spreading, but… Shoh'hau killing Shoh'hau? Such acts had not occurred, on such a scale, for tens of thousands of cycles.

The Brohv'ii. It is the Brohv'ii making us kill each other. All the more reason to erase their kind from the universe.

A deep hum filled his chamber. Words flashed across the wall screen. The Guiding Council wanted to meet with him.

Hashzh crawled through the corridors, wondering what other foolish orders they could give him. When he entered the Council's chamber, he halted and lifted his tentacles above his body.

"The honor is mine to be in the presence of the Guiding Council."

"Greetings, Supreme Guardian Hashzh," answered Supreme Councilor Frtun. "You are welcome in our presence."

He slid closer to the leaders of the Shoh'hau race. "You wish to see me, Councilors?"

"Indeed," said Frtun. "It has been decided that, given the current situation, we will act on your numerous requests for more weaponry."

Surprise took hold of Hashzh. The feeling didn't last long, not when he thought of all the territory and cities the Brohv'ii had captured and destroyed.

If you had initially approved my requests, the Brohv'ii would not be on our planet. But dwelling on what could have been was a waste of thought.

"Thank you, Councilors. How many new weapons can I expect and when?"

Councilor Yrvul answered, "Within fourteen rotations, you will have fifty new tripods, twenty new armed shuttles, and five new planetary defense batteries."

"That is all?"

"Several of our factories have been destroyed or captured by the Brohv'ii, and the majority of our resources must be directed toward completion of the Final Project. We have spared as much as we could for the building of new weapons."

"We will need far more new tripods, shuttles, and planetary defense batteries to deter the Brohv'ii," Hashzh explained.

"I find your comments surprising, Supreme Guardian," Rezdv noted. "You have requested more weaponry on numerous occasions. Now that we give them to you, you complain."

"I am not complaining, Councilor Rezdv. I am merely stating a fact. Our losses have been high. These new weapons will hardly make up for the ones the Brohv'ii have destroyed."

"Enough of your worry, Supreme Guardian," Ehjah said in a harsh tone. "We have seen your reports. The Brohv'ii are no longer advancing. They have realized we are superior to them, and they cannot possibly defeat us. They will soon leave Shoh."

Hashzh stared at Ehjah in disbelief. Why would the Brohv'ii leave when they had control over several regions? They likely halted their forces to save them for an all-out assault on the Final Project.

All the other councilors looked at Ehjah. Hashzh sensed their concern. Perhaps they now believed what he had felt for so many rotations. Ehjah's brain had malfunctioned.

A part of Hashzh felt pleased. Ehjah would be put to death. He knew he shouldn't think such thoughts about a member of the Guiding Council, but his malfunctioning brain was a detriment to them. They couldn't afford that in a time of war.

Supreme Councilor Frtun returned his gaze to Hashzh. "That is all the new weaponry we can provide you. If you cannot defeat the Brohv'ii with the forces you have here, then you must delay them until the Final Project is completed."

"Yes, Supreme Councilor."

Hashzh considered Frtun's words. Given all the losses the Guard Force had suffered, that might be the only strategy he could employ. Concentrate his forces here, strengthen their defensive positions, and let the Brohv'ii come to them. There could be no retreat. They had to hold to the last Shoh'hau. He recalled some of the Brohv'ii's military records he had studied. Hundreds of cycles ago, when they fought with swords and arrows, they would lay siege to strongholds. Sometimes it took them many, many rotations, even half a cycle, before the defenders would succumb, either from too many deaths or too little food, or a combination of both.

Hashzh and his Guard Force did not have to hold out that long. Perhaps twenty-five rotations at most. By then the first part of Guiding Council's Final Project should be ready.

Also, *his* final project should be ready by that time. Then the Brohv'ii would never threaten his race again.

RETALIATION

NINETEEN

"You! Corporal! Five-dollar fine. Now button that uniform."

Lieutenant Colonel Patton watched the young, redheaded soldier cringe, then button the top two buttons of his fatigues.

"Yes, sir. Sorry, sir."

Patton sent a harsh gaze at the corporal, then looked down the table of the mess hall aboard the troop landing ship *USSS Fossil Creek*. Other soldiers turned away and tried to straighten their uniforms as inconspicuously as possible. The muscles in Patton's face strained as if trying to hold back his rising anger.

Those muscles failed

"Five-dollar fine! Five-dollar fine! Five-dollar fine!" He stomped along the table, pointing at various soldiers. Then he halted. Everyone stopped eating and stared at him with a mixture of shock and fear.

"To hell with it! Every single man at this table is fined five dollars! I'm looking at sergeants, lieutenants, and captains who didn't bother checking their men to see if they looked presentable before coming to the mess hall. What the hell good are you dumbshits if you don't use your damn authority?"

Patton stalked away, grumbling to himself. He felt the eyes of his artillerymen on his back.

More like burning through my back.

He knew most of the men hated him and thought he was crazy for maintaining a dress code.

"We're in spacesuits half the time," he'd heard one private gripe. "Who the hell cares if our boots are shined and our top button is buttoned? We ain't in a fashion show."

Idiot. This wasn't about fashion. This was about discipline. This was about taking pride in yourself as a soldier in the United States Army. It was more important than ever to maintain high standards after sitting in the same damn place for two weeks. If they grew lax at camp, they would become lax in the field. That led to mistakes, and mistakes got people killed.

That's not going to happen while I'm in charge.

After lunch, Patton and his 214th SPA Regiment marched out of the ship and bounded over the Martian surface. Their armored vehicles were a mile away, sitting in trenches. The closer he got to them, the more aggravated he became. He glanced over his shoulder at the habitats and landing ships grouped together.

Why don't they hang up a neon sign that says, "Martians attack here"?
Jackasses.

"Hold your positions." That had been the last order his regiment received from the ASEF brass. Every time he asked the commander of the 32nd Infantry Division, Major General Willey, when they were going to start blowing the shit out of the squids again, he'd give him the same answer: "As soon as ASEF Command Staff orders us."

At this rate, that might not be until Judgment Day.

Patton had his men inspect their SPAs to make sure they were in working order. When they had taken care of any needed repairs, he ordered the vehicles moved to other prepared positions. He'd be damned if he'd keep his SPAs in the same place for too long. Why make things easy for Martian artillery?

The day dragged by with Patton staring across the rust-colored Martian landscape. He chafed at the thought of the squids building up their defenses while his men sat on their asses. Or worse, those alien sons-of-bitches launching their own offensive.

You don't win wars by holding your position. You win by attacking. He understood that. Why the hell couldn't his shit-for-brains superiors?

Then again, these were the same people who couldn't recognize the offensive potential of SPAs.

The next day brought some excitement. A squadron of stubby, swept-winged Wright F3F Panther jet fighters flew overhead, headed north. Fifteen minutes later columns of smoke appeared on the horizon.

"Looks like the flyboys are getting some action," said Corporal Fuller, the radioman on Patton's SPA.

"Yeah." The gunner, Private Simpson, nodded. "You hear about that one flier, Rickenbacker? They say he shot down four squid shuttles in one day."

"No shit," said Fuller. "I hope they give the guy a medal for that."

"To hell with Rickenbacker and all those other damn flyboys," Patton snapped. "You think they're real warriors? They zip around the sky for a couple of hours, drop some bombs, then go back to base, get blind-stinking drunk, and act like big shits. They're not in the field every minute of every damn day. They don't have bullets flying around them. They don't sleep in ditches. They're not the ones who plant a flag in the ground and conquer territory. We are! Remember that next time you fawn over some damn pilot like a Hollywood starlet."

"Yes, sir." Both Fuller and Simpson hung their heads, reminding Patton of his daughters Bea and Ruth when he scolded them.

His foul mood continued the next day, and he took it out on his men. He had them run around the camp twenty times, then do lots of push-ups and sit-ups. Next, they did loading and aiming drills on the SPAs. He was busy yelling at one crew for taking too long to traverse the vehicle when its commander, a staff sergeant, said hesitantly, "Um, sir," and pointed behind Patton.

He turned to find a spacesuited figure bounding toward them. He quickly recognized the man with the thick, dark mustache and a prominent forehead.

Brigadier General John F. O'Ryan, the deputy commander of the 32nd Infantry Division.

"Ten-hut!" Patton snapped to attention. The men around him did the same.

"At ease." O'Ryan gazed at the SPAs and their crews. "How's your regiment fairing, Colonel?"

"Fine, sir, despite the fact we're just sitting around instead of killing the enemy."

O'Ryan didn't respond. His eyes narrowed, and his mouth tightened. The reaction didn't surprise Patton. He hadn't exactly endeared himself to the division brass over the past couple of weeks. He couldn't count how many times he asked General Willey or General O'Ryan or the division operations or intelligence officers when they'd get back in the war. Patton knew he was annoying the hell out of them. Not that he gave a damn. Sometimes if you wanted shit done, you had to rattle some cages.

O'Ryan's shoulders rose and fell with a slow, audible breath. The anger on his face faded. "Orders just came down from ASEF Command. We all need to be ready to move out in the next twenty-four hours."

Patton's chest swelled. "Where to?"

"We don't know yet."

"Does this mean we're getting back in the fight?"

"I don't know, Colonel." O'Ryan didn't try to keep the annoyance out of his voice. "The orders said to be ready to move out within twenty-four hours, so stop wasting time asking questions and get ready."

"Yes, sir." Patton snapped him a crisp salute.

O'Ryan returned the salute, grunted, and bounded away.

A smile crept over Patton's face. This was it. They were going to attack the Martians. He could feel it. Enough of this "hold your position" shit. It was time to do what soldiers did best.

Fight.

Unless they want us to hold someplace else.

Patton groaned. Wouldn't that be just like the Army?

RETALIATION

TWENTY

Twenty-four hours had passed since General O'Ryan told Patton to be ready to move out. Their gear was stowed, their rucksacks filled, and all the SPAs were in good condition.

Still, they remained in place. For twenty-five hours. Twenty-six. Twenty-seven.

Patton stalked up and down the regiment's fighting positions, ready to explode. He eyed the SPA crews, looking for any kind of infraction. He needed to take out his frustrations on someone. Much as he wanted to, he couldn't do it on the ones who really deserved it—the damn generals.

Another worry took hold of Patton. What if O'Ryan had lied about the redeployment? What if he said that to mollify him? Even worse, what if other units were headed off to fight while the 214th continued to sit here? Maybe this was his punishment for being such a pain in the ass. It wouldn't surprise him. The Army had its share of petty and vindictive officers.

Thirty hours had passed. Patton headed back to the *Fossil Creek* to sack out. Actually, he expected to just lay in his bunk and stare at the ceiling. He was too enraged to fall asleep.

He had started up the ramp when a lieutenant he recognized as one of General Willey's aides came up to him.

"Colonel Patton."

"What?"

"General Willey has called for a meeting of all regimental commanders in the command habitat at twenty-three hundred hours."

Patton smiled and nodded. *Finally.*

He entered the command habitat twenty minutes early, beating everyone else there. He unlatched his helmet and took it off, inhaling the mechanically generated air. Next Patton removed his gloves and wiped the sweat from his face. He took another gulp of air.

"It does feel good to take off that fishbowl, doesn't it?"

Patton turned around and saw a stocky, dark-haired man enter the tent, his helmet tucked under his arm.

"It gets to the point I feel like I've got a hot towel wrapped around my face, for hours," he said to Lieutenant Colonel Brad Jones, the commander of the 167th Battlewalker Regiment.

"Tell me about it." Jones came over and sat next to Patton. "So you think they're going to let us go back out and fight the damn squids again?"

"If they're smart they will. The squids aren't going to exterminate themselves."

"Hear, hear." Jones nodded.

The other regimental commanders filed into the command habitat. At precisely 2300, General Willey and General O'Ryan entered the briefing room. Patton and the other commanders stood at attention.

"As you were." Willey waved them to sit down. Some enlisted men wheeled in easels with maps and photographs taped to them.

"Gentleman, I know it hasn't been easy for you, being cooped up in camp all this time." Willey's gaze rested on Patton. He took it as a not-so-subtle reminder that he'd irritated the hell out of him these past few weeks.

Patton met Willey's gaze, not blinking, not showing any sign of being intimidated.

Willey gave a barely audible grunt and continued. "Well, that's about to end. Orders just came down from ASEF Command. We're going to launch a new offensive against the Martians."

Several of the colonels nodded or muttered, "Yeah."

"Hot damn!" blurted Patton, tacking on a wide grin.

General Willey shot him an annoyed look. Before he could reprimand him, Patton asked, "So where are we going, sir?"

Willey took a slow breath before answering. "The Arcadia Plain. We're to secure Tharsis City and the smaller Martian cities nearby, then move north into the plain itself. ASEF intelligence believes there is an underground base in that region housing something of vital importance to the Martians."

"Do we know what it is, sir?" Jones asked.

"No. It could be some secret weapon they're working on, it could be where their Guiding Council has taken shelter. Whatever it is, it has to be important for the Martians to pull so many of their forces from other fronts and send them there."

The corners of Patton's mouth curled. It sounded like the intel weenies were gazing into crystal balls or reading tea leaves instead of coming up with actual information. Regardless, they had the bulk of the Martian military in one place. It was the perfect set-up for a decisive battle.

Maybe that's what the damn squids want. The possibility delighted Patton to no end. If the ugly bastards wanted a decisive battle so bad, he'd gladly give it to them.

* * *

Despite having barely slept during the night, anxious energy surged through Patton. He clamped his hands down on his knees and leaned forward in his chair as much as his straps allowed him. His eyes didn't waver from the digital clock mounted to the bulkhead of his quarters. 0360. He gave a brief chuckle at the unusual time. Since a Martian day lasted thirty-nine minutes longer than an Earth day, those extra minutes had to go somewhere.

C'mon, c'mon. He willed the clock to move faster. He couldn't stand inactivity anymore, not when he knew that soon, very soon, he'd start dropping shells on the damn Martians.

The clock blinked to 0361. The intercom blared, "One minute to liftoff. All personnel, secure for liftoff."

Patton's heart slammed against his chest. He clenched his teeth, imagining shells from his SPA exploding amongst those tentacled freaks, ripping their bodies apart.

He didn't want to wait another second longer. He wanted to kill those bastards now!

A rumble went through the *Fossil Creek*.

"Ten seconds to liftoff. Five, four, three, two, one."

A loud groan filled Patton's ears. An invisible hand pressed down on him as the ship rose into the sky. He looked out the porthole at the lavender-blue night.

We're coming, you shit-sucking squids.

Ten minutes passed before *Fossil Creek* reached the edge of the atmosphere and leveled out. Patton unbuckled himself from his seat and made his way to the cargo hold, along with the rest of the 214th. He climbed into his SPA, strapped himself into the commander's seat, and waited again.

My God, he hated waiting.

He felt the ship descend. Patton took a quick, deep breath and looked around at his crew. "This is it, boys. We're finally back in the fight."

"Yes, sir," they replied, though not with the enthusiasm he'd expected.

A tremor went through *Fossil Creek* when it landed. Deckhands rushed about, unchaining the SPAs. Patton unbuckled himself from his seat and went to the front of his vehicle. He held his breath, staring intently at the cargo hatch.

Tingles raced through him when it began to lower. The Martian surface stretched before him.

"Forward!" His right arm shot out.

The SPAs rolled down the ramp. Distant flashes of light caught Patton's attention.

Lightning?

He turned to the left. It wasn't lightning. Heat rays from orbiting ASEF ships streaked down from the sky. Columns of smoke billowed up from Tharsis City thirty miles to the west. More heat rays hit Oceanus, a smaller city twelve miles north of Patton's position.

Using the barrel of the gun to balance himself, Patton took out his binoculars and put them up to his visor. Despite his best efforts, they slid around the glass surface.

"Shit!" The eggheads could build ships that fly across space, but they couldn't come up with binoculars you could use with spacesuits.

He finally managed to keep the binoculars steady enough to see the gully a mile ahead of where they were to set up their firing positions. A few miles beyond it lay Hill 5768, the 32nd Infantry's objective. Patton pictured the Martians hunkered down there, and wondered how terrified they'd be when shells from his regiment started falling around them.

Do Martians even get scared?

Patton chuckled to himself. *They will when we're done with 'em.*

The SPAs rolled up to their positions. Three buggies darted past them, carrying the soldiers who'd set up their forward observation posts.

"Fuller." Patton stuck out his hand and motioned for the microphone. The radioman handed it to him.

"Razorback, this is Warhorse One. We are in position."

"Acknowledged, Warhorse. Standby."

Patton growled. *You've gotta be kidding me.* He'd done enough waiting the past few weeks. Now he had to do more of it in the middle of a battle?

"Colonel." Fuller pointed to the sky.

Dozens of jets soared overhead. F3F Panthers and F5F Hellcats. They dove on Hill 5768. Bombs fell from their bellies. Rockets flashed from beneath their wings. Flames and smoke sprang up from one end of the hill to the other.

Damn flyboys. Trust them to get the first crack at the squids.

"Warhorse, this is Razorback," headquarters radioed.

"Warhorse here."

"Commence bombardment."

"About damn time, Razorback. Commencing bombardment."

He radioed the rest of the 214th. "All guns, prepare to fire on my mark."

The battery commanders acknowledged the order.

Patton looked to his gunner. "Simpson. Ready to rip a piece out of the squids' asses?"

"Yes, sir."

He smiled. That was a much more enthusiastic answer than he got from Simpson before *Fossil Creek* landed.

"All guns... fire!"

Muffled *booms* filled the air. Patton stared through his binoculars at Hill 5768. Puffs of flame and smoke erupted from its surface.

"This is only the beginning, you sons a'bitches," he muttered to himself before radioing the regiment. "Fire at will. No mercy for these bastards!"

The guns thumped away. The regiment mixed the fragmentation rounds with a few germ shells. Patton hoped the Martians didn't have enough protective suits to go around. Let them choke on plague and anthrax. Or maybe the unprotected ones would get bumped off by their buddies who did have suits. He'd heard reports that the squids were killing their own that they thought might be infected.

Nice when the enemy does our job for us. He grinned.

The forward observers constantly called in with new coordinates. Every couple of minutes Patton ordered his SPAs to new positions. It had saved them a few times when Martian counter-battery fire came down on the gully. All the squids hit were patches of red dirt. A few SPAs had shrapnel ping off their hulls. None had been damaged enough to take them out of the fight.

Within minutes, a haze of smoke and dust settled over Hill 5768. The counter-battery fire slackened. The 214th never let up. Patton intended to put the Martians through hell until HQ ordered him to stop.

They did a half hour later.

The battlewalkers moved forward, along with the infantry. Patton scowled as he watched them advance toward Hill 5768.

We should be going with them. But no. The brass was content to have them sit here, to waste the potential of the SPA. What the hell would it take to make those idiots understand how the SPA's mobility and firepower could be used in close quarter combat?

Well, having a brain would be nice. Unfortunately, it seemed those stars that got pinned to your collar sucked out all your intelligence. It sometimes made Patton wonder if he wanted to become a general.

The ammunition carriers arrived just as the infantry and walkers began their assault. Patton let his second-in-command handle the resupply so he could watch the battle unfold. Heat rays flashed through the air. Fountains of dirt burst up and down the hill. Clouds of smoke formed by hundreds of rifles and machines floated over Americans and Martians alike. Several minutes into the fight he made out the domed, tentacled forms of alien tripods marching down the hill.

So they did keep those things out of sight.

The battle raged for over an hour. The heavy enemy fire kept the 32nd from advancing. They made repeated calls for artillery support. Many of the 214th's newly unloaded shells slammed into Martian positions.

Unfortunately, it didn't help. The Americans retreated.

"Dammit!" Patton roared. "How the hell can we let the Martians beat us like that?"

Fuller, Simpson, and the rest of the SPA crew just stared at him in unsure silence.

Patton growled at them. He started thinking of how he might execute the attack when headquarters called. They ordered another bombardment of Hill 5768.

The SPAs sent more shells crashing down on the hill. By now all the smoke and dust made it impossible to accurately target Martian positions. All they could do was hope they got some lucky hits and killed enough Martians for the infantry to break through.

At least the smoke and dust also affected the Martians. Their counter-battery fire didn't come anywhere close to the 214th's positions.

After a half hour, HQ ordered a halt to the bombardment. Patton and the others watched more jets bomb the hill while they waited for the ammunition carriers to arrive with more shells.

The second assault on Hill 5768 proved as unsuccessful as the first. Again, the 214th got numerous requests for artillery support. Again, it made little difference. The 32nd Infantry couldn't break through the Martian lines.

"This is bullshit." Patton stomped over to Fuller. "Gimmie that thing!"

The radioman looked back at him, eyes wide with fear. He handed the microphone to Patton, who snatched it from him.

"Razorback, this is Warhorse One. What the hell's going on?"

A pause. "Say again, Warhorse."

"Why the hell can't our boys advance up that hill? We've dropped enough shells and bombs on it to blow it to Uranus."

"Um, Warhorse. The enemy is well dug in. There's not much cover for our troops. They tried advancing with the battlewalkers, but that isn't working."

"Well, of course it isn't working," Patton hollered. "Only an idiot would try that. Those things have too long a stride. Foot soldiers can't keep up with it. Hell, a few of them probably got stepped on by accident."

The soldier back at HQ didn't reply. Patton took his silence as confirmation he was right.

"Look, put me on with someone who can actually make decisions. I have an idea to break through the Martian lines."

"Um, I don't know, Warhorse. The command staff is—"

"If you want to win this damn battle, then get me someone with stars on their collar! *Now!*"

"Y-Yes, sir."

A full minute had passed before Patton heard the familiar voice of General Willey through the speaker.

"Warhorse, what is this? We're busy here."

"We're busy here, too, sir, trying to take that hill. I have a plan to do that."

"What?" Willey snapped.

"The infantry needs cover. Send my SPAs forward. Our soldiers can stay behind them while we advance. The SPAs can withstand rifle fire, and soldiers can keep up with them easier than they can a battlewalker. Hell, we can bring our guns to bear at point blank range and blow the shit out of the squids."

Patton stared at the speaker, waiting for Willey to respond. The seconds passed without a word from his superior. Patton tensed. Could this be good or bad? It had to be good. Willey was thinking about it. Surely he would see the logic in this and—

"Warhorse, artillery is for support, not attack. I can't risk our fire support on some half-assed plan."

"It's not a half-assed plan! If you want that hill—"

"Stay where you're at, Warhorse!" Willey cut him off. "That's an order. Provide fire support for our infantry when it's requested. Razorback out."

Patton glared at the radio set. He bared his teeth and threw the microphone down.

"Stupid, thick-headed son-of-a-bitch!" He spun away from the radio and threw up his arms. "We're going to lose more of our boys, and we wouldn't have to if Willey would get his head out of his ass and listen to me!"

The crew stared at him, terror on their faces. Simpson swallowed and stammered, "Y-y-yes, sir."

Patton grunted and turned back to the battle.

The Martians repelled the second attack. The artillery continued to bombard Hill 5768 for the rest of the afternoon and into the night. The next morning, the 32nd brought in its reserves, along with a battalion of Marines and a brigade of Australian soldiers who happened to be nearby.

The third assault on Hill 5768 began late in the morning. After four hours of heavy fighting, the Allied force finally broke through the Martian lines and took the hill.

The sun began to set when the 214th was ordered to take up position on Hill 5768 to support the advance on Oceanus.

"Oh my God," Fuller said in barely a whisper as the SPAs climbed the hill.

Patton looked around, jaw clenched. A lump formed in his throat.

A mass of human bodies and body parts covered the ground like some macabre carpet. Burned out battlewalkers and tripods littered the battlefield. He wondered if Colonel Jones's walker was among them.

Patton lowered his head. How many American and Australian boys died on this damn hill? It had to be in the thousands.

He felt nothing but hatred for General Willey, for all his kind. So entrenched in doctrine that they refused to accept any new ideas.

That arrogance, that stupidity had cost countless lives.

Patton wondered how many more young men would die before the damn generals realized their ways were wrong.

RETALIATION

TWENTY-ONE

A dull *thump* went off on Rommel's right. A fountain of smoke and red sand shot into the air. He clenched his teeth as more explosions burst around his fleeing SPAs.

Schnell. Schnell! He urged his vehicle, all the vehicles in the 12th Schaumburg-Lippe Self-Propelled Artillery Regiment, to go faster.

He caught a flash of orange to his left. An SPA flipped over, trailing a tongue of flames. The crew spilled out of the open compartment, the vehicle rolling over them.

Rommel gritted his teeth. Another SPA lost. How many did that make? Nine?

More Martian rockets burst around them. More geysers of smoke and sand rose and fell. A chill took hold of him. Would one of those rockets hit his SPA? Worse still, there was not a thing he could do about it. He had no way of shooting down enemy rockets. All he could do was rely on prayer and luck that his vehicle would be spared. Him and every other member of the regiment. Sometimes those prayers were answered. Other times...

He suppressed the urge to yell for his driver, Corporal Ehelechner, to go faster. The young man already pushed the SPA to its top speed. So did all the other drivers as they put Icarium far behind them.

Anger punched through Rommel's fear. He despised retreating. They should be going forward, especially after a half day's worth of shelling and bombing the Martian city. Yet the aliens pushed back the infantry and battlewalkers and sent the survivors running for their lives.

Something buzzed above him. Cold fear swept over Rommel.

"Down!"

He threw himself flat on the SPA's deck. So did Privates Frosch and Kopitz. Ehelechner scrunched down in the driver's seat as much as possible.

The buzz grew louder, like a large beehive hanging overhead. Rommel held his breath. *Miss. Miss.*

A quake rattled the SPA. Rommel gasped. He thought someone screamed. Kopitz?

Something pelted the back of Rommel's spacesuit. He shivered. Shrapnel?

Long seconds had passed before he realized his spacesuit hadn't been torn and he wasn't bleeding. It must have been just dirt that hit him.

His muscles loosened as the SPA sped across the desert. He rolled on his back and gazed up at the Martian sky. Even with the armored belt around the compartment, he felt exposed. Was it too much to ask to put some sort of armored roof on these damn things?

A minute went by without another explosion.

"They've stopped," Kopitz said in a shaky voice. "Thank God." He crossed himself.

"That is not necessarily a good thing."

Rommel ignored the private's puzzled gaze and scanned around the dull red desert. The end of the bombardment did not mean an end to the danger.

"Iron Horse Three," an SPA commander shouted over the radio. "Three tripods to the east!"

Rommel spotted the three large machines cresting a hill two kilometers away. He snatched the microphone on the radio set. "All units! Turn west now!"

The SPAs swung away from the tripods. Heat rays tore into the ground, far from his regiment.

The second volley struck closer. The third turned an SPA into a mass of fire.

"Hermod." Rommel switched to the command frequency. "Fox One. We are being pursued by three enemy tripods. Request fire support." He gave the coordinates.

"Acknowledged, Fox One. Support on the way."

More heat rays streaked over the desert. Another SPA exploded.

"It better be on the way soon."

Rommel stared ahead of him, looking for any sort of cover. He spotted a row of small hills, five, perhaps six kilometers away. He wondered how many of his SPAs would make it there.

A yellow bolt whizzed past Rommel's SPA. He held his breath, a chill shooting up his spine. Three or four meters closer and they'd be dead.

He snatched the microphone. "Rear guard elements. Turn about and engage tripods. No more than three rounds per gun. Slow them down."

Rommel watched the trailing SPAs wheel around. A knot formed in his stomach. He prayed he hadn't condemned those crews to death.

If we do not put up some sort of fight, more of us will die.

Smoke belched from the SPAs' 15cm guns. Plumes of dirt shot up around the tripods.

The SPAs fired a second volley. More geysers of dirt burst around the Martian machines. One staggered, but soon righted itself. Heat rays zipped through the air. Rommel flinched as three SPAs exploded.

A third volley of shells bracketed the tripods. A flash of orange leaped off the dome of one machine. Rommel sucked down an anxious breath, hoping it would go down.

The tripod tottered backward, then lurched forward, smoke streaming from its side.

The SPAs spun around and hurried after the rest of the regiment. The tripods let loose with their heat rays. Two vehicles burst into flame.

Rommel's jaw clenched. Had he thrown away the lives of those crews for nothing?

A muffled groan came from the sky. Rommel looked up. His hopes soared as a dozen Fokker 15 jets dove out of the sky. Rockets flew off their wings. Fire sprang from the dome of the damaged tripod. Another tripod blew apart. The remaining one fired its heat ray. One Fokker vanished in a flash of orange.

The other jets circled around. Over a dozen contrails stretched toward the last tripod. It fired its heat, missing.

Five rockets struck the tripod. A fireball consumed the top half. The three smoking legs fell over.

A long breath escaped Rommel's mouth. His shoulders sagged. They were safe, or as safe as anyone could be in a war zone.

He halted the regiment behind the range of hills and called a meeting of his battalion and company commanders. The first thing he asked for was a casualty report. They'd lost seventeen SPAs and seven other vehicles. His stomach sank when he counted what that meant in human terms. Nearly a hundred dead.

I should have had the regiment split up. Or maybe we should have stood our ground and fought the tripods. Rommel wondered if that would have resulted in more deaths.

He shut his eyes. Self-recrimination could wait.

Rommel ordered two SPA companies to form a laager around their position, with the engineer battalion digging holes and creating berms for added protection. He tasked his operations officer to set a sentry rotation and sent his scouts out to look for fallback positions.

"We also have ten wounded, two badly," reported his executive officer, Major Ault. "Headquarters has dispatched ambulances."

"Do what you can for them." Rommel ground his teeth. The thick padding of their spacesuits made it difficult to treat injuries in the field. Cutting through the material to put pressure on a wound just let out more air and would likely kill the man you were trying to help. All they could do was seal the breach in the spacesuit and hope they could hold on until they reached a hospital.

The ambulances arrived shortly after the briefing. Rommel watched the wounded being loaded onto the converted troop transports, his eyes lingering on the large red cross on their hulls. In a human war, the symbol would— usually—guarantee the vehicle and its occupants safe passage through the battlefield. The Martians, however, proved they had no qualms firing on hospitals and ambulances, both during the 1898 invasion and here on Mars.

Why would they, when their goal is to exterminate us?

The ambulances departed. Rommel prayed they'd reach their destination safely.

He walked around the perimeter, inspecting the positions of his SPAs, offering encouraging words to his soldiers. More jets appeared overhead. Some circled their position, providing air cover. Others streaked by, probably to bomb Icarium. It was a shame none of the spaceplane transporters could haul heavy bombers like the Dornier 107. They would do much more damage than the smaller Fokker jet fighters.

Yet another oversight by the General Staff.

He returned to his SPA, where Private Frosch pulled out a plastic tube from his pack. "Time for dinner."

The words made Rommel's stomach grumble. He hadn't eaten since this morning.

Frosch held the tube up to his fishbowl helmet. "Mm. Orange flavor."

Ehelechner snorted. "Orange, peach, strawberry. Like it makes a difference. It all tastes like shit."

"I wouldn't go that far, Corporal." Rommel reached into his own pack and pulled out a food tube. "Baking powder would be more accurate."

"Whatever the case, sir, it's still horrible."

"True, but it is better than starving."

"I'm not so sure about that," Frosch said.

Ehelechner and Kopitz chuckled. So did Rommel. In most units, such banter would never take place between enlisted men and a senior officer. But regimental commander or not, these three were his crew. They had to rely on one another, build trust. It also meant a closer bond than most lieutenant colonels shared with corporals and privates.

Rommel inserted the tube, labeled peach, into a slot in his chest compartment. He then pressed a button on his chest. A straw snaked up from the collar of his spacesuit to his mouth. He sucked down a mouthful of grainy paste that tasted nothing like peach and swallowed. It slithered down his throat, nearly making him gag. He forced himself to finish off his "dinner," then brought up the straw for his water tube and washed it down.

What I wouldn't give for some Sauerbraten *right now.*

Darkness fell hours later. Rommel and his crew lay on the deck. The sharp silhouettes of jets groaned overhead. He was grateful for Mars' lower atmospheric density. It would be hard to fall asleep with the constant, thunderous roar of jet engines like he'd hear on Earth.

He stared past the aircraft, eyeing the little pricks of white light in the sky.

"Herr Oberstleutnant?" said Kopitz.

"Yes, Private?"

"Do you know which one is Earth up there?"

Rommel lifted his right arm and pointed. "A quarter of the way up from the horizon, on the left."

Even with his crew nearby, even with his regiment around him, a dark mass of loneliness settled over him. It always did whenever he looked up at the Martian sky during those respites of fighting and saw the little dot that represented Earth. It made him feel every one of the fifty-four million kilometers between Mars and home. He longed for trees and rivers and fields, for any landscape that wasn't dull red. He wanted real food, cooked by his wife, and a beer. Many beers, after all that he'd been through. And he wanted to be out of this spacesuit and breath real air.

"I wonder what my family is doing back there," muttered Kopitz.

"Worrying about you, like all families worry about their sons when they go off to war." Rommel thought of his own family; he thought of Ilda. Did she lie awake, wondering if he were alive or dead? What he wouldn't give to let his wife know he was all right.

What he wouldn't give to be in bed with her right now.

"What do you think they're telling everyone about what we're doing here?" asked Frosch.

"Knowing the government," said Rommel, "that we are advancing on all fronts and the Martians are trembling in fear at the might of the Imperial German Army."

"If they only knew the truth," grumbled Ehelechner.

"Things will be different next time," Rommel spoke with assuredness. "We will go forward, we will take Icarium, and we will be one step closer to ending this war and returning home."

"Unless the generals decide we need to retreat again," said Ehelechner.

Rommel said nothing. What could he say? Were it up to him, he would not run. He would hit the Martians hard and fast, not give them a chance to regroup, and not stop going forward until Icarium fell.

Unfortunately, it was not up to him.

RETALIATION

TWENTY-TWO

"We're really pounding the hell out of them."

Rommel nodded at Corporal Ehelechner's comment. He and his SPA crew stood in a trench atop one of the hills, staring at the distant form of Icarium. Not that he could see much of the Martian city. A mass of black-gray smoke blotted out whatever buildings remained. Heat rays from orbiting ASEF ships fell from the sky like a non-stop lightning storm. Mixed in with the beams were space-launched ballistic missiles.

"I can't imagine anything surviving that," said Kopitz.

"I imagine many said the same thing of the bombardment before our first assault." Rommel turned to the private. "Yet enough Martians survived to push us back."

Kopitz frowned and lowered his head.

"I'm certain there will be plenty of them left alive, even after this," Rommel continued. "They're probably hiding in tunnels all over the city." He paused, face scrunched in thought. "What we need are missiles that can penetrate deep underground before exploding."

"Another idea you can send to the General Staff, Sir," said Ehelechner.

"*Ja*, so they can ignore it like all my other ideas."

Rommel and his crew left the trench and headed downhill. The 12th Schaumburg-Lippe Self-Propelled Artillery Regiment was no longer the only unit here. Vehicles, troops, and habitats of Army Group Duke Albrecht of Wuerttemberg stretched across the plain, now the staging area for the next assault on Icarium.

The sight of so large a force in one place made Rommel wince. All he could think about was what a tempting target this would be for the Martians.

But no enemy attack came. Two days of constant aerial and orbital bombardment probably made it difficult to carry out any pre-emptive strike.

He ordered his SPA crews to inspect and clean their vehicles and weapons. It had been rather windy over the past day, and the damn Martian sand tended to seep into equipment.

Rommel didn't spare himself from the task. It was his SPA, too. Besides, how would it look if the regimental commander's gun failed to fire during a battle?

He swept sand from the ammunition compartment, now fully stocked. The two days of bombardment allowed his regiment to be re-supplied. He'd also gotten replacement SPAs and crews, bringing his unit close to about three-quarters its original strength. He'd asked for more, but division HQ informed him none were available. Other artillery units had suffered worse losses than the 12th and needed replacements to get them up to at least half strength.

Rommel looked up at the sky, to the only other place he could get more SPAs—Earth, nearly a hundred and twelve million kilometers away.

Once the SPAs had been cleaned and inspected, he ordered his men to the kitchen habitats for lunch. At least now they could eat real food, or what the army cooks passed off as real food. It was still better than sucking down that horrid paste.

They could also remove their spacesuits, though there were disadvantages to that. Operating in the field for any length of time made it impossible to bath. It didn't take long for the habitats to reek of unwashed bodies.

Rommel was still standing in the serving line, tray in hand, when word came down. All units were to move toward Icarium immediately.

"They could have at least waited until after lunch," a young lieutenant complained as men hurried out of the officers' mess.

"War waits for no man, *Leutnant*," Rommel told him. "Nor his stomach." Still, it would have been nice to have some actual hot, or even barely warm food, before heading into the field.

Our ships and planes couldn't keep bombarding the city for another ten minutes.

He slipped on his spacesuit and met his crew at their SPAs. Engine humming to life, the vehicle set off across the desert, followed by the rest of the regiment. Along with checking the formation and watching for threats, Rommel sucked down a few mouthfuls of blueberry paste that tasted nothing like blueberry.

The 12th soon reached their firing pits, dug out by the engineers two kilometers from the outskirts of Icarium. The crews covered their SPAs with brown and red camouflage netting as armored troop carriers and battlewalkers advanced on the city.

Rommel checked with his battalion commanders to make sure all his guns were ready and that each battery had posted a sentry. He didn't want Martian soldiers emerging from the ground and taking them by surprise. Next, he contacted the Arado 45 serving as the regiment's airborne artillery spotter. The small aircraft was ten minutes away from Icarium.

All was in place, or nearly in place. Nothing to do now but wait for requests for artillery support to come in.

And come they did. All the bombs, missiles, and heat rays may have turned Icarium into a massive pile of charred rubble, but that rubble made an effective cover for Martian troops. One German infantry unit after another found itself pinned down by the aliens' stubborn resistance. Rommel's guns flung high explosive shells at the city every few minutes.

"How many squids can still be alive there?" Kopitz shoved another round into the breech, followed by the propellant charge.

"Every shell we fire means a few less Martians among the living," said Rommel. "So if we keep doing this, sooner or later there will be no more of them alive in Icarium."

"I like your logic, sir." Frosch smiled as he made his final adjustments to the gun. He yanked the lanyard. The gun thumped. "And there you have it. A few less Martians."

Rommel chuckled.

The guns fired well into the night. Rommel stayed in close contact with Major Baxmann, the regimental supply officer, to make sure they had plenty of ammunition. He had no desire to tell soldiers fighting for their lives in Icarium, "I'm sorry. We have no shells."

The 12th Schaumburg-Lippe Self-Propelled Artillery Regiment continued to field requests for fire support throughout the next day and the day after that.

"I'd hate to be in the infantry right now." Ehelechner shook his head, staring at the smoky horizon. "They must be going through hell in there."

"It hasn't been easy for us, either," said Kopitz. "Being chased by tripods."

Rommel's eyes flickered between the driver and the loader. The battles with those alien machines would have gone easier had the SPAs been designed as a true fighting vehicle instead of a simple tracked platform with a cannon attached to it. They might even be able to provide direct support to the infantry within the city. Certainly better than any battlewalker could. At least SPAs could operate among the troops, unlike battlewalker crews who sat eighty feet above them. They were as likely to squash them as help them.

Perhaps the General Staff would realize all this one day. Given their resistance to new ideas, Rommel didn't hold out much hope.

The requests for fire support diminished on the fourth day of fighting, and more on the fifth. Martian resistance finally appeared to be withering.

On the morning of the sixth day, division HQ radioed Rommel with new orders.

"Break down the netting," he ordered his crew. "We're moving out."

"Where, sir?" asked Ehelechner.

"Inside Icarium, or what's left of it. Part of the southern portion is on a rise. Division wants us there to provide support for the infantry as they push deeper into the city."

Ehelechner's jaw tensed. "Will we be able to get there? The streets must be filled with rubble."

"I'd be surprised if there were any streets left," said Frosch.

"I was told the engineers have cleared a path for us." *At least I hope they have.* "Now move."

His crew and all the others in the regiment broke down their camouflage netting. Within ten minutes, the SPAs were on the move.

"Mein Gott," Kopitz whispered as they drew closer to Icarium.

Rommel gripped the armored side panel, gaze aimed straight ahead. A sea of scorched rubble stretched before him. What few structures that remained standing appeared on the verge of collapse. Columns of smoke rose from the ruin and merged into one large cloud that hung over the city. A shiver went through him as he remembered the similar sights as a child when the Martians burned city after city in his native Württemberg. The terror he'd felt back then bubbled up in his soul. He heard his mother's sobbing as clearly now as he had running from the tripods twenty-six years ago. He closed his eyes, feeling his father's arms around him as the man carried him away from the aliens.

"Are we going to die?" he had asked over and over in a shaky voice, tears streaming down his face.

His father held him tighter and assured him they would not.

And we didn't.

Rommel forced the memories away. He was no longer a scared six-year-old. He was an officer in the Imperial German Army. He now visited death and destruction on the Martian's home world.

"Sir." Ehelechner pointed ahead of him. Two men stood next to a buggy parked near a pile of rubble, waving.

The SPA pulled next to the smaller vehicle. Rommel leaned over the side and introduced himself. "I assume you are to be our guides through Icarium."

"Jawohl, Mein Herr," replied the stockier of the two. "Corporal Ginter, 20th Guard Pioneer Battalion."

Rommel nodded, then extended his hand toward the battered Martian city. "Lead the way. We are anxious to send more shells the enemy's way."

A grin spread across Ginter's round face. *"Jawohl."*

The engineer hurried back to the buggy. Once his partner settled into the passenger seat, the little vehicle hummed toward the city. Rommel and the rest of his SPAs followed.

He gave credit to the engineers. They had done a fine job clearing a path for his regiment. What debris hadn't been pushed to the side had been used to fill in the craters on the road.

The bombardment left a lot of craters.

The ride was anything but smooth. Rommel's SPA rose and fell and dipped and bounced. He doubted the other gun carriers fared much better. Not that he worried too much. The vehicles had been designed to negotiate rough terrain.

He scanned all around him. Scorched, blasted metallic rubble stretched before him. Here and there the remnants of buildings stood. Dark stains covered some of the debris. Blood, both human and Martian.

The buggy turned a corner. The SPA followed.

"Mein Gott," Kopitz muttered.

Rommel followed the young loader's gaze. He swallowed as nausea burned his stomach.

A row of human shapes covered in tarps lay along the side of the road. At least eighty. Graves registry still had yet to claim the bodies. At least their comrades had laid them out with some measure of respect.

The same could not be said for the Martian dead. Many had been left where they'd been shot or blown up. Others had been pushed off the roadway with the rest of the debris. Had this been a human enemy, Rommel would have demanded the bodies be treated with respect.

He had no interest in showing the same regard to the Martians. They were not even men. They were monsters. Monsters who had no interest in talking to or understanding mankind. All they wanted was its extermination. He refused to waste any sympathy on them.

"Any units! Any units!" A panicked voice burst from the radio. "This is Pioneer Seven Five Four. We're pinned down by Martians." He read off his grid coordinates.

Martians? So much for this area being secure. Rommel checked his map. "That's barely a hundred meters from here," he said aloud. On Earth, he'd be able to hear the gunfire. Not on Mars.

"Pioneer Seven Five Four, this is Fox One, SPA regiment," he radioed the soldier. "Give me target reference."

He relayed the coordinates for the Martians, then gave his own position relative to the enemy. Rommel scowled as he eyed his map.

"Dammit." Barely twenty meters separated the aliens from the soldiers. "Can you move further away from the Martians?"

"No!" the soldier screamed. "They'll cut us down."

Rommel clenched the microphone. Any artillery strike would risk killing Germans as much as Martians.

He stared at the gun, then at the SPAs behind him. "Pioneer Seven Five Four, hold on. We're coming to you." He switched to the regimental frequency and looked at the two SPAs behind him. "Fox Five, Fox Fifteen. Follow me to grid reference one zero two four. We are going to help those soldiers pinned down. The rest of you proceed to our new position."

Rommel had Ehelechner take the next right, followed by the other two SPAs. This road had not been cleared or patched up by engineers. Ehelechner did his best to avoid the larger craters and debris piles. One time when the driver rolled up the side of a mound of rubble, he gripped the sides of his command chair, throat tightening, fearing the vehicle would tip over any second.

It didn't.

Ehelechner crested a debris field. Rommel leaned forward. Ahead of them, he spotted three Martians behind the remains of a wall, firing down on the engineers huddled in a crater. About five meters from them stood the remains of a building, its entire front sheered off.

Rommel grabbed the microphone. "Fox Five, on my left flank. Fox Fifteen, guard our rear."

"*Jawohl,*" replied both vehicle commanders.

The SPAs rolled closer to the Martian position. One of the engineers popped up, fired his Mauser rifle, then ducked back down. The round apparently didn't hit any of the aliens.

One of them turned his way. Then another.

"Driver stop!" Rommel shouted. "Gunner. High explosive on the Martian position."

Kopitz rammed the shell into the breech, followed by a powder charge.

The barrels of the Martian rifles flickered. Bullets thunked off the gun and the hull.

"Shit!" both Kopitz and Frosch blurted and ducked. Rommel bit back the same curse and also ducked. He crawled to one of the compartments on the deck and threw it open. He yanked out a stubby MP-18 submachine gun. From one knee, he fired at the Martians. He didn't think he'd hit them. So long as he forced them behind cover, Frosch had the chance to adjust the gun.

Rommel fired one short burst after another. The Martians slid behind the wall. Frosch lowered the 15cm gun, then told Ehelechner to turn seven degrees to the left.

"Fire!" Frosch hollered. He yanked the lanyard. A tremor rippled through the SPA as the gun thumped. A second later, Fox Five's gun went off.

The wall exploded. One of the Martians spiraled through the air, two tentacles torn off, rifle slipping from its grasp.

"*Ja!*" Frosch slapped the side of the gun.

"Good shooting, Private," Rommel complimented him.

"*Danke, Mein Herr.* It's like you say, there are more uses to the SPA than shelling the enemy from kilometers away."

"Remember that if you are ever promoted to the General Staff."

"Ha! I think I have a better chance of marrying Princess Victoria Louise than becoming a—"

Dull *thunks* hammered the SPA.

"Down!" Rommel dropped to the deck. He inserted a fresh magazine into his MP-18 and slid over to the armored siding. More blows drummed against the hull. He peeked over the side.

A pair of Martians lay on the third floor of the blasted building, firing down on the SPAs.

Something tugged on his left leg. He tensed and felt down his calf. His gloved hand ran over a slight tear. He must have got hit by a ricochet. Thank God it wasn't worse.

He reached for his sealant spray when a gun thumped nearby. A muffled rumble followed.

Rommel peered over the side. The third floor collapsed, taking the two Martians with it. Wisps of smoke curled up from Fox Fifteen.

"Dammit." Rommel got into a crouch. "This is why I told the General Staff we need a fully enclosed vehicle. We're too vulnerable to attack from above. Maybe now they'll—"

His mouth hung open wordlessly as he saw Kopitz kneeling, tears sliding down his cheeks. Rommel swallowed and looked down.

Frosch lay on the deck unmoving, two bloody holes in his chest.

TWENTY-THREE

The first thing Supreme Guardian Hashzh noticed when he crawled into the Guiding Council's chamber was eight members lying before him instead of nine. After the traditional greeting, he asked, "Where is Councilor Ehjah?"

"It has been determined he suffered a brain malfunction," answered Supreme Councilor Frtun. "Therefore, Councilor Ehjah was removed."

A feeling of satisfaction came over Hashzh. Ehjah's removal was something that should have occurred long before now. Still, the useless lump of flesh was gone. That's all that mattered.

"When will Ehjah's place be filled?"

"That may not be possible until the current crisis has been resolved," Frtun informed him.

Hashzh contemplated the statement. *That assumes the war will be resolved in our favor.*

"Tell us, Supreme Guardian," Councilor Yrvul spoke. "What are you doing to resolve this crisis?"

"We are forming defensive perimeters around the site of the Final Project. We have also armed as many shuttles as possible. Unfortunately, the vast majority of our shuttles have been destroyed by the Brohv'ii. More than half of our fighting machines have been destroyed or damaged."

"You will have more." The words flew from Yrvul's mouth. "Our factories are building more shuttles and fighting machines."

"True, Councilor, but it will not be enough to replace all the ones we lost."

Yrvul pulled his tentacles closer to his body. "Are you suggesting the Brohv'ii may defeat us?"

Hashzh paused. "That is a possibility."

Some of the councilors twisted their bodies toward one another. Yrvul kept his large eyes on Hashzh, his tentacles quivering.

"That cannot happen. That must not happen!" Yrvul slid halfway off his mat. "Your task is to protect the Shoh'hau race. But the Brohv'ii have swarmed across our world. They've destroyed our cities, killed millions of our race, and have spread their diseases into our air. You have failed in your duty."

"I must agree with Councilor Yrvul," said Councilor Rezdv.

"Respectfully, Councilors, I will have only failed if the Brohv'ii destroy the Final Project. That has not happened, and I will do all in my power to keep that from happening."

Hashzh took in all the Councilors before focusing on Frtun. "The truth is, we should have had far more fighting machines and warships in anticipation of a Brohv'ii invasion. Many Shoh'hau citizens have volunteered to fight the Brohv'ii, but we do not have time to train them to become proper Guardians. As it stands, the Guard Force is no longer capable of carrying out offensive operations. All our focus must now be on defending our remaining territory, especially the area of the Final Project. Our only hope now is for us to draw out the conflict."

"Draw it out?" Yrvul hollered. "You need to *end* this conflict."

"That is my intention, Councilor, but it may take a high number of rotations for that to happen. We must kill as many Brohv'ii as possible when they attack our perimeters, and we must not yield any ground to them. If their losses become too great, they will have to leave Shoh and return to Brohv."

"And what is to prevent them from rebuilding their forces and returning many cycles from now?" asked Rezdv.

"The first part of the Final Project is at least nine rotations from completion," Frtun explained. "So long as the Guard Force holds off the Brohv'ii until that time, what they do in the future will not matter."

He focused on Hashzh. "Defend this region, Supreme Guardian. Defend it with all the ferocity you and your Guardians can summon. We will send you as many new fighting machines, defense batteries, and armed shuttles as possible."

"Thank you, Supreme Councilor. To that end, may I make a request?"

"You may."

"Those fighting machines that have been assigned to the Final Project itself—I would like half of them released to aid in the defense of this region."

"That cannot be done," said Yrvul. "They are vital to the future of The Final Project."

Hashzh felt his irritation grow. "The Final Project may be doomed if I do not have those fighting machines."

"They are needed to protect the future of the Shoh'hau."

"If the Brohv'ii break through our defenses, there may be no future for the Shoh'hau."

"A valid argument," Frtun said. "Still, once the Final Project is completed, our race could be vulnerable without those fighting machines." He paused. "The Guiding Council will discuss this further and inform you of our decision when we have made it."

Frtun dismissed Hashzh a short time later. He crawled back to his chamber, unable to shake his frustration.

"Discuss it further." How long will that take? Will they continue to discuss it when the Brohv'ii have breached the chamber of the Final Project?

They ask me to do everything in my power to preserve the future of our race, then hesitate to give me the weapons needed for that task. Never did he expect such illogical behavior from a Shoh'hau, especially the ones on the Guiding Council.

Perhaps Ehjah should not have been the only one removed.

When Hashzh returned to his chamber, he studied the computerized display of his defenses in the northern region. At least, those areas still under Shoh'hau control. Most of the major cities had fallen. Truthfully, they had been reduced to smoldering rubble.

He looked at his perimeters and the positions of the Brohv'ii armies. A few areas to the west and north of the Final Project should be strengthened. But that would mean taking away forces from other areas, thus weakening them.

Yet if I don't do that, the Brohv'ii may break through those perimeters.

Having those fighting machines from The Final Project would solve that dilemma, but he didn't know when, or if, the Guiding Council would release them.

Right now, he could only stave off the Brohv'ii's attack with the weapons and Guardians available to him.

Hashzh lay still, thinking. There had to be other ways to stop the uprights, especially their fighting machines. While not as advanced as the ones the Shoh'hau used, they still proved formidable. If the Shoh'hau fighting machines failed to stop them, what chance would the ground Guardians have?

Yet Brohv'ii land guardians destroyed some of our machines during the Cleansing Mission, despite the primitive weapons they possessed at the time.

Could that be the answer? Hashzh thought about studying the records from the Cleansing Mission, to see some of the tactics the Brohv'ii used against the fighting machines.

He gurgled in disgust. Had things become so desperate he actually considered using ideas from the enemy? Despite their advances over the past thirteen cycles, they were still a primitive race. They did not value intelligence and reason like the Shoh'hau. Even after the Cleansing Mission, they still fought amongst themselves. The Shoh'hau had lived united for thousands of cycles, while the Brohv'ii continued to live in their separate tribes, stealing from and killing one another. Even members of the same tribes committed acts of violence against each other.

The Brohv'ii did not deserve to live. His mind was superior to that of any Brohv'ii. He did not need their ideas to defeat them. He could devise his own.

Hashzh lay on his mat and thought, coming up with a variety of tactics and dismissing most of them. He was considering ways for ground Guardians to destroy the legs of human fighting machines when a purple light on his panel flashed.

Hashzh stared at it, frozen in surprise. *Givrht.* He thought of the Guard Commander Third Order, who had left to oversee *their* final project shortly before the Brohv'ii invaded. He shot out a tentacle and tapped the light. His eyes shifted to one of the screens on the wall. The message was just three words long.

It is done.

For the first time in many cycles, Hashzh experienced joy. His final project had been completed, sooner than expected.

In a few more rotations, Brohv would be no more.

TWENTY-FOUR

It would seem I'm making it work.

Admiral Beatty again recalled the words of Prime Minister Lloyd George as he read the latest report from Mars. The city of Arcadus Six had fallen an hour ago. ASEF forces continued to gather in what remained of Tharsis City, staging for the final push into the Arcadia Plain. By tomorrow, he'd have more troops and warships to throw into the fight. Like sharks sensing blood in the water, the ASEF nations committed nearly all their remaining ships and space-trained troops to what was shaping up to be the final battle. Even that paranoid loon Stalin sent along a good portion of his space forces. Not the number his predecessor had originally pledged, but far better than the piddly force he contributed to the first wave.

He allowed himself to be happy. Victory was within sight.

Beatty's elation was tempered when he thought of the brave soldiers and airmen down on Mars. ASEF's success had come at a costly price. Casualties had been staggering. The squids seemed to realize the jig was up, and they might as well go down fighting.

He felt for those men on the surface. He thought of his own combat experience against the Mahdists in The Sudan. At least there he'd been on a boat, and a well-armed one at that. He didn't have to lie in mud and filth in trenches with bullets buzzing about and shells bursting all the time.

And I put them in that position.

But what choice did he have? None, if he wanted to ensure the damned squids never threatened Earth again.

Beatty left his quarters and floated through the corridors until he reached the Battle Management Center.

"Admiral on deck," Captain Gibbons announced.

"As you were," said Beatty. "Anything to report?"

"We're still pounding the Arcadia Plain." Gibbons pointed to one of the screens. It showed countless ships spewing heat rays and missiles, all headed toward the Martian surface.

Beatty nodded. "How are our tentacled friends responding to it?"

"They're not. In fact, we've hardly had any return fire from the surface the past few days. If you ask me, I think we've knocked out all the squids' missile launchers and heat ray batteries."

Beatty wanted to believe that but tempered his enthusiasm. "Perhaps, but you can't be too sure. Just keep an eye out." He didn't want to get overconfident and botch things.

"Always, sir."

"Captain," Lieutenant Porter called from his combat coordination console. "Replenishment ship *Loch Ness* approaching. They're requesting permission to dock."

"Then we'd best give it to them," Beatty responded before Gibbons could. "Rather difficult to fight without fresh batteries for our guns and food for our stomachs."

Gibbons grinned, then turned to Porter. "Permission granted. Prepare for docking sequence."

King Edward VII moved further away from Mars. The cruiser HMSS *Gladiator* and the corvettes HMSS *Sirius* and HMSS *Minerva* took up defensive positions around the dreadnought to protect it at its most vulnerable.

Ten minutes passed before Beatty heard and felt the dull *clunk* as the *Loch Ness* connected with *King Edward VII*.

"All docking clamps secure," Porter reported. "Ready to begin transfer operations."

"Commence transfer operations," Gibbons ordered.

"Commencing transfer operations."

Fresh batteries for *King Edward VII*'s heat rays were loaded aboard first. Gibbons ordered all weapons shut down so the batteries could be switched out.

Beatty remained in the BMC. He had a few minutes to spare and didn't get a chance to spend much time on the bridge, or in the BMC, given his duties as Supreme Allied Space Commander. At times, the job made him feel more like a bureaucrat than a sailor. Being here helped ease that feeling. Though he wished he could smell the salt air like he did when he served at sea.

He turned his attention back to the main screen, watching with satisfaction as his fleet continued to bombard the Arcadia Plain.

* * *

Will this be my last mission?

Nvif paused as he neared his armed shuttle. He had wondered that the previous forty times he'd flown into combat. He had survived to this point. The vast majority of his fellow pilots had not. Nvif reasoned his skill was what kept him alive. Not that he considered himself an exceptional pilot. How much skill did it take to fly a shuttle?

But his superiors thought him exceptional. Six rotations ago they informed him they intercepted several Brohv'ii communications regarding the death of one of their pilots who flew a red, triangular jet, someone named "Baron." Apparently, he had been a pilot of some renown.

Nvif had been the one to shoot him down. He recalled that moment, returning from a failed attack on a Brohv'ii spaceplane transporter. The red jet just crossed in front of him, seemingly unaware of his presence. Nvif fired three bursts from his energy weapon. The jet fell from the sky, trailing smoke until it hit the ground and exploded.

To his superiors, killing this "Red Baron" earned him a place in this latest attack on the Brohv'ii. *A desperate attack*, he thought.

Nvif crawled into the shuttle and took his place in the oblong-shaped nose. His skin grew hotter in the confining protective suit around his body. He had long grown used to the discomfort. Better that than inhaling Brohv'ii bacteria.

"All shuttles," the controller radioed. "Prepare for launch."

Nvif activated the engines. A steady groan went through the shuttle.

Will this be my last mission?

He shoved aside the thought, concentrating on the attack plan. He twisted his front half to the left, staring out the control deck's window.

Smoke and flames gushed out of the nearby silos. Fifteen missiles rose into the sky.

"All shuttles," the controller radioed. "Launch!"

The engines roared as Nvif's shuttle lifted off. He checked his scanner. Nine other shuttles formed up behind him.

He twisted the controls to the left, lining up behind the missiles, far enough away not to be incinerated by their exhaust. He gazed at his display screens. They showed all systems functioning normally.

The shuttles rose higher. Nvif could now see the bluish-red curve of the Martian sky. It would not be long before they reached the upper atmosphere.

A beeping caught his attention. Nvif looked at his screens. One of the shuttles fell out of formation.

"Shuttle Seven. What is happening?"

"My engines have failed," the pilot said, fear evident in his voice. "I cannot reactivate them."

The shuttle lost altitude and tumbled out of control toward the surface.

Frustration almost overwhelmed Nvif. Shuttle Seven had been delivered from the factory one rotation ago. Unfortunately, many of the new shuttles and fighting machines had been built so quickly they suffered from numerous malfunctions. He'd already seen four new shuttles crash soon after takeoff.

That doesn't help us at all against the Brohv'ii.

There was nothing Nvif could do for Shuttle Seven or its pilot. All he could do was think about the mission.

The blue and red sky faded, replaced by the blackness of space. Several flashes to the port drew his attention. Energy weapon discharges from the Brohv'ii ships, striking his world, killing more Shoh'hau. Nvif wanted to shriek in anger. He restrained himself. Anger would not stop this assault on his world.

Only action would.

* * *

"Martian missiles!" hollered Porter.

Beatty's heartbeat picked up. He looked to the main screen. Over a dozen bright dots streaked toward the ASEF fleet.

"Range?" asked Captain Gibbons.

"Fifty kilometers and closing." Porter relaxed a bit. "They're going to miss us by ten kilometers. Looks like they're targeting the Norwegian squadron. Their ships have been alerted."

Beatty's eyes shifted to another screen. He watched beams shoot from the knife-like shapes of the corvettes *Eidsvold* and *Tordenskjold* and the larger form of the cruiser *Stavanger*. Several incoming missiles flared and winked out of existence. Beatty tensed as the remaining missiles drew closer to the Norwegian ships.

C'mon, lads. Shoot those buggers down.

Another missile exploded. Another. Another. The last missile had got within a kilometer of the *Tordenskjold* before it detonated.

"All missiles destroyed," said Porter. "No damage to any ASEF ships."

"Splendid." Beatty turned to Gibbons. "Captain, send my regards to the Norwegians. Job well—"

"Shuttles!" Porter hollered. "Martian shuttles approaching!"

* * *

Nvif worked the maneuvering thrusters, twisting his shuttle port and starboard. He'd seen earlier what happened to pilots who flew in straight lines toward the Brohv'ii.

They died.

His eyes shifted from the scanners to the forward window. A massive, rectangular form loomed before him. From the amount of transmissions to both Shoh and Brohv, intelligence believed this to be the invaders' command ship. Destroying it would surely impair their fighting capabilities.

Three smaller ships took up position between the shuttles and the command ship. Nvif swerved his shuttle as energy beams shot across the void of space. He fired back. His beams missed.

Nvif glanced at his scanners. One of the shuttle images flared and vanished.

The other shuttles opened fire. A white flash erupted on the front of one escort ship.

Another shuttle exploded.

Nvif shoved his controls hard to the left. He fired his energy weapon. The beam struck the rear of the largest escort. A bright flash blotted out part of the ship.

Two more shuttles exploded.

Beams flashed past Nvif's shuttle. He kept firing the maneuvering thrusters. Side to side. Up and down. He flew past one of the smaller escorts, a large gash in its rear. It wasn't that far to the command ship.

That's when he noticed two things. One, the command ship had not fired any of its weapons. Two, another ship was attached to its side. A resupply ship, he assumed.

What a fortunate circumstance. The command ship was vulnerable to—

A sharp blow struck Nvif's shuttle.

* * *

"Where the hell did those blighters come from?" Captain Gibbons glared at the wall of screens in the BMC.

"They must have come in behind the missiles," said Beatty. "That's probably why we didn't detect them."

Much as he hated the Martians, he had to give them a nod for an ingenious tactic. It also showed him how desperate they had to be to attempt something like this.

"We need to disengage from the *Loch Ness* now," said Gibbons. "We're sitting ducks with that ship attached to us."

The captain looked over at *King Edward VII's* operations officer. "Mister Lampard. Order all personnel out of the docking tunnel, then disconnect docking clamps."

"Sir, we still have two Polaris missiles in the tunnel."

Beatty tensed. Each of those missiles carried a two-thousand-pound warhead. If they went off this close to *King Edward VII*...

"Better to lose a couple of missiles than the entire ship," Gibbons stated. "Give the order, Mister Lampard."

"Aye, sir."

"Mister Porter. Reactivate all weapons systems."

"Aye, sir. Though it will take a couple minutes to fully recharge."

Beatty's throat went dry as he looked back at the screens. The *Sirius* rolled to the port, venting atmosphere. Three Martian shuttles soared past it. *Gladiator* and *Minerva* sent a barrage of heat rays at them. One shuttle vanished in a white flash. So did a second. An explosion went off behind the third shuttle. It slewed to the right.

Beatty released a breath he hadn't realized he'd been holding. Perhaps *King Edward VII* would come through unscathed.

* * *

Nvif battled his fear, fighting to keep his shuttle steady. Several warning lights and buzzers went off in the control deck. Four maneuvering thrusters no longer worked. The energy weapon's power source had been damaged. He could only get half power from the engines.

I'm not going to live through this. A low hum of terror filled his mouth. He couldn't recall ever being so scared. He would cease to exist. Would death be painful? Was there something, anything, he could do to prevent it?

Nvif looked at his display screens. One system after another malfunctioned.

The hum in his mouth grew louder.

Perhaps it is better this way. He hadn't been among those chosen for the Final Project. What did it matter if he died now, or moments from now?

Nvif managed to turn the shuttle starboard. He flew toward the gap between the command ship and the resupply ship. If only his energy weapon still functioned. He could—

He focused on the command ship. An idea formed, an idea only someone with a brain malfunction would conceive. But with his death imminent, it seemed the only logical course.

He pushed the controls left, toward the command ship.

A *thump* vibrated the shuttle. It drifted starboard.

"No!" Nvif hollered.

He pulled at the controls. They wouldn't respond.

Nvif let out a howl as the tunnel between the two ships filled his window.

* * *

"Lord save us," Beatty muttered. He shuddered as the wounded Martian shuttle smashed into the docking tunnel. An intense white flash engulfed the screen. A split-second later a hammer blow battered the entire ship. A grinding roar drilled through Beatty's ears. He spun through the BMC and crashed into the wall.

The world went dark.

TWENTY-FIVE

Bullets hummed over Captain Zhukov's head. Holding his breath, he leaned out from the rock as far as he dared. He glimpsed a Martian partially concealed in a bomb crater, clutching two rapid-fire rifles. Zhukov fired and ducked out of sight. More enemy rounds thumped against his rock.

Someone gasped nearby. A soldier tumbled down the slope, three bloody holes in his spacesuit. Zhukov wondered if it was one of his veterans or a replacement soldier the Red Army had *finally* sent him.

He looked around the line. Soldiers popped up from behind cover, fired, and dropped back down. Machine gunners shifted from one target to the next, firing short bursts.

Zhukov scanned the Martian line. They remained strong in the center and the right flank. On the left flank, he could make out a dozen or so squids in craters or behind rocks.

Nodding in satisfaction, he bounded down the line, bent at the waist. Rifles and machine guns thumped around him. Martian bullets kicked up geysers of dirt along the berm. Another soldier fell backward, his helmet shattered.

"Lieutenant Morgunov!"

"Yes, sir."

"Have your platoon concentrate fire on the enemy's left flank. Kill them all. That is where we shall breakthrough."

"Yes, sir."

Morgunov bounded off, issuing orders to his sergeants. Zhukov briefly recalled their first battle on Mars, when the young lieutenant looked terrified and unsure. Now the man was a lion, someone who might one day command his own company, perhaps even a regiment.

Should he make it back to Earth alive.

The fire from Morgunov's platoon intensified. It reminded Zhukov of tree trunks hit by dozens of hammers. Puffs of dirt sprang all around the enemy's left flank. A Martian went into spasms in a crater. Another slid back behind its rock and didn't rise. Zhukov sighted one Martin poking its body around another rock. He pulled the trigger. Blood gushed from one of the alien's large eyes.

Zhukov fired the remaining rounds in his Mosin-Nagant. He dropped behind the slope and reloaded. He peeked over the top, searching for more targets. There were none.

"First and second platoons! Charge the left flank! Charge the left flank!"

Zhukov hopped over the rise. Dozens of soldiers swept down the slope, a few unleashing war cries.

"Forward, comrades!" someone hollered behind Zhukov. "Smash the imperialist aliens!"

Zhukov glanced over his shoulder. Lavrentiy Beria cheered them on while making no move to join the charge.

Coward.

Zhukov ignored the useless *politruk* and bounced along the red dirt. A few rounds hummed around them. One soldier fell. Then another. The rest bounded past the dead Martians and headed for the center of the enemy line. Zhukov fired from the hip. So did many other soldiers. A few lobbed grenades. Now exposed Martians tried to scramble for cover. Most were gunned down. Two of Zhukov's machine gunners set up in bomb craters and blazed away. The Martian lines thinned out, but they did not retreat.

Something flashed to Zhukov's right. A pair of tentacles grabbed one of his men. The soldier screamed and struggled. Zhukov bounded toward him.

The tentacles slid under the soldier's helmet and pulled. The young Russian's eyes bulged. He clawed at the tentacles, screaming louder.

Zhukov reached out to help him when the soldier's helmet was ripped off.

"No!" Zhukov blurted.

The soldier's mouth opened wide. He tried to suck in air. The skin on his face turned a whitish-blue. Blood vessels started to burst.

Something gurgled. Zhukov looked left. A Martian sprang at him, tentacles flailing.

He slammed the butt of his rifle into the alien's face. It swatted Zhukov with a tentacle. He grunted and stumbled. Another tentacle grabbed his leg. Surface and sky rushed before him.

Suddenly Zhukov was on his back.

The Martian slid closer. Zhukov let go of his rifle and reached for his knife. A tentacle whipped toward him. Zhukov swung his arm. The metal blade sliced through the silvery material of the protective suit and the tentacle beneath it.

The Martian shrieked. Zhukov rose and lunged at it. He plunged the knife into the Martian's face. It shrieked louder. He pulled out the knife and stabbed it over and over until it did not move.

Zhukov let out heavy breaths, steaming up his helmet. Several seconds passed before he pushed himself up and grabbed his rifle.

The helmetless soldier lay just a few feet away, his face frozen. Zhukov didn't recognize him. Probably one of the replacements from Earth.

He looked away from him and moved on. There was no time to mourn. He had a battle to win.

Russians and Martians shot each other at point blank range. A few soldiers thrust bayonets into the enemy's potato-like bodies. Martians fought back with rifles and tentacles. One actually hurled a soldier several feet across the ground. Zhukov shot the Martian dead.

Gunfire tapered off. So did the screams and shrieks. Zhukov surveyed the battlefield. Most of the Martians were dead. He also saw at least a dozen Russians who would never rise again.

Zhukov lifted his right hand and motioned for the rest of the company to come down. Morgunov approached him.

"It appears the Martians are fighting harder the further we push into the Arcadia Plain."

Zhukov nodded. "I am noticing that, too. It makes me think there is truth to the rumors they are hiding something here."

"It must be something very important. I never imagined the squids fighting so fanatically."

Before Zhukov could respond, he heard Beria shouting, "Well done, comrades! Well done! Another victory for the glory of the Revolution."

The *politruk* walked among the soldiers, clapping and doling out congratulations.

Zhukov grunted, narrowing his eyes at the *Cheka* pig. *And where were you when we were fighting and dying?*

He knew the answer. Cowering behind some rock. That's what Beria always did when they fought the Martians.

And that son of a whore has shot other men for their cowardice. Not that anyone could challenge him on it.

Zhukov looked at one of his dead soldiers. If only that could be Beria instead.

* * *

When evening came, Zhukov saw the big breadbox-shaped form of the troopship *Karabulak* descending from the darkened sky. Several soldiers let out subdued cheers. Zhukov also felt a flicker of joy. Troopships were not comfortable by any stretch of the imagination, but at least inside they could get out of these spacesuits, shower, eat a hot meal and sleep in a bunk.

When the ship's rear cargo ramp lowered, the men nearly broke into a mad scramble. Zhukov had to shout a couple of times to get them to halt.

"We are soldiers, not rabble! We shall board that ship as soldiers."

They marched aboard in an orderly fashion. Zhukov then dismissed them to shower and change. Half an hour later, they met in the mess hall. He stood to the side, allowing his men to go ahead of him. That took much discipline on Zhukov's part. After sucking cardboard-tasting nutrition paste through his spacesuit's mouth tube, again and again, he craved actual food.

But a good officer put his men first. He would let them get their meals before him.

Beria, no surprise, did not ascribe to that view. He cut to the front of the line. Zhukov eyed him, infuriated. What had this man done to deserve his supper ahead of real fighting men?

Unfortunately, neither he nor anyone else told Beria different. One did not say no to a *Cheka* man and expect to live very long.

Once Zhukov made his way through the line, he received beef stew with beets and potatoes, a piece of bread and tea. The stew was a bit watery, the bread was a little stale and the tea lukewarm. Still, it was better than nutrition paste.

He scooped a spoonful of stew into his mouth and gazed around the table. None of his men conversed with each other. How could they with Beria sitting among them, watching them with his beady eyes, a notebook, and pen at his side, ready to write down the names of anyone showing a hint of disloyalty? And for him, anything could be construed as disloyal. Complaining about a lack of ammunition or the quality of food, or talking about a victory by another nation's army. Already two of his men had been "reassigned" at Beria's request. Zhukov had enough experiences with the *Cheka* to know what "reassigned" meant.

He felt the fear hanging over the table, so thick it was suffocating. The last time the Russian people were this scared was back in 1908, when a meteorite devastated a huge portion of Siberia. Almost everyone thought it heralded another Martian invasion. Even when it was determined the explosion was a meteorite, the people criticized the Tsar for not detecting it and destroying it. The doubt among the empire's citizens toward their leader was one reason Nicholas II started his foolish war with the Empire of Japan. It resulted in an embarrassing defeat for Russia, with 40,000 of her sons dead and more anger at the Tsar, who would be deposed and executed a decade later.

All because of a rock from space that had scared people for a couple of weeks.

But the fear created by the *Cheka* did not go away. Instead, it became entrenched in Soviet society.

Zhukov stared at his stew, pushing around some chunks of meat with his spoon. He wondered if the fear would ever go away.

When he thought of those men Beria had "reassigned," he wondered if there might come a day when the *Cheka* killed more Soviet citizens than foreign enemies.

TWENTY-SIX

The next morning, Zhukov's company set out from the *Karabulak* before the sun came up. The regimental commander tasked them with searching the caves in this part of the Arcadia Plain for any sign of hidden Martian troops and tripods. Also, the company was ordered to secure any alien technology they found before one of the nearby imperialist armies obtained it to use in the future against the Soviet Union.

Zhukov led a party into the first cave they came across. It was empty. So was the second one. He pulled out his map and checked the location of the next cave when his radioman, Corporal Obukhov, hurried over to him.

"Captain. We have received a message from headquarters. A group of Martian tripods has been located three kilometers from our position. ASEF ships are preparing to bombard them from orbit."

Zhukov felt a nervous twinge. He looked to the north. Hills blocked the horizon, preventing him from seeing any distant tripods. He then looked up at the blue-gray morning sky. The targeting systems on space warships were pretty accurate. So he'd been told. Still, from so high up, one miscalculation and a missile or heat ray could incinerate them instead of the Martians.

Zhukov looked over the topographical map. He noticed a wash about seven-hundred meters west. That would be a good place to wait out the bombardment.

Unless a missile drops right on top of us.

That might happen or it might not. But he most certainly did not want to be in the open when the ASEF ships began firing.

The company hopped across the reddish soil. Just as they neared the wash, Obukhov thrust a finger to the sky. "Look!"

Several soldiers raised their heads, including Zhukov. Streaks of yellow light flashed down from the sky. None came close to their position.

So far.

"Move! Move! Into the wash!"

The men picked up their pace. Zhukov made sure all of them jumped into the wash before joining them. Many looked over the lip to watch the deadly light show. Bright balls of light intermingled with the heat rays. Ballistic missiles. Columns of smoke sprouted in the distance.

The bombardment lasted ten minutes. Another ten minutes had passed before HQ radioed to say all tripods had been destroyed and his company could proceed.

"It appears the space sailors' aim was good," Zhukov said to the men around him. "We are still here."

Several of them laughed.

Not Beria. The weasel-like *politruk*, in fact, sneered, as though a commanding officer sharing a small joke with his men was a mortal sin. Then again, a sense of humor would probably make anyone unfit for the *Cheka*.

The company trekked across the plain. They scaled a hill where they saw the handiwork of the ASEF ships. A few men let out whistles of awe as they gazed at a ground pockmarked by blackened craters. Here and there lay charred wreckage of Martian tripods.

Zhukov took out a pair of binoculars and pressed them against his helmet, scanning for any caves. He had a feeling any he did find would have collapsed from the bombardment. A troublesome thought scratched at the back of his mind. Would Beria make them dig through a cave-in to search for any morsel of Martian technology that *might* exist on the other side? He sure as hell wouldn't put it past the insufferable bastard.

I'd better get the men moving before he thinks of—

"Captain!" Sergeant Zinchenko called out.

"Yes?"

Zinchenko pointed to the east. Zhukov took a couple steps toward him. At first, he thought he was staring at a crater. But it did not appear to have that rough circular shape to it. He leaned forward and squinted.

Part of the ground had collapsed.

Zhukov continued to stare at it, recalling those first days when Martians kept popping out of the ground to surprise ASEF forces. Could this be another ambush in the making?

He ordered the machine gunners to remain on the ridge to cover them while the rest of the company made their way down the slope. Zhukov kept his finger near the trigger of his Mosin-Nagant, his eyes locked on the opening ahead of them. Tension coiled around his muscles, expecting to see Martian soldiers crawl to the surface. Or worse, a tripod.

The two soldiers on point reached the opening first.

"Do you see anything?"

One of the soldiers, Corporal Rybakov, turned and nodded. "I think so, sir. You should come see."

Zhukov headed over to them, with Sergeant Zinchenko right behind him. When he reached the edge, he looked down.

The collapsed ground formed a natural ramp to the bottom. Among the debris of dirt and rocks, Zhukov noticed silvery metallic glints.

The floor of the cavern was metal.

Zhukov turned around. "Lieutenant Morgunov!"

"Yes, sir."

"It appears we have found a Martian base. The ASEF bombardment must have weakened the ground above it. Form a perimeter around the opening. I will lead a party to see what lies below."

"Yes, sir." Morgunov nodded.

Zhukov pointed to Zinchenko, Rybakov, and the other soldier with him, Private Vishnevski. "You three with me. Eyes sharp."

Zhukov stepped onto the incline. He took a few tentative steps. Confident it was stable, he started down, followed by Zinchenko and the two enlisted men. All had their rifles at the ready.

When he stepped off the incline, Zhukov felt and heard the *thunk* of his boot on metal. His brow furrowed when he felt a strange vibration run up his leg. He looked down to find himself standing on a rectangular groove in the floor. He hopped out of it. The vibration stopped.

He looked around and saw two more grooves. He bent down next to one and put his hand on it. Again, he felt the vibration.

"Sir, what is it?" asked Zinchenko.

"I'm not sure." Zhukov got to his feet. "These grooves are giving off some sort of… I don't know what. Stay off them for now, just to be safe."

"Yes, sir," replied the three soldiers.

Zhukov walked forward, swiveling his head left to right. The grooves ran deeper into the cavern, which was rather wide and about twelve meters high.

"Let's see where these lead."

The four continued on. It grew darker the further they went. The only illumination came from small ball-shaped specks of light embedded in the walls. Emergency lighting, Zhukov thought. The main lighting probably went out when the roof collapsed.

They passed a few other tunnels that had the same grooves on the floor. Zhukov's mind churned, trying to figure out what purpose they served. An aqueduct would make the most sense, except for the fact it was bone dry. Maybe the Martians used it as a transportation system, similar to the underground railroads in New York and London. Though they would need some sort of tracks to—

A dull buzz came from down the cavern.

"Captain, do you hear that?" asked Rybakov. "What is it?"

Zhukov didn't answer. He held up a hand, signaling the corporal to be quiet.

The buzzing grew louder.

Zhukov's chest tightened. Could it be Martians? How many?

All they need is one to sound an alarm.

His eyes swept around the tunnel. About eight meters to his left he spotted the darkened maw of another access tunnel.

"This way."

The four soldiers took huge leaps down the cavern. Fear clung tightly to Zhukov as the buzzing increased.

Come on! Faster! He cursed the lighter gravity of Mars.

Finally, he made the turn into the tunnel. Zinchenko, Rybakov, and Vishnevski joined him just as the buzz filled the cavern. They pressed their backs against the metal wall. Zhukov peered around the corner.

A rectangular platform carrying six Martians floated by, directly over one of the grooves.

Incredible. Zhukov forgot his fear as he watched the platform continue in the direction where he and his men had come from. The thing moved without even touching the ground. Whatever kind of propulsion it used, the Martians certainly hadn't brought it with them when they invaded Earth. The Soviet Union would benefit greatly from a technology like this.

Though how he could get it back to the *Karabulak* was beyond him.

When he couldn't hear the buzz of the platform anymore, Zhukov ordered his men out of their hiding place and moved further down the cavern. He made sure to stay alert for the sound of any other platforms, and also noted any potential hiding places should more Martians appear.

The four had to hide twice more from passing aliens. Each time Zhukov looked back up the cavern, wondering about Lieutenant Morgunov and the rest of the company. Once the Martians reached the opening and saw them, a battle would ensue. More Martians would come to reinforce them. When that happened, he wondered if they had any chance of making it out of the cavern without being seen and killed.

Zhukov considered heading back to the opening but dismissed it. ASEF believed the Martians had something important going on in the Arcadia Plain, and he may have just stumbled upon it. He couldn't leave without finding out what it was.

They walked for another kilometer when they came to a bend in the cavern. Zhukov and the others slid along the wall. Holding his breath, he peeked around the corner.

The cavern ended in a large chamber. Several floating platforms of various sizes hovered off to either side. Just beyond them was a large metal door.

Zhukov turned back to his men and told them what he had found.

"What could be behind the door?" Vishnevski wondered aloud.

"Since I have no x-ray machine built into my spacesuit, I cannot answer that, Private."

Vishnevski lowered his head, looking embarrassed.

"Come on. We must try to get inside."

The men appeared nervous. Hell, Zhukov was nervous. Not that he could show it. But they needed to gather intelligence, and that meant finding out what the Martians kept on the other side of that door.

The four emerged from cover. They bounded along the grooves. Zhukov was about ten meters from the door when he heard a muffled thump. Light spilled from underneath the door.

It was opening!

"Get under them!" Zhukov pointed to the platforms on the left.

They leaped toward them. Zhukov and Zinchenko dove under one platform, while Rybakov and Vishnevski took cover under another. Zhukov stared at the door, which rose higher by the second. Bright light flooded the cavern, forcing him to blink repeatedly. Once his eyes adjusted, he saw several Martians crawl into the cavern. A dozen, two dozen, three dozen. All of them carried rapid-fire guns. Many gurgled and hacked in their strange language. Zhukov had no idea what they were saying, but he could sense the urgency in their tone.

The Martians hoisted themselves up on some of the larger platforms. They floated along the grooves and traveled up the cavern.

Toward the opening. Toward the rest of the company.

He hoped Morgunov and the others could defeat them.

Once the Martian platforms were out of sight, the door began to lower.

Zhukov edged out from under the platform.

"Sir!" Zinchenko called out in a hushed voice.

"I have to see what's inside."

Zhukov crawled as quickly as possible, his heart thumping as the gap between the door and the ground lessened. He feared missing his chance to see what was inside more than he did being spotted by the Martians.

The door was just a couple of meters from closing.

He twisted his head to the side, trying to get a good look inside.

His mouth fell open in silent awe.

Mother of mercy.

RETALIATION

TWENTY-SEVEN

A pinprick of light appeared before Beatty. It expanded into a white blur. He sensed himself groaning as he blinked, trying to bring the world into focus.

A bland white wall appeared, as did a light fixture above him. Beatty moved his head to the left. He saw a row of beds, each one occupied by a man. A woman in a one-piece white jumpsuit floated toward him. He noticed a red cross on her upper right sleeve.

"Admiral?" She moved closer to him. "Admiral Beatty?"

"Nurse?"

"Thank Heaven you're awake. You had us all rather worried."

"What... what happened?" Beatty asked in a raspy voice.

The nurse bit her lip. "I'll fetch Doctor Nickerson. He can explain everything."

She turned and floated away, turning into a room at the end of the ward. Shortly after, a slender, middle-aged man with a narrow face and a brown mustache flecked with gray emerged.

"Admiral Beatty. Good to see you awake. I'm your doctor, Colonel William Nickerson."

"Where am I?"

"You're on the hospital ship *Thomas Linacre*. You've been unconscious for two days."

"Two days?" That sent a jolt of surprise through Beatty. He began to rise.

"Easy does it, Admiral." Nickerson placed a hand on Beatty's shoulder, gently pushing him back down.

"Can't take it easy. The war. We're making our big push." He held his breath, remembering a sharp quake, fire, and pain. His last seconds of consciousness in the *King Edward VII*'s Battle Management Compartment. "My ship. What happened to her?"

"I'm sorry, Admiral. *King Edward VII* was destroyed."

Beatty's muscles seized. His mind fought to reject what the doctor had told him. That battle lasted only a few seconds.

He stared up at the bland white ceiling, thinking of the men onboard *King Edward VII*, thinking of the men he'd lost in the Sudan when the Martians blew up his gunboats.

"How many?" Beatty asked in a flat tone.

"Four hundred sixty-seven dead, roughly a hundred others wounded. The *Loch Ness* was lost with all hands, I'm afraid."

Beatty closed his eyes and let out a long sigh. Now he remembered. *Loch Ness* had been offloading munitions and batteries to *King Edward VII* when that Martian shuttle collided with it.

"Captain Gibbons?" he asked about his flagship's commander.

"He didn't make it. Sorry."

"The Command Staff?"

"General von Seeckt made it out alive. Not a scratch on him. God was definitely watching out for him."

"What about the others?"

"General Summerall and General Ducreux were killed. Admiral Thurman was injured, but he's still carrying out his duties, though with a doctor close by."

Beatty digested the news. He had lost his ground forces commander and chief of intelligence in Summerall and Ducreux, but at least he still had his Deputy Supreme Allied Space Commander in von Seeckt and his logistics chief in Thurman.

And you're still alive and kicking, old boy.

"Well, if Admiral Thurman can keep working with a few bumps and bruises, so can I."

"About that." The doctor's shoulders slumped.

"What is it, Doctor?"

Several seconds of silence passed. "It's... you probably don't realize it yet. 'Phantom pain' they call it."

Beatty's brow furrowed. "What are you on about?"

"Admiral, I'm sorry. Your injuries from the explosion were rather extensive and... We did everything we could, but in the end, we had to amputate both your legs."

* * *

Patton knew he should have felt happier. The ASEF forces were advancing quickly through the Arcadia Plain.

Well, the infantry miles ahead of him advanced, while he and his 214th SPA Regiment sat back and waited for calls for fire support. Sometimes they didn't get any, as aerial or orbital bombardment softened up the Martians enough for the ground pounders to dispatch any survivors on their own.

I need to be up front, Patton thought bitterly as his SPAs rolled across the Arcadia Plain to their next firing positions. He pulled out his map, studied it, then checked the compass on his console. Still on course. He estimated another ten minutes to reach their destination.

Where we'll probably sit and do nothing while others kill the Martians.

"Colonel," Fuller, the radioman, called out.

"What is it, Corporal?"

"I'm picking up something on the radio."

Patton got out of his commander's seat and knelt next to Fuller. Fast, incoherent babble came out of the speaker. Whoever was talking wasn't American, or from any other English-speaking country. It sounded like...

"Is that Russian?"

"I think so," Fuller said.

"Do you know what they're saying?" asked Patton.

"Sorry, sir. The only other language I know is French. Took it in high school."

"Well, a fat lot of good that does us here."

"Yes, sir." Fuller frowned.

Patton continued to listen to the Russian on the radio. Even though he didn't understand a damn word, he could tell from the man's tone that he was scared. Very scared. That probably meant they were under attack. He found it hard to feel sympathy for the Russians. That communist philosophy of theirs didn't let people own land or guns. They couldn't call their politicians shitheads for fear of getting thrown in jail or shot. They didn't even believe in God. He felt any nation that turned its back on The Good Lord was doomed to fail.

But the Russians were allies, for now, and eliminating the Martian threat usurped his mistrust of those Godless bastards. And if they were close by, maybe he could save their asses.

"Can you find out where those Russians are?" Patton asked Fuller.

"No, sir. We don't have any radio direction finding equipment. Maybe we can call HQ. They might know."

"Scratch that, Corporal." If they did that, those moron generals likely wouldn't let him come to the Russians' aid. At least, not the way he had planned.

"Dial into the command net. Let's see if they already know about it."

Fuller gave him an odd look but replied, "Yes, sir."

The radioman played with the dials. Soon a steady stream of transmissions came from ASEF command.

"USSS *Grover Cleveland*, we have an air support tasking order for the 12th US Marine Regiment in Sector Twenty-Seven... German 58th Division is encountering fierce resistance in Sector Twenty-Four. Redeploy the Swedish 4th Regiment and the Austro-Hungarian 116th SPA Regiment to reinforce them... We're getting reports of a Russian infantry company pinned down in Sector Eleven."

When the soldier at HQ read off the exact coordinates, Patton took out a pen and wrote them down in the bottom right-hand corner of his map. He checked the position of his regiment and that of the Russian company.

They were eight miles to the west.

A grin spread across his face.

He held out the map so Fuller could see. "Look at this, Corporal. There's a line of hills about five miles ahead of us. They look like they'll be tough to get over. I think it's best if we go around them."

Fuller's eyes shifted from Patton's face to the map. Again, he reacted with a baffled expression. But like any good soldier, he replied, "Yes, sir."

"Contact the rest of the regiment. Tell them we're heading west."

* * *

Lieutenant Colonel Rommel had been tuning the radio in his SPA to the army group net when he came across someone speaking in frantic Russian. Not understanding the language beyond *da* and *nyet,* he contacted one of his battalion commanders, Major Benzing. He had spent a year in Russia during the Tsar's rule, cross-training with their SPA units, and could speak the language fluently.

"They're under attack," Benzing reported. "Apparently a large number of Martians emerged from underground."

"No wonder that man sounds scared. Do you know their position?"

"Yes, he radioed their exact coordinates. "I checked the map. They're about six kilometers northeast of us."

Rommel looked off in that direction, drumming his fingers on the armrest of his chair. It would take them well out of their way. He knew HQ would never approve it, not when they had their own operations to worry about.

But sometimes map coordinates get misread. A landmark gets missed. An entire unit could be sent off course by kilometers.

More precisely, six kilometers.

Rommel smiled. He didn't trust the Russians, not with that lunatic Stalin in charge. But for now, they were allies, and he should help them.

And show everyone the full potential of armored warfare.

* * *

"Mon Sous Lieutenant."

De Gaulle bristled when he heard his driver, Bosquier, address him. *Sous Lieutenant,* the most junior of officers in the French army. All the years, all the work he had done to achieve the rank of *Commandant,* to lead his own battlewalker regiment. In one instant, he had it stripped away, all because the fat, stupid generals behind their desks had been too cowardly to push on to victory in the first assault on Tharsis City. General Couturier had told him he was lucky he hadn't been thrown in prison for insubordination. But with all the casualties suffered by ASEF forces in general and the French, in particular, they needed every man in the fight.

Once the war ended and they returned to Earth, then he could look forward to spending time in a cell.

Couturier, you spineless bastard.

"Mon Sous Lieutenant," Caporal-Chef Bosquier called out again.

"Oui!" de Gaulle snapped.

"Um, I think I see something."

"What?" De Gaulle leaned forward, staring out the cockpit windshield. His battlewalker, along with the two others in his scouting section, stood on a hilltop. Rust-colored valleys and mountains stretched for kilometers.

"I'm not certain," Bosquier answered. "I'll see if I can zoom in with the telescope."

The landscape condensed. Dozens upon dozens of figures crouched or bounded or crawled over a pockmarked section of ground. Human soldiers battling Martians. De Gaulle had no idea which country the soldiers served. Right now it did not matter. He had a chance to kill Martians and save the lives of those soldiers. He could redeem himself in the eyes of his superiors, perhaps get his proper rank, and his command, back.

"Should we report this to *Commandant* Giraudeau?" Bosquier referred to the former *Capitaine* Giraudeau, who received a battlefield promotion and became the new regimental commander after de Gaulle's demotion.

"No." De Gaulle continued to stare at the distant battle. "I think we should move in closer and determine exactly what is going on there."

RETALIATION

TWENTY-EIGHT

"Warhorse One, this is Labrador Four. We're in position."

Patton grabbed the mike when he heard Lieutenant Kline, the CO of his scout platoon, over the radio. "What do you see, Four?"

"Looks like a couple hundred Martians and a company-sized force of Russians. The squids have the Ruskies pinned down. They've taken cover behind some burned out tripods and in bomb craters."

"Any functioning enemy tripods?" asked Patton.

"Negative. The Martians are strictly infantry. No sign of any heavy weapons. Standby, Warhorse."

Kline paused for a few seconds. "There's a big hole in the ground about four hundred yards from our position. I see a platoon-sized force of Martians crawling out of it. Looks like they've got another underground base here, too."

"Roger that." Patton glanced at his map. "We're about three miles away. Keep me posted."

"Affirmative, Warhorse One."

Patton's eyes locked on the distant hills. His heart beat faster with anticipation. This was the kind of fight he'd wanted. Up close and personal. No longer would he wonder if his shells actually killed any Martians. He could look the ugly sons-of-bitches right in their gigantic eyes when he blew their guts all over this damn planet.

When he got within two miles of the hills, Patton radioed Kline. The scout leader provided him with the exact positions of the largest concentrations of Martian soldiers. Patton studied his topographical map. A plan quickly took shape, which he radioed to the rest of the 214th SPA regiment.

"But, sir," said Major Flanagan, the commander of Battery B. "We need to be further away to provide effective fire support."

"No, we don't, Major. Now carry out my order."

"Yes, sir," Flanagan replied with some reluctance.

Patton grew more anxious as he neared the hills. Finally, the opportunity he'd been waiting for. He would show all those idiot generals the true potential of the SPA.

When they reached the base of the hill, he ordered the regiment to halt and load shrapnel rounds. The SPAs then climbed the slope. He kept an ear out for the sounds of battle, but unfortunately, could hear nothing. Damn low atmospheric pressure. Back on Earth, he'd be able to hear the cracks of rifles and the crash of artillery—fuel for a warrior's soul.

The SPAs crested the hill. Before them lay a valley marred by craters and burned out tripods. Russians and Martians engaged one another in a fierce firefight, with the humans badly outnumbered. Dozens of Martians left their craters and crawled toward the Russian line, rapid-fire guns blazing.

Patton waited until they drove about fifteen yards down the slope before ordering the regiment to halt.

"Target the biggest concentration of Martians in your assigned areas. Fire on my mark."

He looked at one group of Martians creeping ever closer to the Russian lines. Their guns spewed a hail of bullets. A couple of Russians who tried to fire back got cut down. The smart ones hunkered down in their holes. It wouldn't be long before they got overrun.

"Merloni," Patton said to his driver. "Traverse ten degrees left." He looked to the gunner. "Simpson. Elevate thirteen degrees."

Both men carried out their orders.

Patton picked up the mike. "All batteries . . . Fire!"

The bass drum thumps of dozens of guns carried through the air. Geysers of dirt and rock shot up among the Martians. Several of them spiraled through the air. Severed tentacles floated to the ground like grotesque party streamers.

Patton scowled when he saw the shell from his SPA fell short of their target by about fifteen yards.

"Simpson! Elevate another three degrees . . . Fire!"

The big gun thumped. An explosion ripped through the center of the Martian unit.

"Yeah!" Patton roared. "Take that, you ugly bastards!"

The barrage continued. Plumes of smoke and fountains of dirt sprang up throughout the Martian lines. Patton scanned them through his binoculars, expecting them to retreat. Instead, they slid into craters and continued firing at the Russians.

He let out a long breath. The Martians' resistance had grown stiffer the deeper they pushed into the Arcadia Plain. Some might even say fanatical. Of course, they were fighting for the survival of their race. He'd heard plenty of stories from the invasion about army units fighting to the last man. They probably knew they had no chance against those tripods, but when faced with extermination, what choice did one have but to fight?

Patton figured the Martians thought the same way.

If they want a fight to the death, that's fine with me.

So long as they're the ones dying.

Shells crashed down on the Martians. Several thrashed about in their craters, blood spilling from their bodies. Some had tentacles missing.

"Warhorse One, this is Labrador Four."

"Go, Labrador."

"We have more SPAs headed our way from the west."

"Whose are they?"

"Unknown."

Patton swung his binoculars west as his SPA's gun fired. He made out roughly twenty tracked vehicles speeding toward the Martian lines. The newcomers suddenly turned to the north. Patton's brow furrowed.

What the hell are they doing?

The SPAs drove little over a mile before they swung to the right and charged the Martians' northern flank.

Patton got on the radio. "All units, be advised, we have friendlies approaching the Martians from the north. Direct your fire away from them."

Several of his SPAs traversed or lowered their guns to make sure they didn't hit the new arrivals. Patton's SPA shook as the gun fired. The shell exploded in a bomb crater. Two Martians flew out of it, their shredded bodies tumbling across the ground.

Patton looked back at the oncoming SPAs. He waited for them to stop and fire. Instead, they kept driving at full speed.

What the hell are they doing?

Some of the Martians covering their northern flank spotted the SPAs and fired. Sparks from enemy rounds flashed off the hulls.

The guns of the SPAs remained silent. They simply rolled through the Martian lines. Several aliens tried to flee, only to be crushed underneath the treads. Strobes flickered from the sides of the vehicles. Patton zoomed in with his binoculars. Soldiers leaned over the open hull, firing submachine guns.

The SPA in the lead made a hard left, running over another Martian. That's when Patton noticed a black iron cross painted on the side.

They were German.

A soldier popped up from behind the hull and fired a burst from his MP-18 submachine gun.

Wait a minute. Patton kept his binoculars locked on the man. The hawkish features looked very familiar. Could it be . . .

The German fired another burst. A Martian near his SPA went into spasms, then lay still. The other SPAs followed, crushing and gunning down more Martians. Russian soldiers rose from their holes and bounded past the carnage left in the SPAs' wake, taking advantage of the opening in the Martian lines.

A smile grew on Patton's face. "Rommel, you magnificent bastard."

Rommel's unit barreled through the Martians' northern flank, while Patton's regiment concentrated their fire on the southern flank.

"Warhorse One, this is Labrador Four," radioed Kline. "We've got three battlewalkers approaching."

Patton looked over his shoulder as huge fighting machines strode over the ridge. Part of him wished the damn machines would leave. This was the time for SPAs to shine.

He turned back to the battlefield. Most of the Martian force was dead or wounded. He glanced back at the battlewalkers with a wry grin.

We can always let those big SOBs mop up after us.

The battlewalkers marched downhill. Heat rays spat from their snail shell-shaped pods. Patton watched several squids get vaporized. Joy shot through him.

See how you like it now, you slimy shitkickers.

The surviving Martians retreated to the large hole in the ground. The Russians charged after them. Patton's regiment also gave chase, as did Rommel's unit and the battlewalkers. He expected the squids to slither back into the hole. Instead, they formed a circle around it and laid down a steady stream of fire.

"All units," Patton radioed. "Break out small arms."

He hurried to the weapons locker and handed out Thompson submachine guns to his crew. Enemy rounds thudded against the SPA's metal hull. Patton leaned over the side, spotted a Martian and fired. Miss. He fired again. The alien's tentacles flailed, then dropped to its sides. It did not move again.

A heat ray flashed out the corner of Patton's eye. The beam incinerated a pair of Martians. Russians continued to bound over the pockmarked landscape, firing their rifles from the hip.

Patton, Simpson, Fuller, and the SPA's loader, Dunn, fired burst after burst from their Thompsons. Rommel's SPAs continued to flatten Martians.

Soon every single squid around the opening was dead.

"Looks like they really wanted to keep us out of that hole." Patton surveyed the torn and crushed bodies of the Martians. "Makes me wonder what they have in there that's so damn important."

He hopped over the side of his SPA, still clutching his Thompson. Some of the Russians said, "*Spasiba,*" whatever the hell that meant.

"George? Is that you?" someone said in German-accented English.

Patton turned to the short man walking toward him. "Erwin. Looks like you proved SPAs are good for other things besides lobbing shells from miles away."

"As did you." Rommel stuck out his hand, which Patton shook. "Good to see you again, *mein freund.*"

"And you. That was a good idea, firing submachine guns over the side."

"Yes, but I think we would be better served by mounting one or two machine guns on our SPAs for situations like this."

Patton tilted his head, thinking. He turned back to his SPA, imagining a Browning or a Lewis Gun on it. Those weapons, along with the main gun and some thicker armor, would make the SPA a far deadlier war machine.

And if they could ever make heat ray batteries small enough to fit in an SPA . . .

The babbling of one of the Russians broke his train of thought. Patton turned to a narrow-faced, brown-haired young man. He spoke urgently in that brutal-sounding language and gestured to the big hole.

"Hey! I'm American." He tapped the stars and stripes patch on his upper left sleeve. "A-mer-i-can. I don't have a damn clue what you're saying."

The Russian spoke louder and stabbed his finger at the hole repeatedly.

Patton growled. "Yeah. That helps."

"Do not worry, George," said Rommel. "I have someone in my regiment who speaks Russian."

He ordered one of his men to fetch a Major Benzing. While they waited for him, a group of French soldiers from the battlewalkers made their way over, led by a tall dark-haired man. His name tag read DE GAULLE. He eyed both Patton and Rommel and frowned. "So may I assume you heard the same radio broadcast from the Russians as I?"

Patton noted the tone in de Gaulle's voice like he was offended that he and Rommel had shown up and blasted the Martians to hell. Maybe this Frenchie wanted all the glory to himself.

Well tough shit, pal.

By the time Benzing arrived, another Russian had walked up to them, one with a weasel-like face. He spoke to the brown-haired Russian in a sharp tone which made him take a couple of steps back. He looked nervous as he responded in a pleading tone.

"*Tovarishch. Tovarishch.*" Benzing held up both hands in a calming gesture. Both Russians turned to him as he introduced himself, Patton, Rommel, and de Gaulle. The brown-haired Russian identified himself as Lieutenant Morgunov, while the weasel-looking man was called Beria, whom Benzing said was the unit's political commissar. Patton shook his head. He couldn't imagine having some jackass bureaucrat demanding he recite the Constitution and sing the praises of President Wood every day. He'd probably wind up shooting the useless son-of-a-bitch.

Morgunov rattled off a couple of sentences. Benzing repeated them in German to Rommel, who repeated them in English to Patton. "Lieutenant Morgunov wants to thank us for coming to the aid of his unit."

"Tell him we're happy to kill those Martian bastards any time, any place."

After that was translated, Patton said, "Now ask him if he knows anything about the Martian base down there." He pointed to the big hole.

When Benzing translated, Morgunov started to speak, only to be cut off by Beria. "This is the Red Army's sector of responsibility. We shall deal with whatever is down there. Your assistance is no longer needed. Leave."

Rommel grunted. "Pleasant fellow, isn't he?"

"He's an asshole," Patton commented.

"But Comrade Beria," said Morgunov. "What of Captain Zhukov and the others? They are still down there."

"Did you not see all the Martians that came out of that opening, Lieutenant? They must have seen Zhukov and the others. There is no chance they are still alive." Beria turned to Patton and the others. "By the authority of The Communist Party, I claim this area of Mars in the name of the people of the Soviet Union. You must now leave or—"

Muffled thumps interrupted Beria. Patton and Rommel both turned to the opening. De Gaulle also stepped closer, as did Morgunov.

Two men in spacesuits appeared at the bottom of the slope.

"It's the captain!" Morgunov shouted. "Captain Zhukov is alive!"

Cheers went up from several of the Russians. Beria, Patton saw, was not one of them.

Zhukov and the other Russian took a step back onto the slope, brought up their rifles and fired. That could only mean one thing.

More Martians were coming.

TWENTY-NINE

"Erwin, I think we're about to have more unwanted company."

Without waiting for a response, Patton hopped back to his SPA. Rommel did likewise. He ordered Merloni to go down the slope.

"Don't worry," he added when he saw the nervous look on the driver's face. "It should be stable enough to support us."

"Um, yes, sir."

Taking a slow breath, Merloni drove the SPA forward. He turned left and rolled down the slope. Patton tensed, praying he hadn't lied to Merloni.

When the slope didn't collapse, his muscles unwound.

He ordered Simpson to lower the gun when another SPA pulled alongside. Patton turned to find Rommel nodding at him. He nodded back, then looked down the slope. The Russians backed up, firing their rifles.

"C'mon! Move your dumb Russian asses!"

One of the Russians looked over his shoulder. He slapped the other on the shoulder. They bounded past the two SPAs as Patton ordered Dunn to load a shrapnel round. A mass of potato-shaped bodies and flailing tentacles appeared below them.

"Fire!"

The SPA shook. A flash of orange and black burst among the Martians. The gun on Rommel's SPA thumped. Another explosion tore through the squids.

Both SPAs fired again. Two more blasts ripped apart Martians. A few were still twitching. Patton aimed his Thompson and fired. The rest of his crew and Rommel's also raked the Martians with their submachine guns. Several Russians took up position around the SPAs, along with de Gaulle and the Frenchies. Thumps and snaps of small arms fire filled the air as Martians jerked and bled and died.

Patton and Rommel let the foot soldiers clear the slope before they backed up their SPAs. When the two regimental commanders jumped out of their vehicles, another Russian—Zhukov, Patton presumed—stared at his SPA with wide eyes, then looked around at the others surrounding the hole.

"Good. Good," Zhukov nodded. "We will need these. We will need much firepower."

Patton was about to ask what he meant when Morgunov sidled up to Zhukov. "Captain. I can't believe you and Rybakov made it out of there alive." He paused. "Where are Vishnevski and Sergeant Zinchenko?"

"Dead, I'm afraid. We managed to hide in some access tunnels while the Martians passed by on these floating platforms. I guess it was only a matter of time before our luck ran out. Zinchenko and Vishnevski were hit just before we reached the exit."

Zhukov turned back to Patton and Rommel. "We will need your SPAs. The tunnel is too small for battlewalkers."

De Gaulle scowled as Benzing translated for Zhukov. "Your SPAs will fit. We have to get down there now and stop the Martians."

"Stop them from doing what?" asked Patton.

"The rumors about them guarding something important in the Arcadia Plain. They are true. I saw it."

"You what?" Rommel stepped forward, anxiousness radiating from his face. "What is it?"

Zhukov barely opened his mouth when Beria shouted, "Do not answer them, Captain! Whatever the Martians have down there will be dealt with by the Red Army. It does not concern the imperialists."

"Comrade Beria, what I saw concerns all of mankind. We must all unite. It is the only—"

"You wish to join with these people?" Beria waved his arm at Patton, Rommel, and de Gaulle. "You wish to have their capitalistic and decadent ways corrupt the Party and all it stands for?"

"You do not understand!" Zhukov shouted. "You did not see what I saw. If we do not do something, there may be no more Party, no more Soviet Union."

Patton eyed Zhukov. Was this Commie exaggerating? Did he really know what he saw? From what he'd heard, many soldiers in the Russian army came from little villages in the middle of nowhere. Would they even know what some superweapon looked like?

What if he isn't exaggerating?

Beria glared at Zhukov. His face reddened as the silence between them grew second by second.

"Clearly you have cracked under the stress of combat."

"I assure you, Comrade Beria, I am quite sane."

"Then by suggesting we allow the imperialists to accompany us, you have branded yourself a traitor to the Party and the people of the Soviet Union. You would allow these men to study or steal advanced technology they will one day use against our country. I am declaring you unfit for duty and appoint myself commander of this company."

Beria spun around to face Morgunov. "Lieutenant. Take Captain Zhukov into custody. He must be executed for his treason to The Party and to Comrade Stalin. Then you will force these imperialists to leave. If they refuse, sho-"

The thump of a rifle made Patton jerk in surprise. He started to bring up his Thompson when he saw Beria stagger, his mouth wide open.

Zhukov took a step toward the political officer, a wisp of smoke rising from his Mosin-Nagant rifle. He pulled the bolt back and fired again. A bloody hole appeared just under Beria's chest. He stumbled back, pawing for his holster. The wounded man never got a grip on his pistol. With a choking gasp, he fell on his back. Beria looked up at the blue-gray Martian sky with lifeless eyes.

"Holy shit," Patton muttered.

"A tragedy, comrades," Zhukov hollered. "*Politruk* Beria was struck down by Martian bullets defending the people of the Soviet Union."

Several Russians looked to one another, then back to Zhukov. They nodded. Patton swore some of them smiled.

What the hell kind of messed up army is this? One officer shoots another, and all the men are fine with it? He could never conceive of something like that happening in the U.S. Army.

"My apologies," Zhukov said to him, Rommel and de Gaulle. "Beria was no soldier. Just a pig from the *Cheka* sent to spy on us and make sure we are loyal to the Party. An insult to real soldiers."

Patton just nodded, not sure how to respond.

"We do not have time for Beria's nonsense. I must show you what I saw. I need something to draw on."

"Here." Patton handed him one of the maps from his suit's pouch and gave it to Zhukov along with a pen.

The little group walked over to Patton's SPA. Zhukov spread out the back of the map on the hull. He drew a huge oval with four blocks on the bottom, two on the back and four bumps on the top. Patton frowned. The man was no van Gogh.

"What is this supposed to be?" De Gaulle actually sneered at the sketch. Of course, those French were really into art. De Gaulle probably felt a sketch like that should be outlawed.

"I think it is a ship. An enormous ship. The size of a small city."

"Impossible," de Gaulle snapped. "How can a ship be that large?"

"That is the only thing it can be." Zhukov pointed to the blocks. "These are engine exhausts. They can't possibly be anything else. It is a spaceship, the largest one I, or anyone else, has ever seen."

Patton whistled in awe. "If what you say is true, imagine how many missiles and heat rays they can load on that thing."

Morgunov's eyes bulged. "You think the Martians are going to invade Earth again?"

"I doubt it." Rommel shook his head. "After their entire invasion force was wiped out by bacteria, I cannot see the Martians ever wanting to set foot, or in their case tentacle, on Earth again. But they could bombard the planet from orbit."

"And with most the ASEF fleet around Mars," said Patton, "that ship could blast through the few ships around Earth and have plenty of firepower left to flatten most of our major cities."

"Is there anything else you can tell us about this Martian ship?" asked Rommel.

Zhukov nodded. "Yes, something rather strange."

"What?" De Gaulle gave him a curious look.

"I saw the Martians load a big glass tube onto the ship. It was fogged up, but inside I could see another Martian. It was not moving. I thought it was dead, but why would you put a dead Martian on a ship?"

The corners of Patton's mouth curled as he dwelled on that. The Ruski was right. Why put dead Martians on a spaceship?

He glanced at Rommel. The German stared at the ground with a thoughtful expression.

"Looks like you've got something on your mind, Erwin. Wanna share?"

Rommel looked up. "Those tubes Captain Zhukov spoke of. I see no sense in storing already dead Martians on a ship. But..."

"But what?" asked de Gaulle.

"There was an article in a science magazine I read a couple of years ago by Nikola Tesla."

Patton's ears perked up at the mention of that name. Nikola Tesla had been instrumental in the development of spaceships and ebbs. Many considered him the smartest man in the world.

Rommel continued. "He wrote about the possibility of interstellar travel using our current technology."

"And how would that be possible?" de Gaulle wondered aloud. "The closest star system to ours is Alpha Centauri, more than four light years away. Even with fusion engines, it would take at least two centuries to make such a journey. The crew would be long dead before they arrived."

"True." Rommel raised a finger. "But Tesla came up with a way around that. He theorized we could freeze a human being and keep him in what he called 'suspended animation.'"

"Suspended animation?" Patton gave his friend a baffled look.

"Tesla said you could inject a freezing solution into the human circulatory system. While a person may appear dead, they would actually be alive, just barely. Heartbeat, brain activity, circulation, aging, it would all practically stop."

Rommel threw in some scientific babble about how such a machine would work. Most of it went over Patton's head. But Rommel had a knack for the technical stuff. Had it not been for the Martian invasion, his German friend would have made a brilliant engineer.

"By the time the ship arrived at, say Alpha Centauri or even a star system much farther from Earth like Sirius or Epsilon Indi, the crew could be revived by an ebb and not have aged a day, even though hundreds of years would have gone by."

"You believe the Martians are freezing themselves for such a journey?" de Gaulle asked.

"From what Captain Zhukov describes, I would say yes."

"So it's not a big warship they're building," said Patton. "Those sons-of-bitches are building an ark, just like Noah."

"The average lifespan of a Martian is only ten or twenty years longer than that of a human. They, too, will need some way to survive the journey."

"So the Martians will go far away?" Morgunov looked around at the other officers. "This is good. They leave and never bother us again."

"Who's to say the squids didn't load a few missiles on that thing?" Patton pointed out. "Maybe they plan to fly by Earth and blast some of our cities as a going away present before they head off to who the hell knows where."

"If what Captain Zhukov says is true," said de Gaulle, "there is an even more frightening possibility. What if the Martians find a new planet to live on? They would be free to develop their technology to the point where they have engines that can travel between star systems in the same amount of time it takes us to travel from Earth to Mars. They could build weapons more powerful than we can imagine, weapons we will have no defense against."

"But from what you say, that will take centuries," countered Morgunov. "None of us will be around when that happens."

De Gaulle fixed the young Russian with a hard stare. "We will not be around, but our descendants will, and they will curse us for not stopping the Martians when we had the chance."

"I have to say, *Monsieur* de Gaulle here is right." Patton nodded to the Frenchman. "Our orders are to make the Martians as extinct as the damned dinosaurs. After what they did to our planet, the thought of any of those slimy bastards still breathing, no matter how far away from Earth they are, makes me sick. So I say there's only one thing for us to do."

He turned to the Martian tunnel, then back to his fellow officers. "We go down there and blow the hell out of that space ark."

RETALIATION

THIRTY

Hashzh had never seen any Shoh'hau crawl so fast. Yet Supreme Councilor Frtun and the rest of the Guiding Council pulled themselves along one of the ramps extending from the enormous interstellar relocation ship with great urgency.

"Prepare the cryogenic tubes!" Rezdv shouted. *So unbecoming of a Shoh'hau councilor*, Hashzh thought. But given the circumstances, he could overlook Rezdv's lack of decorum.

Brohv'ii soldiers were approaching the launch site.

"Prepare the cryogenic tubes!" Rezdv shouted again. "The Brohv'ii are coming! We must leave at once!"

"Calm yourself, Rezdv!" Supreme Councilor Frtun scolded him.

Rezdv fell silent, but his tentacles quivered in fear as he crawled closer to the large, circular door behind Hashzh. Inside were the tubes that would freeze Shoh's leaders for their journey to whatever distant planet would be their new home. There remained twenty thousand more Shoh'hau that needed to be frozen, many experts in engineering, astronomy, agriculture, and security, skilled beings needed to rebuild their society.

Fear swelled within Hashzh. All their calculations showed that a minimum of 200,000 was needed to establish a viable colony that could sustain and protect itself. Would the absence of those twenty thousand mean the difference between survival and extinction?

They would have to succeed with their smaller numbers. They had no choice.

"Supreme Guardian," Frtun said as he slid toward Hashzh. "My apologies, you will not be able to accompany us on our journey. However, circumstances dictate that you remain here to delay the Brohv'ii. It will take time to freeze and store us. You must keep the uprights away, no matter the cost."

"I understand, Supreme Councilor." Hashzh truly did. He was not pleased with this. He had no wish to die. But as leader of the Guard Force, it was his duty to protect the Shoh'hau race, especially its leaders.

"You cannot fail, Supreme Guardian," Rezdv said. "It is inconceivable that our great race should perish while savages like the Brohv'ii live."

Hashzh looked at the other councilors. Many appeared to have the same fear.

Perhaps I should tell them. He saw no point in keeping it a secret. The Guiding Council would soon be on the relocation ship. He would likely be dead by the time they cleared the solar system.

"You need not worry about that, councilors. No matter what happens to our race, the Brohv'ii will finally be exterminated. I have made certain of that."

"Explain yourself, Hashzh," Frtun demanded.

He told them about his own final project. When he finished, nearly every councilor gargled in astonishment. They turned to one another, tentacles flailing.

"Has your brain malfunctioned, Hashzh?" Frtun's voice rose in anger and shock. "You deceived the Guiding Council and used resources that could have gone to the relocation ship for an unauthorized project. We could have already begun our voyage."

"I had no choice, Supreme Councilor. *You* left me no choice."

"Insolence!" Rezdv blurted. "How dare you speak to us in such a manner?"

"How dare you not provide the Shoh'hau with everything needed to defend our world? For cycle upon cycle, you denied my requests to build more spaceships and fighting machines. Now look at the result. We have killed many Brohv'ii soldiers, but they still overwhelmed the Guard Force. What good are personal weapons against Brohv'ii fighting machines or ships that can bombard us from orbit? Had you approved my requests, we would have repelled the Brohv'ii invaders."

Hashzh felt his entire body shake. Disbelief came over him. Had anyone ever spoken to the Guiding Council in such a manner?

Frtun lay speechless. A great amount of time passed before the Supreme Councilor finally spoke. "What you have done is unthinkable. This defiance is unacceptable. It is good you stay here and die. You are the most unfit being the Shoh'hau has ever produced. Leave my sight!"

Hashzh said nothing. He crawled away from the Guiding Council, sensing the outrage emanating from their large eyes.

How dare they be outraged? The Guiding Council should have put forth a plan to eradicate the Brohv'ii following the failure of the Cleansing Mission. Instead, they feared them so much they ignored the planet, as though that would keep its inhabitants from threatening Shoh.

Dwelling on what the Guiding Council should have done was useless. It wouldn't change the fact the Brohv'ii were nearing the launch site. All Hashzh could do was keep them away from the ship and ensure some of his fellow Shoh'hau survived.

* * *

Patton looked behind him at the flames and smoke billowing from the SPA. Scowling, he turned back to the pile of torn and bloody Martian bodies. They'd blown the slimy squids straight to hell, but not before one of them used a hand-held, or tentacle-held, mortar to take out one of his vehicles. The damn round came straight down in the exposed crew compartment, killing every man inside and disabling the gun.

How many times did I tell those shithead generals SPAs need top cover?

Grunting, Patton waited for Zhukov's soldiers to climb back onboard the SPAs before driving deeper into the tunnels. Clutching his Thompson, he scanned ahead for any sign of Martians. So did the eight Ruski soldiers traveling with him. It made Patton feel like he was riding in a sardine can, but they couldn't let the infantrymen walk alongside them. They'd take forever to reach that space ark. Patton had a nagging feeling they needed to get to it pronto.

He tensed when they came to another access tunnel. The last one they passed, Martians streamed out of it and ambushed them. Would they do the same here?

Patton raised his Thompson, finger wrapped around the trigger. They drew closer to the tunnel. Closer.

No Martians appeared.

The SPAs rolled on. They passed another access tunnel, and another. No Martians ambushed them.

"Be ready, everyone." Rommel's voice came from the radio. "Captain Zhukov says we are close to the entrance to the space ark."

"All right, you heard the man." Patton looked around at his crew and their Russian passengers. "We're almost there. Expect the squids to have a welcoming committee. I don't care how many of those sons'a bitches they throw at us. We're gonna blast through 'em or roll over 'em and make sure that damn space ark doesn't get off the ground. Got it?"

"Yes, sir," his crew responded.

The Russians just stared at him. Shit, did any of these borscht-eaters speak a word of English? Well, even if they didn't, they were still warriors and would surely pick up on the sentiment of his words.

Kill the damn Martians.

The glow of his SPA's headlights revealed an enormous steel door ahead.

Right in front of it were at least a hundred Martians.

The rattle of rapid-fire guns echoed through the tunnel. Rounds pinged off the SPA's armored siding. One Russian's helmet shattered. A mass of blood covered his head.

Patton fired a couple of bursts from his Thompson, then grabbed the radio mike.

"Let the bastards have it!"

The artillery fired, their thumps a little louder in the enclosed tunnel. Shrapnel rounds exploded amongst the Martians, tearing apart their bodies. Russian soldiers leaped out of the SPAs. They stayed behind the vehicles, firing rifles and machine guns. Dunn rammed another shrapnel round into the gun. Patton had the SPA turn five degrees to the left and ordered Simpson to fire. A split-second later a puff of smoke and flame blotted out a group of Martians. Other SPAs behind Patton fired over the top of him. Explosions sent Martian bodies flipping through the air.

Something droned above him. Patton tensed, recognizing the sound.

Mortars.

Two rounds exploded harmlessly. Another landed near a German SPA. Shrapnel tore through a Russian soldier leaning too far around the rear.

Yet another round struck an SPA. Fire and smoke poured from the wrecked gun.

More Martian bullets peppered Patton's SPA. One ricocheted around the interior. Dunn yelped and grabbed his left leg.

"Dunn! You okay?"

The loader hesitantly drew back his hand. A tear showed around his thigh.

"Just a graze, Colonel."

"Good." Patton applied an emergency sealant to the tear. "Now load some more rounds so we can kill these squids."

"With pleasure, sir."

The Martians took out two more SPAs. But firing at near point-blank range, Patton's and Rommel's regiments tore apart the aliens with a rain of shrapnel rounds. The Russian infantry picked off more, as did de Gaulle and his little group of Frenchmen, who could only fight with their Berthier carbines since their battlewalkers had been left at the surface.

The rattle of Martian guns faded. Patton tried to peer through the haze of smoke that had settled in the tunnel. He couldn't make out any squids moving.

"Cease fire," he radioed the other SPAs. "Cease fire."

Zhukov led several of his men forward to check on the Martians, accompanied by de Gaulle and his men. Every so often, Patton heard the thump of a rifle. Some soldier making sure a squid never twitched again.

Ten minutes later, de Gaulle walked up to his SPA. "All the Martians are dead. Once again, they fight to the bitter end."

"Considering what's behind that door, you can't blame them."

Rommel bounded past Patton's SPA and examined the massive door through the haze.

"That looks pretty damn thick, Erwin. I'm wondering if our shells can blast through it."

"I do not think directly, but let me see."

Rommel strode closer to the door, his glass-encased head moving side-to-side and up and down. Patton could sense the engineer inside his German *freund* trying to work out the problem.

Work it out quick. I didn't come all this way just to be stopped by a damn big door.

"There." Rommel pointed up. "Along the top. That should be the weakest part of the door. We will hit it with high-explosive rounds and hopefully dislodge it."

"Hopefully?" Patton tilted his head.

"I believe it is our only option, given what we have on hand."

Patton stared at him. He hoped they didn't have to use too many shells on the door. He wanted to have plenty for the Martians on the other side.

But if we don't bust through it, that space ark goes bye-bye.

Even if it did get away, it would still have to get past the entire ASEF fleet. Surely they would blast it to pieces.

What if they can't? The ark had to be armed, considering it carried the future of the Martian race. It didn't have to stand and fight the ASEF fleet. Just punch a hole through a few ships and speed off to where the hell ever. Then maybe come back hundreds of years from now and start this war over, just like de Gaulle feared.

No way could he risk that.

Patton nodded to Rommel. "Let's do it."

The SPAs backed up and elevated their guns. Once Dunn slammed a high-explosive round into the breech, Patton radioed, "Open fire, and keep firing until that door comes down."

The drumbeat of artillery filled the tunnel. Fireballs flashed around the top of the door. Shattered rocks fell on top of the Martian corpses.

Volley after volley exploded against the edges of the door. Patton ran his eyes over it, looking for any sign of it weakening.

He found none.

More shells burst along the top of the door. Patton ground his teeth. Were they going to use up all their shells before they–

A deep moan came from the door. Patton snatched the mike. "Cease fire! Cease fire!"

The guns fell silent. The moaning grew louder.

C'mon, you bastard.

A huge crack of light appeared atop the door. It grew larger as the door fell backward. Patton practically jumped to the front of the SPA, teeth bared as he watched it fall ever so slowly. Damn this lighter Martian gravity.

With a deep *clunk*, the door hit the ground. Bright light poured into the tunnel.

Patton thrust his arm at the opening. *"Forward!"*

RETALIATION

THIRTY-ONE

They are here. They are actually here.

Shock overwhelmed Hashzh as the Brohv'ii gun carriers rolled into the launch site. He thought of the Cleansing Force, the Brohv'ii bacteria that felled them. That concern vanished. He and all the other Shoh'hau here wore protective suits.

While they might be immune to Brohv'ii disease, they were not immune to their bullets and shells.

He flinched as explosions rumbled throughout the launch site. Guardians and technicians tumbled across the floor and fell from ramps, bloody holes in their suits.

Hashzh grabbed his personal weapon and fired. The dull rattle of other weapons went up all around him. So did the thump of personal mortars. Flames and smoke rose from two gun carriers.

More Brohv'ii shells exploded amongst the guardians. Hashzh reloaded his weapon and turned to the relocation ship. A Shoh'hau guided a walking transportation platform containing a cryogenic tube onto the vessel. That had to be Supreme Councilor Frtun. He scanned the ramp leading to the cryogenic chamber. Another platform carrying a tube made its way toward the ship. Another member of the Guiding Council.

They had to make it safely to that ship. How could a new Martian society function without its leadership?

Hashzh scurried across the floor. He ordered five other guardians to follow him.

When they reached a circular door at the far end of the launch facility, Hashazh raised a tentacle and slammed it against the control panel on the wall. The door opened, revealing three large walking transportation platforms.

Each one carried an energy weapon.

* * *

Rommel grimaced as another SPA burst into flames. He spotted a trio of Martians thirty meters away. One held a mortar and reached for another shell.

"Gunner," he called to Frosch's replacement, a thin private named Dasbach. "Shrapnel. Three Martians. Thirty meters ahead. Driver. Five degrees left."

Ehelechner swung the SPA to the left while Kopitz slammed a shrapnel round into the breech. The Martian with the mortar turned their way when Dasbach pulled the lanyard. The shell burst just behind the Martians. Shrapnel sliced through their bulky bodies, transforming them into a bloody mess.

The SPA rolled forward. A few Russians bounded behind them. Rommel saw explosions along the side of the space ark, tiny pricks of light on the enormous vessel. They couldn't be doing any real damage.

He snatched the radio mike. "All guns. Concentrate your fire on the engines."

Little fireballs soon blossomed on the two large engines mounted on the port side. Rommel's jaw clenched. Were their shells having any effect? Spaceships had to have thick hulls to withstand atmospheric re-entry, as well as spaceborne threats like radiation and micro-meteorites.

How could a standard high-explosive shell penetrate that?

Dread bubbled in his stomach. Would this attack be in vain?

A white beam flashed across the chamber. Rommel whipped his head left. One of his SPAs erupted in flames.

"*Was ist das?*"

He looked to the far end of the launch site. Three walking platforms skittered across the floor, each carrying a heat ray similar to the ones used by Martian tripods.

How did they—

Another SPA blew up.

* * *

Hashzh gazed in satisfaction at the burning gun carrier. The weapon platform to his right fired. The beam missed another Brohv'ii vehicle. The gunner corrected his aim and fired again. Flames consumed the gun carrier.

Hashzh blasted another gun carrier. For a moment, he mentally scolded himself. He should have had more of these platforms constructed. They would have greatly aided his ground guardians in the absence of the larger fighting machines. Instead, all he had at his disposal were these three prototypes.

He ended these useless thoughts. Dwelling on his lack of foresight would accomplish nothing.

Bending the control stick to the right, Hashzh rotated the beam weapon toward another gun carrier.

* * *

De Gaulle watched as another SPA burst into flames.

Shit! He glared at the heat ray platforms as they continued their advance. What he wouldn't give to be in his battlewalker right now.

Down on one knee, he took aim with his Berthier carbine and fired. So did his crewmen, Bosquier and Ponge. None of their rounds hit the Martian on the platforms.

A few SPAs fired their guns. Clouds of black and orange burst from the floor. Not close enough to knock out the platforms. The Martians returned fire. Two SPAs exploded.

Several SPAs backed up. The Russian infantry also retreated. De Gaulle gritted his teeth as memories of Tharsis City came flooding back. He'd be damned if he'd retreat again, not with the Martians about to escape to a whole new world.

Bullets hummed past. De Gaulle looked left. Six Martians crawled toward them, clutching rapid fire guns.

He fired his Berthier. Blood spurted from the eye of one Martian. De Gaulle checked over his shoulder and saw a smaller ramp leading up to a circular door.

"Take cover!" he shouted over the muffled pops of Bosquier and Ponge's carbines.

They got to their feet and bounded toward the ramp. More Martian rounds hummed around them.

A strangled gasp came from Ponge. His arms flew out to his sides as he slowly fell to the floor.

"Ponge!" Bosquier started to turn to his crewmate.

"No!" de Gaulle shouted, seeing huge, bloody holes in Ponge's back. "He's dead. Move!"

The two bounded toward the ramp as fast as Martian gravity allowed. Another volley of bullets hummed past. None hit them.

They dove under the ramp. De Gaulle twisted around and poked his head out as far as he dared. Bullets thudded against the ramp's surface. He sighted a Martian and fired. It staggered. De Gaulle rolled back under the ramp as more bullets came his way. Bosquier then fired and ducked back under cover.

De Gaulle glimpsed a shell detonate near a heat ray platform. Shrapnel tore into the two Martians on it. One toppled off the platform while the other still lay at the controls, unmoving.

One down.

But two more heat ray platforms remained. So did the Martian soldiers charging them.

So did the damn space ark.

* * *

"Son-of-a-bitch!" Patton scowled at the flaming wreck that had been one of his SPAs.

Many of his SPAs and Rommel's kept backing up, trying to put distance between them and the Martian platforms.

"This pulling back shit won't get us anywhere."

Patton got on the radio. "Company A, Company B. Form a line and blast those platforms to hell! Everyone else hit that ark!"

Patton ordered another high-explosive round for the port engine. His eyes flickered between the ark and the platforms. Some of his SPAs had taken up position and fired. A few shells exploded around the platforms. None were hit. Patton bared his teeth. *Hit the damn things!*

White beams flashed across the launch site. Two of his SPAs turned into fireballs. Some of the German SPAs rolled forward to reinforce the Americans, led by Rommel himself. Captain Zhukov followed with his Russian infantrymen, shooting at the Martian soldiers still slinking about the place.

The gun of his SPA fired. More thumps came from the other artillery nearby. Explosions sprouted from the ark's engines. He checked through his binoculars. No sign of any damage.

"Dammit!" There had to be a way to get through that armor. If he only had better shells. Or bigger guns.

He caught movement out the corner of his eye. Another walking platform emerged from a room atop one of the ramps. Instead of a heat ray, it carried one of those freezing tubes.

Patton continued to stare at it, thinking. As big as the space ark was, the Martians couldn't take their entire population. If they had to rebuild their society somewhere else, wouldn't it make sense to bring along their best and brightest? How many scientists, doctors, engineers, and warriors did they have stored away? He wouldn't be surprised if some of those tubes contained members of their Guiding Council.

"Merloni. Spin us around forty-five degrees. Simpson. Elevate gun seventy degrees."

The two soldiers obeyed. Patton ordered Dunn to load a shrapnel round.

At least I won't be wasting any shells here. "Fire!"

The SPA shook from the recoil. The shell exploded a few feet from the platform. Close enough. The squid controlling it flailed then laid still. Shrapnel shattered the glass tube, shredding the Martian inside.

"Put some more through that door," Patton ordered. "They probably have more Martian ice cubes up there."

* * *

Hashzh twisted around when he glimpsed the flash. Fire swept over the weapon platform behind him. His concern escalated.

It was now him against all the remaining enemy gun carriers.

Even with his advanced weaponry, he knew he wouldn't survive. Not against so many. The Brohv'ii would eventually kill him. All he could do was destroy as many gun carriers as possible and safeguard the rest of the Guiding Council and the relocation ship.

Hashzh targeted another gun carrier and fired. It exploded. The guardian driving the platform moved to the right. Two Brohv'ii shells missed them. The shudder from the blasts rippled through his body.

He turned the weapon toward another gun carrier when he saw smoke pouring out of one of the rooms above the launch platform. Shock stilled him when he realized which one it was.

The cryogenic chamber

Hashzh let out a disturbed gurgle when flames burst from the room. *The Guiding Council. They are still in there!*

He noticed a shattered tube on a transportation platform. That had to be one of the councilors. Dead The Guiding Council, Shoh's leaders. Were they all dead?

Hashzh let out an anguished screech. The Guiding Council was dead! Killed by the Brohv'ii. Killed by a race that was nothing but sentient fungus!

He looked back at the gun carriers, wailed, and fired. The beam missed. Two shells exploded close by.

Die! You must die for killing the council!

Hashzh fired again. The beam clipped a gun carrier. Smoke rose from its side.

No Guiding Council. How could Martian society function without its leaders?

Not all the council are dead. Hashzh fired the beam with one tentacle and activated his communicator with another. "Commander Befvg," he called the commander of the relocation ship.

"Yes, Supreme Guardian."

"Launch at once."

"But the rest of the Guiding Council is not yet aboard."

"The rest of the Guiding Council is dead." Hashzh fired the beam weapon, destroying another gun carrier. Shells continued to explode nearby.

"Dead?" Befvg said in a flat tone. "The Guiding Council is dead?"

"Yes."

"What do we do? What can we do without the council?"

"Supreme Councilor Frtun is still alive. He is onboard your ship."

"But we have always been guided by nine," said Befvg. "How can one lead all the Shoh'hau?"

"He will have to!" Hashzh's tentacle slipped off the trigger. All his appendages flailed in anger. "We have no choice. Take off now before the Brohv'ii can damage the ship!"

RETALIATION

THIRTY-TWO

Rommel observed the zigzag pattern of the heat ray platform. Left for a few seconds, then right for a few seconds. Left, right, left, right. The Martian was falling into a predictable pattern.

A fatal pattern.

"Ehelechner. Ten degrees right. Kopitz. Load high-explosive."

The SPA swung to the right. Rommel kept his eyes on the heat ray platform. The Martian controlling the weapon had not fired for several seconds. Instead, it flailed its tentacles. He swore the thing looked agitated.

He stared down the barrel, waiting . . . waiting.

"Abfeuern!"

* * *

"If you do not launch now, you will condemn the Shoh'hau to extinction!" Hashzh shouted. "Do you wish that?"

"No, Supreme Guardian."

"Then la-"

A deafening roar battered his auditory organs. Hashzh cried out as he flew into the air. Intense heat seared his body.

He crashed to the floor. His vision darkened. Bitter cold settled over his body. Hashzh saw the burning wreckage of his weapon platform before his eyes closed, never again to open.

* * *

De Gaulle shoved another five-round clip into his Berthier, leaned out as far as he dared and fired. He missed. The remaining three Martians sprayed them with their rapid-fire guns. De Gaulle ducked under the ramp.

"This is why I opted out of the infantry," Bosquier complained. "I would give anything to be in our battlewalker."

"As would I." De Gaulle leaned out and fired again. Miss.

The Martians crawled closer. Bullets hammered the ramp. De Gaulle peeked around the edge. The damn squids couldn't be more than twenty meters away. They had to—

A puff of orange and black erupted behind the Martians. Blood shot out in a geyser from one of the aliens. The other two thrashed about, wailing like mad.

A small grin formed on De Gaulle's face. Whoever the SPA crew was that fired that shell, he owed them a bottle of wine. Perhaps a whole case.

With the heat ray platforms out of commission, some of the SPAs went back to targeting the Martian soldiers still creeping about, while others fired at the space ark. De Gaulle frowned as shells exploded against the engines of the massive vessel without causing any damage.

"They're not doing anything!" Bosquier waved his hand toward the ark. "It is going to fly off. Ponge and all the others will have died for nothing."

That comment sparked anger in de Gaulle. They could not just accept defeat, not after so many had already died in this chamber.

Think. There must be some way to destroy that ship.

They could do it if they had some battlewalkers. Their heat rays should be strong enough to penetrate the armor surrounding those engines.

Of course, they didn't have any battlewalkers here, nor could the get them through the tunnels.

De Gaulle cursed under his breath as he gazed around the launch site. His eyes came to rest on the one heat ray platform not aflame. Both Martian crew members were dead, but the weapon appeared in good shape.

"Bosquier, come."

"Sir?"

"We may not have a heat ray, but the Martians do." He pointed to the walking platform. "We will borrow theirs."

Bosquier gave him a dubious look, but nodded and said, "Yes, sir."

The two Frenchmen bounded across the floor toward the platform. De Gaulle kept his carbine at the ready, just in case either of the Martians twitched.

They didn't.

De Gaulle and Bosquier climbed onto the platform. They grunted as they pushed the dead Martian away from the controls and off the platform. Even though the controls were designed for Martian tentacles and not human hands, they managed to manipulate them by wrapping both hands wrapped around a single stick.

De Gaulle swung the heat ray toward the ark and raised the barrel. He nudged the stick a couple of times to the left, glancing at the SPAs. He worried one of them might take a shot at the platform.

I think they can easily tell that I am not a Martian.

He blocked out the worry, concentrating on one of the ark's side-mounted engines. De Gaulle found the pressure point on the stick and squeezed.

A white beam shot from the barrel. It struck the point where the engine and hull met. Flames and sparks leaped from it.

De Gaulle gritted his teeth, squeezing the stick harder. The beam continued to burn into the ark's engine. The fire and smoke grew in intensity. He didn't let go of the trigger. He wouldn't. Not until the entire engine blew.

A ball of flame gushed from behind the engine. Just a little longer and . . .

Something buzzed behind him. It grew louder by the second. Dread slithered through him. He knew that sound from his battlewalker training days.

It was a heat ray battery overloading.

No! Not now.

His muscles tensed. He didn't let go of the trigger even as his fingers grew numb.

"Sir, the battery," Bosquier warned.

De Gaulle ignored him and continued to fire. The barrel of the heat ray glowed red.

The buzz became deafening, even with Mars' lower atmospheric pressure. De Gaulle knew only seconds remained before the battery exploded.

"Dammit!" He released the trigger and turned to Bosquier. "Jump!"

The two leaped off the platform and hurried away from it. A bass drum-like thud sounded behind de Gaulle. He and Bosquier dove to the floor. De Gaulle looked over his shoulder. The rear half of the heat ray platform was on fire.

Cursing, he got to his feet and stared at the spaceship's shot. Flames and smoke poured from behind it. Would it be enough to disable it?

Something moaned overhead. De Gaulle looked up. His eyes widened, and his mouth fell open.

"Mon dieu."

The ceiling above the space ark slid open.

* * *

"Aw shit!" Patton glared at the receding ceiling and the Martian sky above it.

"Fox One to all units," Rommel's voice came through the radio. "Evacuate the launch site at once."

"What?" Patton grabbed the mike. "We can't leave! We can't let that damn ship take off."

"Our shells have no effect. The heat ray de Gaulle commandeered is destroyed. If we don't leave now, we'll be roasted by the engine exhaust."

Patton nearly crushed the microphone. Damn that Rommel, but he was right.

He ordered Merlori to turn the SPA around. A few Russian soldiers, including Captain Zhukov, scrambled on board. Patton stared at the fire and smoke billowing from behind the one engine. He prayed that was enough to keep the damn thing grounded.

The SPAs rolled out of the launch chamber as a rumble came from the space ark. Patton's head trembled as he tried to hold in his rage. He was retreating before the job was done. The one thing he hated most, and he was doing it.

And what would you accomplish by staying in there and getting barbecued by that ship?

The SPAs drove through the tunnels as fast as possible. No Martians ambushed them.

They finally reached the collapsed section of the tunnel system. One by one, the SPAs climbed the incline to the surface and kept going. Patton continued to check behind him for any sign of the space ark.

Tremors rippled underneath him. A dark shape rose from the ground.

"Dammit, no!"

The shaking of the ground grew more violent. The three unmanned battlewalkers from de Gaulle's squad toppled over. The space ark continued to rise. Smoke belched from the port side engine. Not that it mattered. The massive ship cleared its underground launch chamber.

Patton smashed a fist against the armrest of his commander's chair. They failed! The damn squids would get away and make a new world their home. He pictured a whole new Martian invasion centuries from now, with weapons no one could even dream of.

I'll see you bastards then. Patton wondered who he would be reincarnated as when humanity next fought the Martians. Obviously a great leader. After all, he had been Hannibal and a field marshal in Napoleon's army during some of his previous lives.

I guess I should start thinking how—

A gigantic fireball burst from the damaged engine.

"Look at that!" Patton pointed. His crew all turned their heads.

"Holy shit!" Fuller blurted.

The space ark slewed to one side. It struggled to stay in the air but fell back toward the opening.

"It's going down!" shouted Dunn.

The ark slammed against the edge of the opening. Another tremor went through the ground. The ark tilted to port and fell until it vanished from sight.

Patton raised his fist and roared in triumph. Americans, Germans, Russians, and French in the other SPAs did the same. He then got on the radio and alerted ASEF command of their situation.

Less than a half hour later, dozens of triangular shapes appeared above them. Fighter jets of various types and nationalities. They dove on the opening, dropping bombs and firing rockets. Several columns of smoke merged into one.

After twenty minutes of bombing and strafing, the jets flew away. Heat rays and missiles rained down from orbiting ASEF ships. Plumes of smoke and flame belched from the opening, reminding Patton of pictures he'd seen of volcanoes.

Patton ordered Fuller to switch the radio to Rommel's frequency. Grinning from ear to ear, he said, "Well, Erwin, those sons a'bitches wanted a new place to live, now they got their wish. Because we just sent them all to Hell!"

RETALIATION

THIRTY-THREE

Beatty held the sheaf of papers in his hand as he lay in bed aboard the hospital ship *Thomas Linacre*. He had insisted on receiving regular reports regarding the fighting on Mars. Not just to stay on top of things, but to take his mind off the fact that he was a legless cripple.

It didn't work. Beatty's eyes constantly drifted from the reports to the blankets, which lay flat where his legs ought to be.

What do I do now? He had imagined following their victory on Mars, he would be appointed to the Lords Commissioners of the Admiralty. Beatty couldn't see that happening now. Who would follow someone who was just half a man? And his wife, Ruth. He had issued orders that no one tell her the nature of his injury. But she would see it for herself when he returned home. Would Ruth go from wife to nursemaid? Fetching his clothes. Bringing his meals to him. Taking him to the loo. Doing every damn thing for him because he was incapable of doing it himself?

How long would she do that? Did she want to stay married to a man as helpless as a newborn babe?

He thought of his sons. David II, age nineteen and a cadet at the Royal Navy College, and Randolph, age thirteen. They both looked up to him. Could they do that now with the knowledge their father was weak and useless?

Beatty slammed the papers on his bed and stared up at the ceiling. *Why did this happen?*

He'd lost count of the number of times he'd asked himself that question. The answer was simple. It was war. Men lost limbs in war. He'd seen it with veterans of the Sudan and the Martian invasion. Beatty had always looked upon them with pity.

Now people would do the same to him.

The intercom by Beatty's bed buzzed. Sighing, he reached over and pressed the button. "Yes?"

"Sir, General von Seeckt wishes to speak with you. He says it's urgent."

"Very well." Beatty noted how flat his voice sounded. He didn't care.

Seconds later, he heard the voice of his Deputy SASC. "Admiral. How... um, how are you?"

"Managing," he muttered. "What is it?"

"Our telescopes on the Moon detected an asteroid on a collision course with Earth."

Beatty sat up, staring at the intercom. "Where will it hit?"

"It's projected to strike the Arabian Peninsula."

"That's mostly desert. There shouldn't be too much damage. Why the concern?"

"Admiral, the asteroid is nearly a kilometer in diameter."

The news paralyzed Beatty. *One mile?* The world saw what a relatively small asteroid could do in 1908 when one hit the Tunguska region of Siberia. But one this large...

Fear took hold of him, fear that he had never known before, even in combat.

"Admiral, the telescopes detected something else about this asteroid."

"What?"

"Exhaust from a fusion engine."

"On an asteroid? How the bloody hell..." The realization hit him. "The Martians. They strapped a bloody engine on that rock."

"That appears to be the case," said von Seeckt.

"What's being done to stop it?"

"The ASEF Supreme Council is discussing the matter as we speak. But... but most of our warships are here at Mars. Only a few ships remain on Earth. I... I do not know if they have enough firepower to destroy the asteroid."

Cold sweat broke out all over Beatty's body, what body he had left. "Understood, General. I'll contact the Council. We'll try to come up with some plan. Meanwhile..." Beatty bit his lip. Good Lord, he couldn't believe he was about to suggest this. "Meanwhile, you'd best prepare for a permanent stay on Mars. It will be up to you lot to keep the human race going if the worst . . . the worst happens."

"There are many nurses on the hospital ships," said von Seeckt. "Hopefully the Martian wildlife is edible. We will find a way to survive."

"God's speed to you, General. All of you."

"Thank you, Admiral."

Beatty clicked off the intercom. His hands trembled. He pictured Earth in his head, a blue and white ball hanging in the void of space. He narrowed his focus to England, to London, to his home in the County of Cheshire.

To Ruth and their two boys.

Beatty tore off the restraints keeping him in the bed. He pushed away the blankets as he began floating. He threw out his arms and made like he was doing a breaststroke. Instead of moving forward, he twisted around in mid-air. Without legs, he couldn't push off anything and propel himself.

"Dammit!"

"Admiral? Admiral!"

He turned his head and saw a young, raven-haired nurse at the other end of the ward. Lieutenant Hill.

"Sir, what are you doing out of bed?" She floated toward him, so effortlessly.

Of course, she still had her legs.

"You need to get back in bed."

"I need to get to the bridge."

"But, sir, you—"

"Dammit, Leftenant! The Martians have got a bloody enormous asteroid headed for Earth, and if it hits, this," Beatty waved a hand around the ward, "is going to be your new home."

Hill gaped at him, the color draining from her face. Many of the patients looked at him, then at each other, in disbelief.

Much as it pained him, Beatty forced himself to say, "Now, Leftenant help me to the bridge."

"Yes, sir."

Hill put an arm around Beatty's shoulders and guided him out of the ward and through the corridors. His heart beat furiously. Why couldn't she push him faster? The faces of his wife and children hovered in his mind's eye. He had to do something to save them, to save the entire human race.

They finally made it to the bridge. All eyes turned to him in surprise. The captain, a pot-bellied man named Conroy, gaped for a few seconds, then shouted, "Admiral on the bridge."

"Oh, stuff formality." Beatty responded. "Who's your communications officer?"

"Here, sir." A skinny, brown-haired young man raised his hand. "Leftenant Fisher."

"Fisher, I need to get in touch with the ASEF Supreme Council at once."

Beatty had Hill guide him over to Fisher's console. By the time he reached it, Prime Minister Lloyd George was on the line.

"Admiral. I didn't expect you to be up and about."

"I don't think now is the time to be lying in bed, sir."

"So you've heard about our crisis."

"I have."

A few seconds had passed before Lloyd George spoke. "Admiral, you are on with the rest of the council, minus Premier Stalin."

"Where is he?"

"The crazy son-of-a-bitch thinks we're pulling his leg." That sounded like US President Leonard Wood. "He thinks we're trying to get him to send the rest of his space fleet away from Earth so the other ASEF nations can invade Russia."

"You can't be serious? Surely Stalin's own astronomers know this asteroid is heading toward Earth."

"Probably," said Wood. "But most times when someone gives Stalin information that contradicts his opinion, that someone winds up dead."

Beatty's face tightened in frustration. The Soviets probably had more spaceships on Earth than any other nation. If Stalin refused to send them after the asteroid, all life on Earth would be in jeopardy.

"What about the rest of ASEF? Do we have enough ships to shoot this thing down?"

"We only have a handful of corvettes in orbit," stated Kaiser Wilhelm II. "The rest of our ships are docked at spaceports here on Earth or on the Moon. By the time we assemble the crews, and they take off, it will be too late."

Beatty gripped the back of Leftenant Fisher's chair and lowered his head. "Is it going to be as bad as I expect?"

"Probably worse, Admiral."

A new voice. Not a world leader, at least of a country. Beatty recognized the man as the world's foremost scientific mind, Nikola Tesla.

"Judging by the speed of this asteroid, when it strikes the Arabian Peninsula, the blast will be twenty million times more powerful than the Tunguska explosion."

Beatty started to shake, his mind was unable to conceive of such power. He barely heard the terrified gasps from Fisher, Hill, and others on the *Linacre*'s bridge.

"The Ottoman Empire will be gone," Tesla continued. "Wiped off the map. So will much of Africa and Eastern Russia. But that is only the beginning. Millions upon millions of metric tons of debris will be thrown into the atmosphere, blocking out the sun for years, perhaps decades. Global temperatures will plummet. No vegetation will be able to grow. Humans and animals will have no food to sustain themselves." His voice quivered. "The Martians will finally have what they always wanted. The end of all life on Earth."

"Surely there must be something we can do," said Beatty.

"The corvettes we already have in orbit simply do not have the firepower to destroy the asteroid."

"What about destroying the Martian fusion engine?" asked Emperor Maximilian I of Austro-Hungary. "Would that not stop it?"

"No, Your Excellency," replied Tesla. "Even without the engine, at this point it is close enough to Earth where it will be pulled in by the planet's gravitational field and still hit us at great velocity."

"Then let's stop talking about what we can't do," suggested President Wood, "and start talking about what we *can* do."

"There is one possibility, Mister President, though it is a rather desperate plan."

"Professor, that big rock is going to hit Earth in less than three hours. So I'll take desperate."

The other leaders voiced their agreement.

"Very well," Tesla said. "It is possible to overload the fusion engine of one of our spaceships and set off an explosion of great magnitude."

"Large enough to destroy the asteroid?" asked French President Maginot.

"Yes. Not completely, mind you."

"Explain," demanded The Kaiser.

"Blowing up the asteroid will create a shower of debris. Many of the smaller fragments will burn up in the atmosphere. Other larger fragments will make it through and strike Earth. They will not have anywhere near the power to wipe out the human race, but we will suffer some damage."

"How many of these fragments will hit Earth?" asked Maximilian.

"Unknown. Dozens, perhaps over a hundred."

"That could be devastating," Maginot blurted.

"Most likely," said Lloyd George. "But it is a disaster we can recover from."

"Then we must do this!" hollered Sultan Yusaf I of the Ottoman Empire. "Blow up a ship and destroy this asteroid before it destroys my empire!"

"We should get in touch with our space forces commanders and see what ships we have that can reach the asteroid in time," said Wood.

A few minutes of unbearable silence passed. Beatty had to clench his teeth to keep from throwing up. Never did he expect to face the end of the world twice in his lifetime. They survived the first time due to divine intervention as bacteria killed off the Martian invaders. Now, now when they had exacted their revenge when they had ravaged Mars as its inhabitants had done to Earth, the bloody squids had one final card to play.

Tears stung his eyes as he thought of Ruth and the boys. Would they freeze or starve to death if the asteroid hit? He almost wished for the asteroid to come down right on Britain. Make the end quick. It was too much to bear to imagine his family suffering a slow, agonizing death.

"Admiral Beatty," Lloyd George radioed.

"Yes, Prime Minister?"

"There is one ship close enough to intercept the asteroid before it reaches Earth."

"Which one is it?"

A pause. "Yours."

A wave of shock swept over him. "But this is a hospital ship, not a warship."

"Which still uses a fusion engine," said Tesla. "That is all we need."

Beatty nodded. "We'll have to evacuate the ship beforehand."

"Of course," Lloyd George responded. "Begin preparations immediately."

"But not everyone can leave the ship."

Beatty furrowed his brow at Tesla's comment. "What do you mean?"

Tesla sighed heavily. "For this to work, some... well, some sacrifice is required."

"What sort of sacrifice?"

"There must be a pilot to land the *Linacre* on the asteroid and an engineer to oversee the collapse of the magnetic containment field and overload the fusion engine. Both, I'm afraid, must remain on board until the end."

THIRTY-FOUR

So this is it.

The surreal feeling came over Beatty as he stared at the ebb screen, studying the diagram Tesla sent him on how to intercept the asteroid. He didn't regret his decision to volunteer. He was the logical choice to pilot the *Linacre* onto the asteroid. As the highest ranking onboard, the ultimate responsibility fell on him.

Personally, he had no wish to spend his remaining days as a burden to his family. Better to go out like this, for Ruth and his sons, for king and country, for all mankind.

Beatty still wished he could see his family, talk to them, one last time.

"Is everything ready, Admiral?" Prime Minister Lloyd George asked over the radio.

"Yes, sir. All ship's personnel and wounded have been evacuated. Nurse Hill strapped me into the helm before she got into her escape pod. I have Professor Tesla's instructions in front of me, and the chief engineer has volunteered to remain aboard to overload the engine."

"What's the chief engineer's name?"

"Weilman. *Lef*tenant Commander Raymond Weilman."

"Does he have a family?"

"Yes. A wife and a daughter."

"I'll see to it they're well cared for. Your family as well."

"Thank you, Prime Minister. And, sir..."

"Yes, Admiral?"

"I was wondering... if you could have someone tell my wife and sons." Beatty tried to push down the lump in his throat. "Tell them I love them, and I pray they understand why I did what I did."

"I'll give them the message personally."

"Thank you."

"It's the least I can do." Lloyd George paused. "Godspeed, David."

"Thank you, sir. Beatty out."

He shut off the radio and let out a long breath. Beatty then hit the intercom for the engine room. "Weilman?"

"Here, sir."

"Shall we get on with it?"

"We'd better, hadn't we? I'd like to still look down on Earth from the pearly gates."

"As would I, Commander. Preparing to accelerate."

Beatty tapped several buttons in front of him. The *Linacre* shot through space. His eyes flickered from one part of the ebb screen to another, noting the ship's current speed and the target speed calculated by Tesla to intercept the asteroid. *Linacre* was actually ahead of the asteroid but needed time to build up enough speed to match that of the deadly space rock on its approach.

He also looked to a projection screen on his right linked to the ship's rear telescope. Already he could make out the bright ball of light that was the asteroid.

Sweat soaked his torso. He checked and double-checked and triple-checked the *Linacre's* speed and course. The smallest mistake would mean death for every living being on the planet.

Beatty glanced at the asteroid. It looked much bigger than it had only a few seconds before. Again, he checked the ebb. Speed and course still looked good, so long as Tesla's projections were on the mark.

They have to be. He's the smartest chap in the world.

Unfortunately, even smart people weren't infallible.

Beatty shivered when he looked back at the screen. The asteroid appeared almost on top of him. He tried to shake off his anxiety as he did another check of the *Linacre's* speed and course. So far, so good.

The asteroid vanished from the screen. A split second later, he spotted it through the bridge window.

It sped further away from him!

"Dammit!" Beatty punched more buttons. *Linacre's* velocity increased. The gap closed between the ship and the asteroid. Not as much as Beatty would have liked. He pushed the engine harder. His heart pounded as *Linacre* drew closer to the asteroid. One-hundred kilometers... Eighty kilometers... Forty kilometers.

Linacre shuddered.

"Sir," Weilman called. "The engine's getting pushed past its limits."

"No choice, Commander. If we don't get to that rock, the Earth's done for."

"Understood, sir, but if you keep pushing the engine like this, it's going to give out."

Beatty tensed, panic swelling within him. If the engine failed, Earth was done for.

What choice do you have?

He coaxed every bit of power he could get out of the engine. Twenty kilometers and closing to the asteroid.

The shuddering grew more violent.

Hold together. Please, Lord, for the sake of all your children, hold this ship together.

Ten kilometers... five kilometers. The brown, uneven surface of the asteroid filled the bridge window.

Beatty deployed the landing struts. He felt like someone had tossed the ship inside a baby's rattle.

So close. Please... hold... together.

Another shudder went through the ship, a different one. They had touched down on the asteroid.

"We're down, Commander! Collapse the magnetic field!"

"Collapsing magnetic field, aye."

A minute after giving the order, a piercing whine reached his ears. The engine overloading. He wondered how long it would take. Hopefully, not too long.

Beatty sat back, looking out at the surface of the asteroid. He let out a sardonic laugh. A big ugly rock would be the last thing he ever saw. Not his wife. Not his sons. Not even the Earth. Just this damn asteroid the Martians flew here to—

A monstrous roar filled the ship. A white light obliterated Beatty's vision.

RETALIATION

EPILOGUE
SIX MONTHS LATER

Captain Georgy Zhukov looked around at the men in the armored troop carrier. The reactions were what he expected. A mixture of nervousness, excitement, even annoyance. That last one best described his mood.

"The imperialists are invading the Soviet Union!" his regimental commander blared less than an hour ago.

Zhukov's infantry company piled into ATCs and set off for Zinovyevsk to protect it from the invaders who at this moment were storming the beaches of Odessa.

If the regimental commander spoke the truth.

Over the past two weeks, Zhukov's superiors had announced an imperialist invasion half-a-dozen times. Men, vehicles, battlewalkers, and jets all headed south to throw the enemy back into the Black Sea.

But there never were any invaders to fight. Each time had been a drill. Zhukov suspected the same this time as well. Not that he could act that way. He needed his troops ready for the day the imperialists really did invade.

If that happens.

Patton, Rommel, and de Gaulle seemed decent enough, for foreigners. Despite their differences in language and culture, they had worked well together. Their efforts led to the destruction of the space ark and the deaths of Martian leadership. Those events broke the will of the Martians to continue the fight. They fled into the deserts and mountains, trying to hide from the ASEF soldiers still on Mars to hunt them down.

But things change. Alliances shift. The wealthy industrialists and their puppet politicians in nations like Britain, Germany, France, and America had a stranglehold on the working class and would never willingly relinquish it. The workers themselves, too blinded by religion and too concerned with materialistic pursuits, would never rise en masse as the Russian people had.

Conflict with the imperialist nations was inevitable.

Zhukov wondered if that conflict would happen sooner rather than later.

"I do not think this is another drill," said a corporal sitting across from him. "I heard there was an explosion near Vinnytsia a few days ago. It has to be the imperialists dropping space rocks on us again."

Zhukov just stared at the corporal, saying nothing. In this part of the Ukraine, that explosion could have been anything from a locomotive's steam engine to a grain elevator. But after the disaster at Novonikolayevsk, stories of any explosion within the Soviet Union made people nervous.

Stalin blamed the destruction of the city along the Ob River, and the damage to four other cities and towns, on ASEF. From what Zhukov heard while still on Mars when the Martians tried to smash a large asteroid into Earth, Admiral Beatty himself managed to blow it up, but much debris had rained down on Earth. Most struck desolate areas or landed in the sea. Some hit cities and villages, including Novonikolayevsk.

Stalin had the Red Army drilling ever since.

"Captain."

Zhukov turned to his radioman, Corporal Gordiouk. "Yes, Corporal?"

"Headquarters reports this was a drill. We are to return to base."

As I suspected.

The vehicles turned around and headed north. The battlewalkers nearby also reversed course. Zhukov gazed out at the green steppes around him. He would have been surprised had the imperialists actually invaded. While they did defeat the Martians, the cost of victory had been high. The British, Americans, Germans, French, and other nations would need a long time to rebuild their militaries. He doubted they were in any shape to begin another war so soon.

The convoy came to a halt just a few kilometers from their base in Cherkasy. Zhukov leaned over the side of the ATC, trying to see what caused the delay.

A buggy rolled beside the convoy, coming toward him. Three men sat inside the vehicle, wearing standard green army uniforms. But something about them sent a tinge of nervousness through Zhukov. That nervousness grew the closer the buggy got.

His stomach clenched when it stopped by his ATC. The three men got out, two of them clutching rifles.

Zhukov's face stiffened, trying to hide any sign of concern. He could tell just by looking at the trio they were not Red Army soldiers.

They were *Cheka*.

His mind flashed back to Mars, to shooting Beria, as it always did in the presence of any *Cheka* pig. His heart thumped harder.

It's been six months. If they suspected anything, they already would have arrested you.

The group leader, a stocky man with a compact, unsmiling face, glared at the men in the ATC. Most averted their eyes. A few swallowed.

The leader took a step forward. His hard eyes fixed on Zhukov. "Captain Georgy Zhukov?"

His stomach turned to lead. *"Da."*

"Come." The leader waved his hand in a demanding manner.

Tremors started up and down Zhukov's legs. He forced them to leave and jumped over the side.

They have nothing on you. Beria's body had been vaporized during the barrage that destroyed the space ark. The survivors of his company swore to keep the truth to themselves till the day they died. They all hated Beria. This had to be about something else.

"Disarm him," ordered the leader.

The two other *Cheka* men stomped forward, ripping away Zhukov's rifle and snatching his pistol.

"What is the meaning of this?"

"The *Cheka* has completed its investigation into the death of *Politruk* Beria on Mars."

Zhukov suppressed a shiver. "Wh-What investigation? Comrade Beria was killed by the Martians."

"Not according to some of the men in your company."

Zhukov froze. Had one of them talked?

Then again, if the *Cheka* wanted you to talk, they had many methods to make certain you talked.

"We have been concerned about all of you because of your association with anti-revolutionary elements on Mars," said the leader.

"You mean the imperialist soldiers? We fought alongside them. We killed the Martian leaders and stopped them from leaving Mars."

"True, but who knows what subversive thoughts they may have put into your head. Why do you think we separated all of you upon your return to Earth? So you would not grow your ranks and plot to overthrow Comrade Stalin."

"That is a lie!" Zhukov hollered. "I am loyal to Comrade Stalin and the Soviet Union."

"Loyal citizens do not murder a *politruk*. Some of your men were... persuaded," an evil grin spread across the leader's face, "to tell us the truth about what happened to Comrade Beria."

Zhukov wanted to throw up. They had him.

He opened his mouth. It had taken a couple of seconds before words came out. "*Politruk* Beria would have sent the imperialists' SPAs away. Without those guns, we never would have stopped the Martian space ark."

"The Red Army could have stopped it without help from the imperialists." The leader's eyes drilled into Zhukov. "Captain Georgy Zhukov, you have been found guilty of the murder of *Politruk* Lavrentiy Beria. The sentence is death, to be carried out immediately. On your knees."

Zhukov took a deep breath and remained standing. If this were to be the end, he would meet it like a man.

The leader scowled. "I said on your knees."

Zhukov spat in the *Cheka* man's face. "Go to hell, stupid son of a whore!"

One of the leader's men rammed the butt of his rifle into Zhukov's back. He gasped and went down on his knees. He closed his eyes, trying to fight the pain, trying to be defiant. He'd be damned if he'd show fear in front of these *Cheka* vermin.

The cocking of a pistol turned his blood to ice. Zhukov shut his eyes tight, and waited for the—

* * *

"A most interesting concept, *Capitaine*. Most interesting, indeed."

"*Merci, Mon General,*" de Gaulle responded to General Louis Franchet d'Espèrey, the Army Chief of Staff. He still stung a bit when referred to as *capitaine*. At times, he thought he should feel grateful that he had gone up two ranks after his demotion on Mars. But when he had been a *commandant* before, given how he had disabled the Martian space ark, he should have been promoted to lieutenant colonel.

One day.

"Of course," d'Espèrey continued, "the biggest criticism I can see is that there is no heat ray."

"But it is still well armed with machine guns and a mortar. Until we can build smaller heat rays, this must suffice."

D'Espèrey silently nodded and went back to studying the diagram.

De Gaulle tried to keep from shifting in his seat. He felt more angry than nervous. Was d'Espèrey trying to find more faults with his proposed miniature battlewalker?

"At four meters in height," de Gaulle said, "it is ideal for operating in tunnels or buildings. It is better armed and better protected to deal with ambushes than a regular infantry soldier. Yes, battlewalkers are powerful, and everyone is enamored by them. But as we saw during the space ark battle, they cannot go everywhere. Even the SPAs proved cumbersome in the close quarter fighting. How many were lost during the battle?"

De Gaulle leaned forward, his enthusiasm and hope rising. "These machines are ideal for supporting infantry at a platoon or company level should support from larger battlewalkers or artillery not be immediately available."

D'Espèrey regarded him in silence for several seconds, then nodded. "You make a good point, *Capitaine.*"

"*Merci, Mon General.*"

"I shall take this to the War Minister and recommend this project be undertaken. If he approves, I will assign you to my staff to help oversee its development. And since this sort of project is not normally handled by a *capitaine*, you would be restored to your original rank of *commandant.*"

"*Merci, Mon General.*" De Gaulle felt ready to burst. This meeting had gone better than he expected.

D'Espèrey got to his feet. So did de Gaulle, who saluted. He had just turned to leave when the general called out, "*Capitaine*. Before you leave, a word."

"*Oui, Mon General?*"

"Your exploits during the space ark battle have made you well known, not only in France, but all over the world. But do not let that fame go to your head."

De Gaulle gave him a perplexed look. "I do not understand."

"This proposal for your miniature battlewalker, you sent it first to Lieutenant Colonel Juin on my staff, no?"

"*Oui.* We served together on Mars. I figured he could get my proposal to you quicker than if I went through normal channels."

"There *is* a reason 'normal channels' exist," said d'Espèrey. "We all must follow the chain of command for the sake of discipline. We cannot have our officers operating outside of established rules simply because they are impatient."

D'Espèrey took a breath. "You are a brave and intelligent officer, *Capitaine* de Gaulle, and an exceptional leader. I believe you have a bright future ahead of you in the army, but you must curb these bouts of rash behavior you are prone to. Arguing with superior officers, circumventing the chain of command, will not win you supporters or help you advance in rank. What happened to you after the Battle of Tharsis City should serve as a powerful lesson."

De Gaulle fought to keep his expression neutral. "*Oui, Mon General.* Thank you for your advice."

He left d'Espèrey's office and strutted down the tiled corridors of the War Ministry. The sneer on his face grew more pronounced as he neared the exit.

"*Follow the chain of command.*" He snorted as d'Espèrey's words echoed in his head. Had he followed the chain of command, his proposal would languish on some toad of a junior staff officer's desk for the next three years.

To hell with that! The miniature battlewalker was something France needed before its next conflict. The Martians may be defeated, but other threats to the Republic loomed. Stalin grew more paranoid with each passing day, and his military did not suffer the high losses that most other ASEF nations did. There was talk of rebellion in some of the colonies in Africa. Many military and political leaders, as well as ordinary citizens, wanted to stick their heads in the sand and ignore these dangers. One war had ended. They did not want to think of another beginning.

That was why France needed forward-thinking men like him to face the new challenges that lay ahead. Men like d'Espèrey were too concerned with rules and procedures. They were cautious. Cautious men did not accomplish great things.

Men of daring did.

De Gaulle slowed his pace as he approached a large, brown, classic-style building. The Second Elysee Palace rebuilt after the Martian invasion. The official residence of the president.

A smile crept across de Gaulle's face as he continued to stare at the building.

Someday.

* * *

"Good to see you again, George." Colonel Rommel extended his hand. "May I personally congratulate you on your promotion. Now you are one step away from General."

"Thank you, Erwin." Colonel George Patton clasped the German officer's hand. "Don't know yet if I'll want to give up my bird for a star when the time comes. I've been cussing out generals for years for being idiots. I sure as shit don't want to become an idiot myself."

Rommel laughed, then looked at the fields and trees beyond them. "I see you have been rewarded well for your new rank."

"Yup. Nearly a hundred thousand acres. All mine." Patton slowly swept an arm across his body, taking in the vast fields of the Fort Knox School of Armored Warfare. "I hope you and your men enjoy it, and remember, don't go easy on my boys."

"I have no intention of doing so." Rommel grinned.

"Ha! I knew you wouldn't."

Patton led Rommel toward his personnel buggy as German SPAs and buggies rolled out of a nearby troop landing ship.

"That's why I wanted you here for these exercises," Patton continued. "After everything you did on Mars, who better to give these boys a challenge then you?"

"*Danke.* I, too, hope your men will give mine a challenge. I do not wish them to become complacent. I fear too many soldiers and politicians are, and barely eight months have passed since the war on Mars ended."

Patton grunted. "Tell me about it."

The two officers climbed into the buggy. The driver started the engine and rolled across the field.

"We already have a bunch of jackasses in Congress who want a major demobilization," Patton groused. "Are they ignoring that nutcase Stalin over in Russia? The crazy son-of-a-bitch still thinks we deliberately blew up that city of his, Novo-whatever-the-hell. He keeps calling for a worldwide communist revolution, for the workers to rise up. How the hell can anyone think that guy isn't a threat? Then there are the Japs. They're starting to build up their navy, even more than their space forces. They're up to something, I tell you. Sneaky bastards."

"Mm." Rommel nodded. "I think there was a small, naïve part of me that hoped the invasion and our retaliation would finally bring all the peoples of the world together. Obviously, that has not happened."

"You can have the vast majority of the people wanting world peace, but the truth is, there are always going to be evil SOBs out there making trouble. That's why people like us will always be needed."

The buggy pulled up to a tent. Patton and Rommel got out and walked into it. After offering Rommel a seat, Patton opened his footlocker and pulled out a bottle of whiskey and two glasses.

"To your promotion, *mein freund.*" Rommel raised his glass.

"And to yours." Patton nodded, noting the tabs of a full Imperial German Army colonel on Rommel's collar.

They knocked back their drinks. Patton poured another round when Rommel said, "I propose we next toast the acceptance of our newly designed SPAs by our superiors."

"Exactly what I was thinking." Patton smiled wide. "All these years of bitching and hollering, we finally got what we wanted. A brand new SPA. Enclosed chassis and thicker armor for better crew protection, three-hundred-sixty-degree rotating turret, machine guns. Too bad about the main gun, though. A thirty-seven millimeter is gonna seem like a pea shooter compared to what we had on our SPAs."

"True, but I'm sure through trial and error we will be able to upgrade the main gun in a few years."

"Yeah, hopefully before the Ruskies or the Japs decide to pull something," Patton grunted. "I also hope the shitheads at the War Department come up with a better name for it."

"What are they calling it?"

"The Direct Infantry Support Gun, which the military geniuses shortened to DISGU."

"*Ach!* A terrible name."

"You'll get no argument from me."

"As much as I have criticized the General Staff," said Rommel, "at least they came up with a better name for our new SPA."

"And what would that be?"

"We call it the 'panzer.'"

Patton cocked his head to the side. *Panzer.* He liked it. The name invoked a sense of speed, strength, and lethality, everything he had envisioned in this new type of SPA.

"Erwin, my friend, I say DISGU is dead." Patton raised his glass. "Long live the panzer."

AUTHOR'S NOTE

The following is a list of historical figures used in this story and an overview of their accomplishments in the real world.

George S. Patton (1885–1945): American general. Led successful campaigns in North Africa and Sicily in WWII.
Erwin Rommel (1891–1944): German field marshal. Legendary panzer commander in WWII. Implicated in the assassination plot against Hitler and forced to commit suicide.
Charles de Gaulle (1890–1970): French general, leader of the Free French Forces during WWII, President of the French Fifth Republic.
David Beatty (1871–1936): British fleet admiral. Commander of the British Grand Fleet in WWI.
Georgy Zhukov (1896–1974): Marshal of the Soviet Union during WWII. Played a pivotal role in driving the German Army out of Russia.
Lavrentiy Beria (1899–1953): Head of the Soviet NKVD, the forerunner of the KGB. Executed following a 1953 coup led by Nikita Khrushchev and Georgy Zhukov.
David Lloyd George (1863–1945): British Prime Minister 1916–1922.
Leonard Wood (1860–1927): American general. Served in the Spanish-American War and the Philippine Insurrection. Unsuccessfully ran for president in 1920.
Andre Maginot (1877–1932): French Member of Parliament and Minister of War. Advocated a string of forts along the border with Germany that would become known as the Maginot Line.
Maximilian I, aka Archduke Maximilian Eugen of Austria (1895–1952): Son of Archduke Otto of Austria, brother of Charles I, the last emperor of the Austro-Hungarian Empire.
Heinz Guderian (1888–1954): German general, considered a pioneer in armored warfare.
Alphonse Juin (1888–1967): French General. Led Free French forces during the Italian campaign in WWII.
Charles Summerall (1867–1955): American general. Fought in WWI, served as US Army Chief of Staff 1926–1930.
Hans von Seeckt (1866–1936): German general. Commanded the German Army after WWI.
Eddie Rickenbacker (1890–1973): American fighter ace of WWI.
John F. O'Ryan (1874–1961): American general. Commander of the New York National Guard, commander of the US 27th Division in WWI.
William Nickerson (1875–1954): Member of British Royal Army Medical Corps during WWI. Recipient of the Victoria Cross.
HMS Thomas Linacre: The hospital ship featured in this story was named after the British physician who lived from 1460 to 1524. He founded the College of Physicians in London.

Louis Franchet d'Espèrey (1856–1942): French general. Led successful campaigns in Eastern Europe during WWI.

Some prominent historical figures of this period were absent from the story. Given the devastation of the Martian invasion, no doubt many of these people would have been killed, been crippled, or chosen different paths in their lives.

RETALIATION

JOHN J. RUST

John J. Rust was born in New Jersey. He studied broadcasting and journalism at Mercer County Community College in New Jersey and the College of Mount St. Vincent in New York. He moved to Arizona in 1996, where he works as the Sports Director for KYCA radio. Rust has published five other novels and several short stories.

Other Books by John J. Rust:
Sea Raptor
Fallen Eagle: Alaska Front
Dark Wings
The Best Phillies Team Ever
Arizona's All-Time Baseball Team

RETALIATION

MARK GARDNER

Mark Gardner is a US NAVY veteran. He lives in northern Arizona with his wife, three children, and a pair of spoiled dogs. Mark holds a degree in Computer Systems and Applications and is the Chief Operator for KYCA radio. Gardner has published three other novels, three novellas and several short stories.

Other Books by Mark Gardner:
Champion Standing
Sixteen Sunsets
Days Until Home
Body Rentals
Forlorn Hope
Brass Automator

 SEVEREDPRESS

facebook.com/severedpress
twitter.com/severedpress

CHECK OUT OTHER GREAT
SCIENCE FICTION BOOKS

DERELICT: MARINES
by Paul E. Cooley

Fifty years ago, Mira, humanity's last hope to find new resources, exited the solar system bound for Proxima Centauri b. Seven years into her mission, all transmissions ceased without warning. Mira and her crew were presumed lost. Humanity, unified during her construction, splintered into insurgency and rebellion.

Now, an outpost orbiting Pluto has detected a distress call from an unpowered object entering Sol space: Mira has returned. When all attempts at communications fail, S&R Black, a Sol Federation Marine Corps search and rescue vessel, is dispatched from Trident Station to intercept, investigate, and tow the beleaguered Mira to Neptune.

As the marines prepare for the journey, uncertainty and conspiracy fomented by Trident Station's governing AIs, begin to take their toll. Upon reaching Mira, they discover they've been sent on a mission that will almost certainly end in catastrophe.

ALLIANCE MARINES
by John Mierau

One by one, all of Earth's colonies have gone dark and silent. Reach, the last colony, teeters on the verge of civil war against its Earth-loyal overlords...and Reach-born rebel Lee Zhang has sworn to push the planet over the edge.

As the colony descends into total war, a convoy from Earth races across the galaxy, carrying news of a threat unlike anything mankind has faced before. The colonies have all been destroyed by a vast alien horde, and now Earth has fallen, too. Time is running out for sworn enemies to learn to trust and unite, or the human race is extinct. The Takers are coming to destroy mankind. If we don't do the job for them first.

SEVEREDPRESS

facebook.com/severedpress
twitter.com/severedpress

CHECK OUT OTHER GREAT SCIENCE FICTION BOOKS

SPACE MARINE AJAX
by Sean-Michael Argo

Ajax answers the call of duty and becomes an Einherjar space marine, charged with defending humanity against hideous alien monsters in furious combat across the galaxy.

The Garm, as they came to be called, emerged from the deepest parts of uncharted space, devouring all that lay before them, a great swarm that scoured entire star systems of all organic life. This space borne hive, this extinction fleet, made no attempts to communicate and offered no mercy.

Humanity has always been a deadly organism, and we would not so easily be made the prey. Unified against a common enemy, we fought back, meeting the swarm with soldiers upon every front.

PLANET LEVIATHAN
by D.J. Goodman

The cyborg commandos of the Galactic Marines are the greatest warriors in the galaxy, but sometimes one will go bad. Too unstable to be let back into the general population and too powerful for a normal prison to hold them, there is only one place they can be sent: Planet Leviathan.

SEVEREDPRESS

facebook.com/severedpres
twitter.com/severedpress

CHECK OUT OTHER GREAT SCIENCE FICTION BOOKS

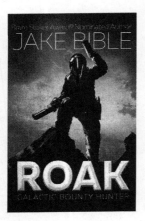

ROAK
by Jake Bible

There are thousands of bounty hunters across the galaxy. Solid professionals that take jobs based on the credits the bounties afford. They follow the letter of the law so they can maximize those credits.

Licensed, bonded, legal.

Then there's Roak.

Deadly, unstoppable, invisible.

SIEGE
by Gustavo Bondoni

This is humanity's last stand. Threatened on all sides by enemies they can't fight and often can't even comprehend, the human race has taken refuge in an inhospitable corner of the galaxy. A tiny pocket of habitable space concealed by black holes and dust clouds, hiding a cluster of colonies where the last humans in the galaxy reside, preparing themselves for a war of annihilation against all comers. Crystallia is a hidden military base that guards the access route to the colonies. The main mission of the soldiers there is to remain undetected for as long as possible, to spot any incursions from the outside and to hit them with everything in humanity's arsenal. No one is quite convinced that this strategy will be enough to save the colonies or even to create enough of a delay for some of the colonists to escape. The best bet for the human race is to remain concealed. Unfortunately, something has found them.

Made in the USA
Middletown, DE
10 June 2017